THE CAT'S PAW

The 9 Lives Cozy Mystery Series

Book Two

Louise Clark

Book design by eBook Prep
www.ebookprep.com

January, 2017
ISBN: 978-1-61417-996-2

ePublishing Works!
www.epublishingworks.com

ACKNOWLEDGMENTS

Writing a book is never a solo project and I want to thank several people who took a critical look at this story and helped me to make it better. Any errors, of course, are mine, because in the end I'm the one who makes the decisions on what to and what not to change.

I asked Patricia Spice to review the text from a lawyer's point of view. She identified several scenes that needed amending, then was kind enough to back and forth with me until I got it sorted out in a way that worked to both our satisfaction. "After all," she said, "if you're going to write about the Canadian legal system, you may as well get it right." Yup, and a very good point!

Mary MacGregor, an avid mystery reader and an academic whiz, pointed out that no academic advisor would be so much into a student's life as Dr. Peiling was involved in Brittany Day's. Her comments made me dig deeper into *why* Peiling acted the way he did. Thank you for that, Mary!

Thanks also to my excellent editor, Alethea Spiridon, who edited both this book and *The Cat Came Back*, the first volume in the 9 Lives Cozy Mystery Series. I love the way Alethea edits. She leaves my style alone, but catches my mistakes. The best kind of editor!

Finally, I'm sending hugs and major thanks out to my family—Dave, Forrest and Alex—for their patience and for not complaining about the piles in the living room…and the dining room…and the kitchen…and the hallway…and…and…You get the picture. You're the best!

CHAPTER 1

At six forty-five on a Wednesday morning in November, Christy Jamieson was standing staring at the coffee machine in her kitchen. She was wearing a fluffy tiger-striped dressing gown her late husband Frank had given her two Christmases before, because he said it would help her bond with Stormy the Cat. Her hair was sleep-tousled and uncombed. Her mind dozed as she waited for the single brew coffee to drip into her cup. When the doorbell sounded, she frowned. She was not at her best before her first cup of coffee, but she was the mom of an active eight-year-old, so she was surprisingly good at switching on awareness when needed.

Doorbells at six forty-five in the morning did not bode well.

She cast a last, longing look at the dripping coffee and headed for the door, speculating on who was on the other side of it as she went.

She hoped it would not be the obnoxious social worker, Joan Shively. The woman claimed she had the right to drop in at any time to ensure that Christy's daughter, Noelle, was being properly cared for, but at six forty-five? If she thought she could barge into the house for an inspection, she had another thing coming.

Could be Quinn Armstrong, her neighbor and…friend. Since they had only known each other a short two months, Christy wasn't sure she was ready to call him her boyfriend, but they were close and getting closer. Quinn understood her need for an early morning hit of caffeine, so he rarely came by before Noelle was in school. She did a quick finger-comb of her hair and hoped the layered ends would fall into place, just in case he had decided to drop in. She smiled to herself. If he'd changed his pattern today she wouldn't be upset. They could chat over coffee.

The route from her townhouse kitchen to the front door was through the living room and down half a flight of stairs. She'd hardly finished her happy daydream about a quiet morning visit with Quinn when she reached the shallow landing. She hauled open the door, then stared.

Standing in front of her, looking annoyed, was not the child services lady or Quinn. It was Noelle's great-aunt, Ellen Jamieson, dressed in an expensive suit with a pencil skirt and a man-tailored jacket. The cloth was finely woven and charcoal in color. The blouse underneath was pearl gray. The outfit had probably cost Ellen a fortune.

Christy blinked, wondering if she had dozed off in front of the coffeemaker. Ellen Jamieson didn't come to visit. She hardly spoke to Christy and only to Noelle when she thought it was necessary to convey family traditions, or to show Jamieson solidarity.

What was she doing on Christy's Burnaby doorstep?

"Well," said Ellen. "Are you going to invite me in?"

An errant defiance, born of Christy's recent success in thwarting the embezzlement plans of one of Ellen's longtime friends and a trustee of Noelle's inheritance, blew away the fog of a pre-caffeine morning and teased a smile onto Christy's lips. "It's rather early for a social call, Ellen. I have to get Noelle ready for school. Why don't you come back later? Shall we say—ten forty-five?" Ten forty-five came out of nowhere. Probably the forty-five reflected in the current time. Why ten? Who knew? It didn't matter, Christy thought, as she watched Ellen's eyes widen with surprise.

Then those brown, gimlet-hard eyes narrowed.

Uh-oh, Christy thought. *Trouble ahead.*

"This is not a social call!" Ellen announced, drama injected into every word. "I am here to claim sanctuary."

Okay, maybe she was asleep. *Sanctuary? Ellen?*

At that point Stormy the Cat sauntered down the stairs, probably alerted that something unusual was up by the sound of the doorbell. Cats were naturally curious creatures, always interested in the smallest detail, but Stormy shared his body with Christy's late husband, Frank Jamieson, and Frank liked to poke his nose into everything. As Ellen made her dramatic announcement, Stormy reached the top of the half-flight of stairs. He hissed and all the hair on his back stood on end as he arched.

It's six forty-five in the morning. What the hell is she doing here?

"Claiming sanctuary," Christy said. With Frank now on the scene and loudly broadcasting his aversion to his aunt, things were about to get complicated. "You'd better come in, Ellen," she said, holding the door wider.

No way! Indignation shivered through the words.

The front door opened onto a landing that had half staircases leading both up and down. It was small space so Christy turned and led the way up, leaving Ellen to handle the front door. She resisted the urge to sigh as she scooped up the hostile cat when she reached the top of the stairs. She wanted him out of Ellen's way when she finally made it up the stairs. With Stormy in her arms, she turned to see that Ellen was manhandling a large suitcase onto the landing.

Frank noticed at the same time. The cat stiffened in her arms and began to wiggle. *After what she's done she figures she can move in? I don't think so!*

"Ellen."

Ellen succeeded in getting her suitcase into the house. She looked up at Christy as she closed the door.

"Why do you have a suitcase?"

"I told you," Ellen said impatiently. "I need sanctuary. Now, if you will show me to my room—"

Furious, Stormy fought Christy's hold. He extended his claws and tried to scramble free. Christy was a seasoned cat owner, however. She shifted her grasp so that she had both hands around the cat's ribcage, just below his front legs. Holding him tightly and away from her body, there wasn't much the cat could do to escape. He slumped, his limp body extended to its full length. Subdued, but not defeated.

Still at the bottom of the stairs, Ellen observed them with a frown. "I trust you will cage that beast while I am in residence."

Over my dead—

"Yes, well. Ellen, you have a perfectly good condo in a great location downtown. Why are you here, in Burnaby?" Burnaby was one of Vancouver's suburb municipalities, the next town over and about half an hour from downtown by car, but a suburb nonetheless. Ellen didn't do suburbs.

"My condo has been robbed. I have been violated!"

Christy sucked in her breath. Even the resistance leached out of the cat. "You'd better come up then. Have you called the police?"

"Yes," Ellen said, abandoning the suitcase in front of the door as she climbed the stairs.

Christy dropped the cat onto the floor then led the way into the kitchen, where the coffee had finished dripping into the cup. With a pang, she passed the mug to Ellen, who accepted it, then set up the brewer to make a second cup for her. "What did the police say?"

"Nothing," Ellen said bitterly. "I haven't seen them. The 9-1-1 operator said a constable would visit later in the day, since the burglars had already left. I told them my housekeeper would let them into the apartment. I wasn't remaining, to wait on their convenience."

She's crying wolf, Frank said, with considerable disgust. *What's all this bull about being violated?*

The coffeemaker hissed and gurgled, then spat coffee into Christy's cup. While she waited for it to finish brewing she went to the pantry cupboard to grab a can of cat food for Stormy.

"Why don't you tell me *exactly* what happened," Christy said, opening the can and dishing the contents into Stormy's bowl. Frank seemed to get as much pleasure out of Stormy eating as Stormy did, so she hoped that if she provided food, Frank would forget about Ellen. For the moment, anyway.

"I woke up just before dawn thinking I heard some strange noises," Ellen said. "Where do you keep your sugar?"

Christy pulled a spoon out of a drawer and used it to point to a bowl on the kitchen table. Ellen took the spoon, her cup and herself over to the table. She liberally scooped sugar into the cup, then sat down facing Christy who still stood by the coffeemaker.

"What kind of noises?" Christy asked as the machine finished and she picked up her mug. She took a large, revivifying gulp of coffee. This conversation wasn't one she should be having before finishing her first cup of the day.

Ellen sniffed, both hands around the mug. "The kind that shouldn't be there at five thirty in the morning. Thumps. Footsteps. Grunts. I lay there, listening, but I was half asleep and not sure that what I thought I heard, I actually did hear."

Ellen's description was close enough to the sounds Christy had heard when her home was broken into just a few weeks before that she shivered.

She's grandstanding. Always has to one up me and mine. Pay no attention to her, Chris.

"If you didn't hear the sounds again, what makes you think you were broken into?" Christy asked, ignoring Frank.

For once, Ellen looked uncertain. "I must have drifted off to sleep, but I dreamed I heard voices. That startled me and I came completely awake. I got up and that's when I discovered that the mirror in the hall was broken, as well as one of the legs on the little console table below it. I realized then that I hadn't been dreaming or imagining the sounds I heard. Someone had been in my home!"

The distress in her voice and on her face was very real. Christy said gently, "That's when you called the police."

"That's when I packed a suitcase," Ellen said grimly. "Whether the police came in minutes or the hours it will apparently take them, I wasn't staying."

Stormy's nose was still deep in his food bowl, but Christy's ploy to keep Frank out of the conversation wasn't working. *She's not staying with us. Period.*

"Why come here?" Christy asked. "Why not a hotel? There are lots of good ones in the city."

"Jamiesons don't live in hotels," Ellen said.

"Live? Not stay?"

"I am not going to return to that apartment," Ellen said, thrusting up her chin.

"But surely…after the mess has been cleaned up—"

"I will be putting the condo up for sale," Ellen finished smoothly. She lifted the cup and sipped. When she put it back down on the table her voice was decisive. "I will not live there again."

Stormy finished his breakfast and licked his chops, before settling in to clean face and chin with tongue and paws. Frank's mental protest came with a gritty edge that expressed both anger and desperation. *She is not moving in. This is our home, not hers. She can't stay.*

"I get that," Christy snapped. She gulped more coffee.

Ellen stared at her, brows raised. "There is no need for hostility. This house is part of the Jamieson Trust. As such I have as much right live here as you do."

The cat's tail was swishing angrily from side to side as he stood defensively over his bowl, staring at Ellen. *If she stays, I go.*

"We'll see what the police have to say. Once we've heard from them, we can make a decision."

Ellen sniffed as Frank broadcast an equally dubious sound. Christy resisted the urge to sigh. The role of the peacemaker was never smooth. "Have you eaten, Ellen? I'm about to make bacon and eggs for Noelle. Would you like some?"

"Yes," said Ellen and Frank at the same time.

By eleven o'clock Christy was exhausted. Her usual smooth morning schedule, honed to a nanosecond, had gone completely off the rails. As a result, she'd rushed breakfast, shoved her body into the first clean clothes she could find (jeans and a long-sleeved T-shirt) and she and Noelle had to run all the way to the school to make sure Noelle was in her classroom before the start bell rang. Back home, she discovered that Ellen expected help settling into the spare bedroom. They argued—again—about Ellen's decision to move in until Ellen announced that she was emotionally drained and would be taking a nap. Relieved, Christy retreated to her front steps, where she sat in the mid-morning quiet in the hopes of soothing her frazzled nerves.

The weather was no brighter than her emotions. A solid bank of gray clouds covered the sky. It wasn't raining yet, but it was November and in British Columbia's lower mainland, November and a solid mass of cloud meant that it soon would be. In the flower box beside her front walk the Shasta daisies drooped, their bright heads heavy on stalks that were no longer putting energy into new growth, and the Japanese cherry tree had shed its purple-red leaves.

Several pale yellow birds with big bills and black masks landed in the tree and went to work on the remaining few small, bitter fruits, swallowing them whole. Christy watched their energetic fluttering and thought with a kind of rueful amusement that she had been flitting around with the same kind of energy as the birds since Ellen's arrival, but a lot less efficiently.

She'd only been sitting there five minutes when Quinn settled in beside her. She sighed and put her head on his shoulder as he slipped his arm around her waist.

Quinn Armstrong had begun as her enemy, then became her ally and now was a friend and, she very much hoped, eventually her lover. He'd helped her prove that her husband, Frank Jamieson—heir to the Jamieson Ice Cream fortune—had not abandoned her and their daughter, Noelle, but was actually dead. During that investigation she had discovered Quinn was a man who was both sexy and honorable, a combination that touched her emotions even as his dark-lashed gray eyes and kissable mouth had her thinking thoughts she wasn't quite ready to act on.

"I hear Ellen Jamieson has come for a visit," he said. He rubbed his cheek against her hair and moved a little closer.

"Let me guess. Frank told your father."

She felt Quinn's chest rise and fall in a sigh. Frank communicated telepathically with Christy, Noelle and Roy, Quinn's father and a bestselling novelist, but for some reason Quinn couldn't hear him. Frank swore it was Quinn's fault, and maybe it was since Quinn was very much a grounded, facts-oriented kind of person. But Frank had a possessive streak when he was alive. Christy wouldn't rule out the possibility that Frank was deliberately excluding Quinn because of her attraction to him.

"Yeah. Dad said he came over to vent because he couldn't do anything to stop her." Quinn kissed the hair he had just nuzzled, making it very clear that he was more interested in how Christy was taking the arrival of Ellen, than what Frank was feeling.

It was Christy's turn to sigh—hers with pleasure. She loved the feeling of having a man to lean against, a man whose first concern was for her.

"Frank says that she was burgled. Is that true?"

Christy straightened reluctantly. She needed to look into Quinn's eyes and she couldn't do it cuddled up against his chest. Quinn, being an award-winning journalist, would be able to make sense of Ellen's dramatic announcement. "She claimed it happened while she was in bed, asleep or half-asleep. Which," Christy said, a frown puckering her forehead, "makes it a home invasion, not a burglary, I guess."

Quinn frowned too. "Is she sure it actually happened?"

"There was a broken mirror and table, so, yeah, it happened."

"Frank was not clear on that point," Quinn said. "He thought the story was an excuse so she could move in and make his life miserable."

A little bubble of amusement welled up inside Christy. "She doesn't like cats. She told me to lock Stormy into a room."

Quinn laughed. "That must have gone over well."

"I was relieved when Frank slipped away just after breakfast. By that time Noelle was down. She must have opened the door for him while I was trying to convince Ellen that she didn't want to sell her condo because of a little break-in."

"Anything stolen?" Quinn asked.

"Not that Ellen noticed." Christy searched his face, basking in the warmth—and yes, worry—in his eyes. "Quinn, why would someone break in, shatter a mirror and a table, but steal nothing?"

"Noise," he said promptly. "The sound made by the breaking mirror and furniture would be loud in the predawn quiet. The thieves were probably frightened they would be discovered and took off."

"Maybe," Christy said.

Quinn stroked Christy's red brown hair away from her face. "I came over to see if you were okay."

He was afraid Ellen's burglary would remind her of the home invasion she'd fought off here in her own home so very recently. Stormy had been injured, but she and Noelle had been fine.

And Quinn had come to her rescue, while his father had taken the injured cat to the twenty-four hour vet. She smiled at him, leaned forward and kissed him lightly on the lips. "I'm fine," she whispered.

He changed the kiss into a more intimate one. At least, as intimate as two people could get while seated on the front porch of a small townhouse located in a high-density development in the suburbs. When he drew away he murmured against her lips, "I worry about you, you know."

She did know and it warmed her all over. As he straightened, his gaze a caress, she said firmly, "Ellen will get tired of living here and she'll hire a service to thoroughly clean her condo, then move back there. It won't take her long."

His caressing gaze morphed into one of amused disbelief. "Are we talking about the woman who said she'd been violated because someone came into her condo and broke a mirror?"

"I know Ellen Jamieson. A townhouse in the burbs won't cut it. She'll be gone within days." Christy heard the ragged edge of desperation in her voice and hoped Quinn hadn't.

But he was laughing at her now, his eyes bright with affectionate mirth. "If you say so."

She had the unfortunate feeling that he'd nailed it and Ellen Jamieson was here to stay.

CHAPTER 2

They called her because a Jamieson was involved.

Detective Billie Patterson of the Vancouver Police Department eased her car to a stop in front of the modern, glass-and-steel building which housed Ellen Jamieson's condo. Located close to English Bay and a short walk to the Granville Island Ferry, the low-rise structure featured large open terraces on the top three floors. Jamieson's apartment was on the fifth floor; not quite a penthouse, but pretty damn close.

The building access included a doorman, apparently there to help owners with parcels and to vet guests during the day and evening, and a reasonable, but not state-of-the-art security system in the underground parking garage. Patterson took note of that and added the information to her growing mental case file.

On the fifth floor, a patrolman greeted her at the condo entrance. "The body's on the terrace, Detective. You enter it through the living room."

"I'll look around first." If she hadn't already been aware of the Jamieson wealth, Ellen Jamieson's apartment would have alerted her to it. The flooring was real wood, a dark walnut that gleamed with a high-gloss finish. The area rugs strewn throughout were authentic Persian carpets, with intricately woven patterns in vivid blues and reds, lovely to look at and expensive to buy. The furniture was antique, most of it solid Victorian pieces built by top craftsmen. Even though she poked through the entire apartment, there wasn't a recliner, or modern squishy, comfortable, sofa in sight.

Starchy, proper, and stiff. That's what she remembered of Ellen Jamieson from her investigations into the disappearance and later death of Frank Jamieson, and her apartment confirmed it.

So what was she doing with a dead body on her terrace?

Jamieson had claimed she heard the sounds of a scuffle, glass shattering and then voices. When she'd discovered the broken mirror and table, she had called 9-1-1 then vacated the premises. The bedroom testified to her hurried departure. The bed was unmade and the cupboard doors were open. Clothes were strewn over the bed and a small reading chair by the window—evidence she had packed, and had done it quickly.

Patterson swung back to the entryway with the broken mirror and ruined console table. The patrolman guarding the door straightened. "Do we have a name yet?" she asked, referring to the victim on the terrace.

He nodded. "Brittany Day," he said quickly. Then he pulled out a notebook. "Of Calgary. Currently studying at English Bay University."

Brittany Day, Patterson thought. *Well, well, well. Wasn't that interesting?*

"Who found the body?"

"I did, sir. As a result of a 9-1-1 call, I was sent to check the residence. The occupant, a Ms. Jamieson, had left the premises, but had authorized the doorman to access the apartment. He unlocked the door and I came in to assess the damage. In my inspection of the unit, I found the woman's body on the terrace. She was already dead and had been for some time."

Patterson nodded, then headed out to the crime scene.

The terrace was designed to be outdoor living space. Flower boxes held an assortment of annual plantings that must have been beautiful during the summer months, providing vivid color against the elegant slate flooring. An awning covered a modern patio set—six padded chairs around a rectangular, granite-topped table. Near the furniture grouping was an outdoor heater, further proof that this area was meant to be used pretty much year-round.

Not surprising, Patterson thought. The view of English Bay and beyond was spectacular. She could imagine sitting here after a shift to chill out and let the beauty of the area flush away all the crap she brought home with her. It would be awesome.

She doubted Ellen Jamieson had a lot of crap to flush out at the end of her day, though. And she probably hardly ever used the terrace. Ironically, the outdoor furniture looked to be the most comfortable in the whole apartment and Jamieson didn't seem the type to appreciate comfort, if the rest of the furniture was any indication.

The terrace buzzed with crime scene techs taking evidence, but most of them were around the body, which was wedged behind the patio heater.

She cornered the medical examiner for time of death first. "Early this morning," he said.

He was a burly man who had once been a linebacker during his university days. He looked like the kind of guy who would say only what needed to be said, but she knew that if she got him started, he'd talk her ear off. She didn't want to get him started. "How early is early?"

He shrugged, but his expression was thoughtful. "I can't be certain from the kind of cursory examination I can give on the scene, of course, but—"

Yeah, yeah. Spit it out, Patterson thought, careful to allow no evidence of her impatience into her expression. That only made him worse.

Miraculously he actually came to the point. "I'd say no earlier than five o'clock and no later than eight."

"Great," Patterson muttered. "That gives me nothing."

"Detective, you know my process. I am thorough, and I do not make mistakes. I will not commit unless I am certain."

Yeah, yeah, Patterson thought again, but she nodded politely. The guy pissed her off, but he was right. He did good work.

She stared down at the earthly remains of a young woman with brown hair, matted and darkened with blood from a head wound, and a curvy figure that had probably had labeled her as sexy in life. She was wearing a tank top and a pair of buttercup yellow pants, made of some sort of flowing material. Patterson crouched down to feel the texture.

Long-legged and lean, the detective was dressed in dark slacks, a simple cotton shirt and a brown leather jacket. She liked the pants, so she was careful to keep away from the puddle of blood near the victim's head. She rubbed the fabric between her fingers. It was soft, with almost a silky feel to it. Not a normal material for street clothes. More like the kind used for pajama bottoms or lounging pants.

She looked over at the medical examiner. "Was she wearing a coat or a jacket of some kind?"

He shook his head. "What you see is what you get."

Patterson grunted, resisting the urge to run her fingers through her hair, which was pulled back from her face. Instead she rubbed the scar that ran down one side, from eye to jaw, and frowned.

Jamieson murders tended to be brutal and involved head wounds. Though they hadn't yet found Frank Jamieson's body, he was reported to have been bashed on the back of the head before being bundled into the trunk of a car, then taken for what amounted to an execution.

Whoever had killed this girl wanted to be sure she did not survive the assault. She'd bled copiously from the head wound and the indent in her skull was clearly visible. As Patterson studied the body, she thought that the injuries looked almost…personal. She grimaced and stood up.

Of course it was personal. Brittany Day was one of Aaron DeBolt's girlfriends. DeBolt had been charged as an accessory in the murder of Frank Jamieson and he was currently being held without bail because he was considered a flight risk due to his links with Vancouver's seedy underbelly of crime lords and drug kings. His socialite mother and respectable, old-money father had tried to convince the judge that bail should be granted, but to no avail. DeBolt was still in lockup and would remain there until his trial.

If there was a trial. Patterson shoved her hands into the pockets of her brown leather jacket as she stared moodily down at the body of the once-pretty victim.

A week ago, Brittany Day had come forward claiming that DeBolt had been with her on the night of Frank Jamieson's death. Patterson didn't believe the alibi was true, but she had to investigate it all the same. So far, everything she'd learned fit and the alibi held up. It looked like DeBolt would walk, even though Patterson's gut told her that the man was guilty as sin.

Now Brittany Day was dead and it seemed that someone—probably Ellen Jamieson since this was her apartment—wanted to make sure that DeBolt didn't weasel out of doing hard time for his part in Frank Jamieson's murder. The blunt object and the energy used to wield it indicated anger, and maybe fear. Powerful emotions that would push a person into violent acts he or she would never normally consider.

Patterson gazed down at Brittany's face and wondered why the woman had come to Ellen Jamieson's apartment in the first place, dressed so casually. Had Ellen offered her a bribe to retract her statement that she had been with Aaron DeBolt on the night in question? Had it been Brittany who offered to change her testimony for a generous payment? Had she come to the apartment to pick up her cash?

Either was possible, Patterson thought. Ellen Jamieson's fortune didn't come from the Jamieson Trust, currently on the cusp of bankruptcy. No, her wealth came from family money and investments in the Jamieson Ice Cream Company, and since Jamieson Ice Cream was still a thriving business, she had plenty of cash to spare.

Patterson looked around the open terrace, glad the November day was mild and it wasn't raining. She could leave the crime scene geeks here and in the apartment to do their work collecting every scrap of evidence they could find while she followed Ellen Jamieson out to Burnaby where she'd retreated after she'd heard the break-in earlier today.

At that thought Patterson grinned, the smile adding a mischievous glow to her attractive features as it warmed her brown eyes. She'd bet that Christy Jamieson wasn't happy just about now, not with having her husband's aunt descending on her. From what Patterson knew of the complicated Jamieson family relationships, Christy and Ellen didn't get along. Not surprising, considering Ellen Jamieson was one of the four trustees whose hostility had made Christy's married life miserable.

She suspected the coming interview would make for an entertaining afternoon.

"Hi, Mrs. Jamieson. Is Ms. Ellen Jamieson here by any chance?"

Christy stared at Detective Patterson. She looked like an ordinary twenty-something attractive woman, smartly dressed in a leather jacket, crisp black slacks and a tailored shirt, her sand-brown hair drawn back in a stylish French braid. She had what Christy thought of as her "cop face" on, though: serious, to the point of being unreadable. Why would the police force send a plainclothes officer to Burnaby to talk to Ellen about the burglary at her condo? Surely an ordinary constable would be appropriate. "Sure," she said. "Ellen's in the living room. Come on up." She stepped aside to let Patterson enter, then led the way up the stairs.

Ellen Jamieson was sitting on the sofa, her back to the big bay window and the view of the greenbelt behind the townhouse. On the coffee table in front of her resided a rectangular tray containing a china tea set that had been a gift to Frank's parents on their tenth anniversary. The china was eggshell-thin and patterned with roses, daisies and other flowers. On the tray were a teapot, teacup and saucer, desert plate and a platter of small sandwiches. She was in the act of pouring tea for one when Christy and Detective Patterson entered the living room.

She set down the pot carefully and frowned. "Who is this, Christy?"

"You remember Detective Patterson from the police department," Christy said. She kept her voice even and careful. She and Ellen had been rubbing against each other since Ellen had shown up and her temper was wearing thin. She had a healthy respect for Patterson's deductive capabilities, though, and didn't want to parade family squabbles in front of her.

Ellen raised her brows in a way that could only be called haughty. She made a deliberate show of checking her watch before she said, "It is one forty-five in the afternoon, Detective. I contacted the police before six this morning."

"There have been developments in the case, Ms. Jamieson," Patterson said. Her voice was even, her eyes assessing.

Christy thought that if she'd walked into a house and been greeted with the kind of hostility Ellen was producing, her tone would be a lot sharper than Patterson's was. "Detective Patterson, would you like a cup of tea? Or coffee?"

Patterson smiled at her in a friendly way and said, "If coffee isn't too much trouble, I'd prefer that, Mrs. Jamieson."

"Of course." As Christy headed into the kitchen she thought that there had been amusement in Patterson's eyes and maybe even a trace of sympathy. She set about brewing the coffee, at the same time resisting the urge to sigh. Hopefully Patterson brought good news that would send Ellen back to her condo sooner rather than later. She

tuned out the quiet hum of voices from the living room
until she returned there with Patterson's coffee, plus a plate
and napkin so the detective could share the sandwiches.

The voices stopped as she entered the room, so she said
cheerfully, "I brought a plate for you, Detective Patterson.
The sandwiches on the tray are egg salad or ham." Ellen
had wanted watercress. Christy didn't stock watercress in
her fridge and she'd resisted Ellen's demand that she
immediately rush to the grocery store to pick up several
bunches.

"Thank you for the offer, Mrs. Jamieson," Patterson said,
accepting the sturdy mug Christy handed her, "but I
finished a sandwich before I came."

"Not a problem," Christy said. She smiled at Patterson,
then glanced at Ellen. She was frowning, but her expression
wasn't the usual grim disapproval she aimed at people who
didn't meet her exacting standards. There was dismay and
an edge of fear in the expression. Christy resisted the urge
to ask what the problem was. Instead she said, "I'll leave
you to your discussion, then. I'll be outside in the garden, if
you need me."

"Stay," Ellen said.

Patterson wrapped both hands around the coffee mug as
she raised it to her lips. Over the rim her eyes were
watchful.

Christy hesitated. "But—"

Ellen raised her arm and pointed. "This policeman—"

"Person," Patterson said.

"Is making unthinkable suggestions. I want a witness to
the answers I give to the questions she is asking."

Christy put the unwanted plate on the coffee table as she
sank down on one end of the sofa. Ellen was far from her
favorite person, but she knew all about how devastating
allegations and innuendoes could be. "What's going on?"

"A body was found on my terrace and she—" Ellen
pointed dramatically at Patterson. "Believes I put it there."

"A body?" Christy said. She could feel her eyes widening

and her mouth dropping open. "You mean, like a human body? A dead body?"

Patterson nodded and Ellen said, "Yes!"

"What's a body doing on your terrace?" Christy asked, staring at Ellen.

"An excellent question," Patterson said. She drank more coffee and watched the interplay between Christy and Ellen.

Ellen quivered with anger. "Are you helping this person, Christy? Are you so abandoned to your responsibilities to your family that you would take the authorities' side and help them railroad me into prison?"

"Whoa! Wait a minute," Christy said. She held out a hand, palm up in the classic "stop" position. The statement was typical of Ellen, caustic, self-centered, dramatic. She shouldn't be shocked by it, but she was.

Patterson said, "I am only here to discover the facts of the case, Ms. Jamieson. Your burglary is now an open homicide investigation. Questions need to be asked and we are starting with you, because the body was discovered on your premises."

"Who…" Christy paused to clear her throat. "Who was killed?"

"A young woman by the name of Brittany Day." Patterson looked from Christy to Ellen. "Do you know her?"

Ellen sniffed. Christy said in a low voice, "I do. She was a friend of Aaron DeBolt."

Ellen peered at her. "Aaron? Are you sure?"

"Yes. She was one of his harem of babes who always trailed him around."

"Something more than that, Mrs. Jamieson," Patterson said. "Ms. Day was a grad student at English Bay University. Her father is the president of a petro-chemical company in Calgary. And…" Here she paused, deliberately stretching out the moment. "Brittany Day was with Aaron DeBolt on the night your husband was alleged to have been murdered. That means DeBolt has—had now—an alibi for that night."

Christy stared at the detective, feeling sick. She knew her husband Frank had been murdered, because his essence had taken up residence in the body of Stormy the Cat after his death. Frank had told her that Aaron lured him into an alley, where he was clubbed and pushed into the trunk of a car for a drive that ultimately led to his death. But Frank only communicated with a few select people. Patterson and the police department didn't have access to his thoughts and information. Real physical proof had to be gathered. An alibi from a living human being would go a long way toward clearing Aaron.

Now the woman who was providing the alibi had been murdered. On Ellen Jamieson's terrace. And Ellen, as Frank's oldest living relative, could be expected to have a stake in seeing those who were accused of killing him brought to justice. That meant she had a very good motive for murdering Brittany Day, the one person who could prove Aaron's innocence.

Ellen was right. She was in deep, deep trouble.

"I think, Detective Patterson, that you should leave now," Christy said. "Ellen won't answer any more questions unless she has a lawyer present."

CHAPTER 3

Patterson didn't go without asking a few more questions, but Christy managed to keep Ellen from blurting out anything that came to mind. Ellen was clearly shocked by the realization that her burglary had resulted in a death. Christy wasn't sure she actually understood that she was currently the prime suspect in that death.

As she saw Patterson out, Stormy the Cat hopped up the front stairs.

Is the cop here about Aunt Ellen's home invasion?

"I hope you are not seriously considering Ellen for Brittany's murder, Detective," Christy said. She didn't look at the cat. Patterson already thought there was something odd about Stormy. She didn't want to increase her speculation by talking directly to him.

There was a moment of silence after she finished speaking, then Stormy hissed and arched his back, puffing up his fur and generally doing his best to look dangerous. Patterson raised her brows—at the cat's antics or her question, Christy couldn't be sure—and said, "We have to follow all avenues in an inquiry, Mrs. Jamieson. I'm sorry you feel it is important for Ellen Jamieson to have representation before she can speak to us."

Good call, babe, Frank said. *Fill me in on what's going on after this chick leaves.*

Christy had an absurd desire to laugh. Detective Patterson was about as far from a "chick" as a woman could get.

The cat shot Patterson one more baleful look, then stalked into the house. Christy said, "Detective Patterson, you used the same phrase on me when I was a suspect in Frank's disappearance. You were wrong then and you are wrong now. Ellen Jamieson isn't any more guilty of this murder than I was of helping Frank embezzle from his trust fund."

Patterson grimaced, then shrugged. "I'll be in touch, Mrs. Jamieson."

Christy watched her run lightly down the steps then on to her car. She waited until Patterson's vehicle had driven away before she headed back into the house.

In the living room she found the cat sitting on the couch beside Ellen, eyeballing the platter full of sandwiches. "Off," Christy said. She picked up Stormy and placed him on the floor near the kitchen doorway. "Eat your own food. The sandwiches are egg salad. You know they give you indigestion."

I smelled ham. The voice sounded miffed. Ham was one of Stormy's favorites.

Christy grinned and was about to reply when she saw Ellen staring at her oddly.

"You know when your cat has indigestion?" Ellen said.

"Some foods give him gas," Christy said hastily. "It's easy to figure out."

"Really." Ellen shot a disapproving look at the cat.

Thanks for getting me into trouble, babe, Frank said grumpily. Stormy sat on his haunches and licked a paw.

Christy turned to Ellen. "Patterson will be back. You should get yourself a lawyer as soon as you can."

"Normally I would go to Edward Bidwell," Ellen said. "But…"

But Edward Bidwell was one of the discredited trustees from the Jamieson Trust. Not only was he charged with embezzlement from the Trust, but the law firm where he had once been a partner had forced him to resign. Edward Bidwell was no longer a useful connection in a time of trouble.

"I'll talk to Quinn. He and Roy probably know someone you can contact."

Ellen perked up at the sound of Roy Armstrong's name. "An excellent idea." Christy began gathering up the used cups and plates. She almost dropped them when Ellen added, "That way whoever you choose will be comfortable working with you and that reporter son of his." Her lip curled as she said the word, *reporter*. There were some things Ellen couldn't let go, even if her life depended on it. Hostility toward the media was one of them. "You can all work together to clear my name."

Very carefully, Christy placed the fragile china back onto the silver tray. The cat sashayed over to the couch, then jumped onto it and sat down, paws primly together, tail neatly tucked around them.

"Ellen, I'm not a private investigator," Christy said cautiously.

You figured out who killed me. That was pretty good work. If that cop thinks Aunt Ellen murdered someone, she really does need a private dick.

"No, of course not. But Quinn Armstrong is reputed to be excellent at his job. He'll know how to proceed," Ellen said. "You can help him."

Aunt Ellen can be clueless about some things, but when it comes to self-preservation she's pretty sharp.

"Ellen, Brittany Day was murdered. I don't want to get involved."

"I'm involved," Ellen said. "Your husband's aunt. Your daughter's great-aunt. That woman is determined to charge me with murder. And if she does, the media will have a feeding frenzy. Do you want them here, camping out on your doorstep? Here, where there are no gates and no security guards to protect you?"

No, she did not.

But she also didn't want to go hunting a murderer. Her final confrontation with Frank's killer was still fresh in her mind and the knee she'd twisted as she tried to escape his furious rage still twinged if she pushed herself too hard—a constant reminder that she wasn't trained for confrontations with killers.

"Ellen, I…"

"Please, Christy. I must have been there when the murder happened. I was in my bed, asleep, but who would believe that I could sleep through someone's death? Patterson thinks I'm guilty, I'm certain of it. I'm not, but I have no way of proving it. I need help."

Christy had never heard panic in Ellen's voice before, but it was there now. She was surprised how deeply Ellen's vulnerability moved her.

Ellen's right, without you and Quinn she's toast. I hate to say it, but you've got to help her, babe.

"Please," Ellen said again.

With a sigh, Christy caved. "All right. I'll ask a few questions and see what I can find out. But just a few questions! I'm not chasing murderers."

Ellen nodded and whispered, "Thank you."

The cat licked her hand and began to purr.

When Christy picked Noelle up at school about an hour later, Mary Petrofsky, Noelle's best friend, announced that this was her mother's day off and Noelle should come to her house to play then stay for dinner. Noelle was enthusiastic, so Christy agreed, provided Mary's mother was okay with it. They waited at the school for Mary's mother to arrive, then, with the playdate and dinner confirmed, the two girls and their mothers walked home together. Christy liked Mary and her mother, Rebecca, so she cheerfully kissed Noelle when they neared the Petrofsky house and waved her good-bye. Then she went inside her townhouse and called Quinn to tell him about the developments. He suggested a strategy session. In the background Christy could hear Roy suggesting dinner and offering to cook. Christy said she and Ellen would be there at five thirty.

The cat came too, of course.

Ellen insisted they change for dinner, so Christy put on a pretty teal-colored dress with a V-neck, long sleeves, and a skirt that came well up her thighs. Ellen's choice was a flirty number that showed she had a great figure for a woman in her fifties. They had both dressed for the Armstrong men, Christy noted with amusement when she saw Ellen. She thought Quinn would notice and approve, but she wasn't sure how much of an impression Ellen would make on Roy.

When Frank saw her she heard a wolf whistle in her mind as he pretended she'd chosen the dress for him. As they left the house, she thought it was a good thing Quinn and the cat couldn't communicate.

They assembled in the Armstrongs' vivid orange kitchen, Ellen and Christy at the table with glasses of wine, while Roy presided over the cooking area and Quinn did a stint as host, organizing pre-dinner nibbles as well as the drinks. Ellen was clearly bemused that they had centered themselves in the kitchen for the discussion, which amused Quinn, but Roy simply ignored it.

"What do we know about this girl, Brittany Day?" Quinn asked, his eyes lingering with approval on Christy after he had set a bowl of tortilla chips and another of store-bought salsa in the center of the table.

The cat, curled up on Christy's lap, popped his head up over the tabletop and eyed the bowls. "No. Not for you," Christy said. Frank projected a distinctly annoyed sound. Roy laughed.

Ellen said, "That animal!" and shook her head.

Quinn raised his brows and looked at Christy. She shrugged and cocked her head at Ellen. Quinn grinned, evidently pleased that he was no longer the only one who couldn't hear Frank.

Ellen took a chip and gingerly dipped it in the salsa, before she nibbled delicately at the edges.

"Brittany Day," Christy said, dunking her own chip in the salsa, "was one of the girls with Aaron DeBolt the night of the Infant Heart Transplant Foundation Gala. Do you remember, Quinn?"

"They were smoking weed," Quinn said. "Yeah, I remember. I figured DeBolt had some kind of kinky sex thing going on with the two of them."

"Kinky sex?" Ellen said, her voice disapproving. "Aaron DeBolt? Why, he is a fine young man from a good family. He wouldn't indulge in such behavior."

"Maybe not when he's sober," Christy said. When Ellen frowned at her, she added gently, "He deals drugs, Ellen, and uses them. He was almost always stoned when I met him with Frank." She crunched her chip, enjoying the bite of the spicy salsa on her tongue.

Ellen stared at her. "Impossible. I will not believe it."

Don't forget, Natalie DeBolt is her best bud. My dear Aunt Ellen can be loyal when she wants. Just not to me, her nephew and the kid she helped to raise.

Christy lifted her wineglass and sipped. She wasn't going to acknowledge Frank's rather bitter comment. Nor was she going to argue with Ellen about Aaron DeBolt. Their discussion tonight centered on the murder victim. Time to get back on topic. "Detective Patterson said that Brittany Day came from Calgary and she was an EBU student. Her dad is apparently the president of a petrochemical company, so it sounds like there's money in her background."

"There, you see?" Ellen was clearly not going to let the issue of Aaron's respectability go.

Christy resisted the urge to sigh.

"EBU is the place to start, then," Quinn said. He pulled out one of the empty chairs at the table—the one nearest Christy—and sat down. "We'll begin with the registrar's office and see if we can find out who her professors were.

Then we go and talk to them. It may take some time, though. EBU has a huge undergrad population."

"It may not be that much of a problem, because she was a grad student." Christy said. She scooped up more salsa with a chip. "But privacy laws are pretty strict about what information can be released about students," she added, thinking of conversations she'd heard between her parents, who were both practicing academics. "The registrar's department may not be cooperative."

"Good point," Quinn said. He shot her a look of approval that warmed her all the way to her toes. "We'll start with social media, then. See if we can discover any clues online. If we can find out what grad program she was in, it shouldn't be too difficult to find her advisor."

"Okay. I'll get going on the computer research tomorrow morning, after Noelle is at school."

Quinn nodded acknowledgement, then his gaze drifted to Ellen. "Even if we find out Brittany's role at EBU, it's only one element. The more important issue is why would she be in your apartment so early in the morning, Ellen?"

"I have no idea," Ellen said stiffly. She pursed her lips. "That is what I asked Christy to help me find out."

Quinn smiled disarmingly and nodded. "I understand, but Patterson is a smart detective. She's going to be focused on that why and digging into the how, if she hasn't started already. What kind of answer do you think she'll come up with?"

"I don't know! I doubt I ever met the girl! I certainly would question how she got my address. And why the daughter of a Calgary oil man would stoop to breaking into my apartment."

"Maybe she didn't break in." Quinn's low, quiet voice slashed through Ellen's rant, leaving her gaping.

Then she rallied. Her voice was cold when she said, "What are you suggesting?"

"Nothing. Everything. Would Brittany Day, daughter of a prominent family, EBU grad student, have the skills to pick a lock?"

"Probably not," Christy said. "Which means someone helped her."

"Or opened the door when she rang," Quinn said, his gaze still focused on Ellen's face.

Her brows snapped together in a frown. "What you are suggesting is absurd. Why would I admit this young woman to my apartment in the pre-dawn hours?"

Quinn drank wine, regarding her over the rim of his glass. "Maybe you admitted her the night before—"

Ellen gasped and her cheeks flushed scarlet. "That's disgusting! You know nothing about me. You have no right to speculate about my private life."

"And maybe you wanted to break off your relationship with her and she threatened to expose you. She was, what? Half your age? Maybe thirty years younger?"

The cat, who had been curled in Christy's lap, sat up. *He's on the wrong track. Aunt Ellen's straight as they come.* His whiskers twitched, distracting him. *Is that shrimp I smell?*

"Yes," Roy said. "It's almost ready."

"For your information, Mr. Armstrong, I am not gay," Ellen said. Her voice was steel. "Nor do I seek romantic partners who are the age of my friends' children." She stood up. "I think it best if I leave now. If you will excuse me?"

"Sit down, Ellen," said Roy, who was dishing the fresh shrimp into a large bowl. "Quinn, come here and cut the bread for me, will you?" He brought the bowl of shrimp to the table and set it down in the center. Then he took both of Ellen's hands in his and looked deep into her eyes. "My son means well, even if he is a little heavy-handed."

Quinn, now on the other side of the counter cutting a loaf of fresh Italian bread, snorted. The cat, whiskers twitching, cautiously put a paw on the edge of the table. Roy ignored them both.

"Quinn is trying to show you the kind of danger you're in, Ellen. And if you think Quinn's questions and assumptions are intrusive, you'll find the questions the police ask unbearable. Better to face them here, amongst friends, and decide how to deal with them."

Ellen said nothing for a moment. Her eyes searched his, while her expression went from hot anger to a vulnerable fear. Then she nodded. "I understand," she said in a voice that had the hint of a shake to it. Slowly she sat back down.

Roy smiled, nodded and turned to the cat, who now had both front paws on the table and was squirming in Christy's grasp. "No filching from the table. I've got a plate set aside for you."

Stormy wriggled free and did a nosedive onto the floor. *Thanks old man. The cat figured there was too much talk and not enough food. I didn't know how long I could hold him. Nice work with Aunt Ellen. By the way, you know she's got the hots for you, don't you?*

Roy went beet red and Christy choked back a laugh. Ellen eyed them both curiously and Quinn sighed as he placed the plate of freshly sliced bread onto the table. Roy put down the plate of shrimp for the cat, had Quinn refill wine glasses and brought two bowls of salad to the table. By the time he said, "Dig in, everyone," Ellen appeared to have forgotten the odd behavior.

"Does Natalie DeBolt know much about her son's friends?" Roy asked as he ladled shrimp onto his plate.

"She and Aaron are quite close, so I would assume so," Ellen said. She pointed to the seafood on Roy's plate. "The shrimp haven't been shelled."

Roy liked to go down to the docks in the old fishing village of Steveston and buy shrimp fresh off the fishing boats tied up there. A quick steam and the shrimp were ready to eat. Add freshly baked bread and you had a feast. In Ellen's world, the Jamieson world, shrimp were used in fine cuisine; cleaned, beheaded, and sauced. "You can eat the shells, and the heads too," Christy said, deciding to be helpful.

Ellen opened her mouth, on the verge of saying something disapproving, Christy thought, then closed it and visibly changed tack.

"Really?" She scooped up three shrimp and put them on her plate. Then she added a piece of bread and a great deal of salad. She eyed the shrimp, but dug into the salad.

"Ellen, why don't you talk to Natalie and see what you can find out about Brittany?" Roy suggested. He popped a shrimp in his mouth, head and all.

Ellen's eyes widened. Then she looked down at her plate. "Yes. Yes, of course." She stabbed her fork into the body of the shrimp. "I intended to phone Natalie anyway, to tell her about the break-in." Her knife hovered over the plate, as if she planned to cut away the offending head and shell. "I see no reason why I would not ask her some questions about the young woman." Instead, she put the shrimp in her mouth, head included, then slowly, almost reluctantly, began to chew.

Christy felt her eyes widen. She looked over at Quinn. Amusement was clearly written on his face. He glanced her way and winked. She wondered if he'd be so cheerful if he'd heard Frank's comment about Ellen's feelings for his father. She pushed the thought away.

"I'll see what I can find out about Brittany's family, especially her father," Quinn said. "He shouldn't be hard to track down." He cleaned a shrimp, shelling and beheading it with his fingers before he ate it. "What about you, Dad?"

"I'll talk to Three and see what he thinks. He retired a couple of years ago and lives on Salt Spring Island now, but he can probably arrange for someone from his former firm to look out for Ellen's interests."

Ellen's eyes widened. "Three?"

"An old friend," Roy said, smiling at her. "He's actually called Trevor Robinson McCullagh the Third. I call him Three because he's got such a pretentious name."

"I know the McCullagh law firm," Ellen said. Her bemused expression said she didn't see anything pretentious about Trevor's name. "How do you know him?"

"My late wife Vivian used to work with him. He provided his services *pro bono* for protesters who got into trouble."

"I see." Ellen cut the head off a shrimp, then scraped off the shell before she put it in her mouth.

Having consumed his portion of shrimp, the cat was now washing his whiskers and Frank was back in the conversation. *Looking into Brittany Day's background is a good start. Finding Aunt Ellen a lawyer is a priority. We can reconvene same time tomorrow and share what we've learned.* Stormy jumped up onto Christy's lap, evidently focused on the shrimp remaining in the bowl.

"How…how managerial," she said as she put the cat back onto the floor.

"Yes, very organized," Ellen said. She beamed at Roy.

Roy smiled back, then winked at Christy. He'd heard Frank's comments too. "And not a bad idea."

CHAPTER 4

When the doorbell rang at one fifteen, Christy was ready to do anything to escape being shut up with Ellen for a minute longer. The worries of yesterday seemed to have been forgotten as Ellen complained about the size of the bedroom she was using, Christy's choice of breakfast foods, the absence of a three-course, beautifully plated, luncheon meal, and Christy's insistence on performing mundane tasks like loading the dishwasher, vacuuming, and laundry. Fifteen minutes before, Christy had suggested Ellen dust the joint living/dining room and received a blank stare in reply.

It was just too much. Christy wanted Ellen to leave, and this after one day and in the midst of a major investigation.

It didn't help that Frank had been broadcasting snarky comments all morning. Content ranged from how Ellen behaved to what she said and her whole attitude toward life. Ellen was blissfully unaware of the comments, but every sneering, bitter observation grated on Christy's nerves.

When she opened the door to discover Quinn on the other side, her heart did a little flip and her breath hitched. He was wearing a leather jacket, jeans and a sweater. Nothing special, but he looked all male to her, and her immediate reaction was one of pleasure.

"Hi," he said. "I wondered if you would like to go for a walk with me?"

There was a faint smile on his mouth and his gaze was filled with intensity. Christy was reminded of the night they had gone to the IHTF gala, when she'd stood in this doorway and kissed him after he'd brought her home. His gaze now was filled with the same smoldering desire that had shaken her that night and had brought a mutual need roaring to the surface.

"I'd love to," she said, glad that the jeans she was wearing hugged her hips and the V-necked sweater she'd chosen that morning was a cashmere and silk blend that caressed her skin and clung in all the right places. "Just let me get my jacket." Her voice sounded low and husky in her ears. Sensual. Something flashed in his eyes and his smile deepened. Her muscles tightened in response. *Keep it light,* she thought, a little desperately. She couldn't kiss Quinn here, in her doorway, with Ellen lurking somewhere in the townhouse. She didn't want to expose her feelings for Quinn and have Frank's aunt tear them apart. They were too new, too fresh to handle a thorough critique by a disdainful in-law.

She shouted to Ellen that she was going for a walk, then shrugged on the jacket and slipped out the door. Before she could close it, paws thundered down the stairs as the cat bolted for the opening.

If you're going out, so am I. Aunt Ellen has been driving me crazy all morning and the cat doesn't like her.

Quinn raised his eyebrows as Stormy rushed past him, then disappeared into the bushes on the opposite side of the street. "Problems?"

Christy closed the door. Quinn took her hand in his as they headed down the steps. The intimate gesture warmed Christy in a way that lightened her mood. She smiled up at him as she said, *"Problems* isn't exactly the right word. Ellen is being a princess who expects to be waited on constantly and Frank is annoyed about everything she does. Stormy isn't happy with her either."

"What's the cat's problem?"

Since the morning when she'd gone to confront Frank's killer and Stormy had tried to communicate her danger to Quinn, he seemed open to the potential that there was something more to the Jamieson family pet. Not that he had fully accepted that Frank's essence had taken up residence in Stormy, it was more that he was willing to suspend judgment.

Christy laughed. "Stormy jumped up on Ellen's lap this morning when she was sitting in the living room. Frank said Stormy expected to have a tummy rub, or at least have his ears scratched, but Ellen just sat there, stiff as a statue and didn't touch him. I think she's cat-phobic. Eventually Stormy jumped off and left her alone." The cat could have been the poster image of an annoyed feline as he stalked away, tail up and shivering with irritation, his back stiff. Ellen didn't seem to care, though, which annoyed Stormy even more. At least, that's what Frank had told her.

She and Quinn were heading up the street now, toward a path through the treed greenbelt behind the townhouse complex. Quinn evidently had a destination in mind. "So Stormy doesn't approve of humans who don't cater to his every need and Frank doesn't like Ellen because she was one of his trustees. How about you?"

They turned on to the dirt path that meandered through the dense trees. It skirted a couple of complexes before it reached a connecting path that led to the school, then continued on to a park with a playground. Beyond that another intersecting path led to an open area with tennis courts, a soccer field and yet another playground. When the kids were out of school it would be busy, but now, in the middle of afternoon classes, Quinn and Christy were pretty much alone, except for the odd new mom pushing a buggy or ambling along with her toddler-aged child.

"She's been driving me crazy. I needed this break," Christy said. The lush conifer woods of a Pacific Northwest rainforest bordered the dirt path and closed around them as they walked. Laced through the evergreen of the spruce, cedar, and pines were the skeletal arms of deciduous trees that had dropped their leaves for the winter. On the ground beneath their feet lay the fading colors of the fallen leaves, the orange and scarlet of maple, the gold of cottonwood and birch.

"Poor sweetheart," Quinn said. He drew her off the path into the trees. Then, sheltered by a large hemlock, the tips of its long branches drooping toward the forest floor, he slipped his arms around Christy's waist and drew her against him.

She gazed up into his eyes to see him studying her expression, searching for her reaction. Putting her hands on his shoulders, she rose up onto her tiptoes, offering herself. His eyes gleamed with something she thought was satisfaction, then his mouth was on hers and her eyes were closing with the pleasure of his touch.

They kissed for a minute or an eternity, making love with their mouths because nothing more was possible at this moment in time. He used teeth and tongue to tease and tempt until Christy was throbbing with a pleasure she couldn't have. When he finally drew away they were both breathing hard.

"You know how much I want you," he said, leaning his forehead on hers.

"Yes, but—"

"I know. You have Noelle and Frank, and now you have Ellen, too. I understand."

An iron restraint echoed in every word and Christy was both torn and touched. She reached up to stroke the dark hair off his forehead. "I'm rebuilding a reputation too," she said huskily. She swallowed hard. "Otherwise I'd arrange for your father to babysit Noelle and I'd ask you to take me to a hotel for a night."

"I don't want a one-night stand with you, Christy. I want more. I want a future." He straightened and with a little laugh, said, "I can wait...I think." He took her hand and they resumed their leisurely walk.

Christy was very aware of his larger, muscled body beside hers. She wanted to lean against him and cuddle closer, but she didn't think it was fair to test his restraint. Seeking a neutral subject, one that would take both their minds off of the demands of their bodies, she said, "I found the program Brittany Day was in, and I have the name of her advisor."

"Well done." The approval in Quinn's eyes made her blush with pleasure. "What was she into?"

"She was enrolled in a collaborative research-based program that has a combined math and chemistry focus. She was a master's-level student, but there are also doctoral students in the program." Christy shook her head as she thought about the languid, bitchy woman she'd last seen at the IHTF gala. "Not exactly what I expected. I also found the names of some of the people she knew through Aaron DeBolt, but I thought I'd approach the advisor first."

"Good idea," Quinn said. They passed the school, quiet now with the children inside their classrooms. "I tracked down her father's company, but I wasn't able to make contact with him. I spoke to his secretary and offered condolences, but she was very protective and wouldn't put me through. I did some digging on the company. It has a good reputation for its business practices, including its environmental policy. Roger Day is considered to be a progressive CEO who runs a clean, well-managed operation."

"Were you able to learn anything about the rest of Brittany's family? Or about her background?" The trees surrounded them again, wrapping them in a cocoon of green quiet. Christy felt as if she and Quinn were the only two people in the universe, a feeling that created a special serenity as they walked, even though they were discussing a murdered girl.

Quinn shook his head in answer to her question. "His personal information is closely guarded and secret. I'll have to dig a little deeper to find it."

But he would. Christy was quite sure of that.

"One thing I did learn. There's plenty of money in the family. The company's last annual report to shareholders cited Day as having a base salary of close to a million dollars. That didn't include his bonus and stock options. I don't think Brittany was suffering a shortage of cash."

"Fits with the way she was dressed at the gala," Christy said. "Her gown was beautiful and probably cost her several thousand. Then there was the jewelry she was wearing and her shoes! Big bucks. Everything she wore shouted money."

"Aaron struck me as the kind of guy who wouldn't bother with someone who didn't have a trust fund behind them."

"You got that one right," Christy said, with a little laugh.

They walked along in silence for a while, aware of each other and communicating mutual desire in the quiet way of the brush of shoulder on shoulder, a shared look, the warmth of hands held. They reached the park and there decided to turn around.

"I wonder if Brittany was a princess, always demanding, worrying about status and her place in things?" Quinn said as they retraced their path. "Or was she was a dedicated, rather naive student who got mixed up in something she didn't know how to handle?"

"I hope her advisor will be able to tell us," Christy replied.

"When you make the appointment with him—or is it a her?"

"Him."

"Okay. When you make the appointment to meet with him, I'll come out to the university with you."

"I hoped you would," Christy said. She smiled up at him and when he smiled back her heart did a little flip.

She sighed when their walk was over and he left her at her door. Spending time with Quinn invoked both pleasure and a guilty confusion in her. She desired him. She enjoyed being with him. She respected him. She thought she was falling for him, and she so wanted that. But they still had not buried

Frank, who lived with her and was in her head every day. And she was Noelle's mom, which she loved, but which also had responsibilities. She wasn't sure how to integrate a man—a lover—into her life at this moment in time.

She was wrestling with these thoughts as she shrugged off her jacket and hung it in the little closet by the front door.

A voice—critical, imperious, and yes, fretful—interrupted her. "You were gone a long time."

She looked up to see Ellen standing at the top of the stairs. The expression on her face was disapproving. Christy resisted the urge to sigh. "It's a beautiful day and I thought I'd take advantage of it."

Ellen sniffed.

Christy wasn't sure whether she disapproved of a person walking in the crisp fall sunshine, or Christy not being there when Ellen wanted her. "What's up?"

"I spoke to Natalie. She is devastated by Brittany's death." Ellen paused. Hesitated in a most un-Ellen like way. "She's coming to visit tomorrow. She'll be staying for lunch."

"Visit? Here?"

Ellen nodded.

"In my house?"

Ellen flushed at the incredulous note in Christy's voice, but she tilted up her chin and said in her arrogant way, "In the Trust's house."

"Oh, my," Christy said, so shocked at the thought of entertaining Natalie DeBolt that she didn't even flinch at the barb about the ownership of the townhouse.

She didn't want to make nice with Natalie, tomorrow or any other day. So it was that later that afternoon, when she called English Bay University and spoke to Dr. Jacob Peiling, Brittany Day's academic advisor, she arranged to meet the man at eleven forty-five in the morning. Since it would take her at least an hour to drive from Burnaby out to the EBU campus on the west side of Vancouver, she would be well away before Natalie arrived.

Thank God.

* * *

Dr. Jacob Peiling, Brittany's academic advisor, was a tall, gangly man with a prominent Adam's apple. He looked younger than Christy expected, with wavy brown hair, a beak of a nose, and glasses he tended to push up on that nose while he spoke. Dressed in jeans and a checked, button front shirt, he could have been in his forties, but Christy knew from his extensive list of publications that he was past fifty. He greeted her and Quinn graciously, urging them to sit in simple metal frame chairs with black leatherette seats and backs.

"You wanted to ask me about Brittany Day," he said, his Adam's apple bobbing disconcertingly. He arched a brow above the heavy brown frame of his glasses. "I don't know how much I can tell you since you're not family."

On the long drive across town to EBU Christy and Quinn had talked about what strategy to use to get Peiling to talk. From her experience with academics, Christy figured a sideways approach was best. Get him chatting, disarm him, see what precious bits of information he dropped. Quinn wasn't sure how far they'd get, but he agreed that it was a way to set the conversation in motion.

"We'd appreciate anything you can tell us, Dr. Peiling," Christy said now. "Brittany's body was found at my aunt's home and she is distraught about it. Not only did a young woman die, but Aunt Ellen doesn't know anything about her."

Peiling looked thoughtful. He gazed above Christy's head at the plasterboard wall behind her and shoved his glasses higher up the bridge of his nose. His office was a large cubicle in a steel-and-glass building constructed in the seventies when universities were doing their best to erase their elitist ivory-tower reputations. Utilitarian inside and out had been the order of the day, and the style hadn't aged gracefully. He said, "She was from Calgary."

Christy nodded encouragingly. Quinn said conversationally, "I understand her father is in the oil business."

Peiling's throat bobbed as he swallowed, and he nodded. "He's a geological engineer of some repute. We went to university together."

Roger Day was an engineer. When he and Jacob Peiling attended university there were only a few institutions in Canada with big-name reputations in the field. A little tingle of hope had Christy saying, "Oh, what university was that?" When he named the institution where both her parents worked, she was able to say, "What a coincidence! My father is in the math department there, and my mom is an English prof."

As she'd hoped, that broke the ice with Peiling. He looked at her with more interest and said, "Brittany was a master's student in the mathematical chemistry project I chair. This would have been her second year in the program. She was an excellent student. Not brilliant, but hardworking and thoughtful. I will miss her."

Somehow Christy couldn't fit the image of Brittany as hardworking scientist that Dr. Peiling was painting with what she knew of the woman. "Did she have problems keeping up with her work?" When Peiling frowned, she changed direction. "I mean, she was a friend of a friend and when I met her socially, she didn't seem academically inclined at all."

He shrugged. "I don't know what she was like away from the university. I just know that here she was a student who was an asset to my research team."

"You mentioned the program was split between two disciplines. What was her focus?" Quinn asked.

"She was a math major." He nodded at Christy, working his glasses up his nose. "Like your father, Mrs. Jamieson. As I said, she was competent, if not inspired. Though inspired wasn't what was required for her part in the project. I needed her to do her work and provide background materials for my PhD students to use."

"So she can be easily replaced," Quinn said.

Christy looked at him, wondering if he was searching for more details or trying to get under Peiling's skin.

The professor's mouth tightened and his throat worked as he swallowed. "Not true," he said finally. "I had great respect for Brittany. As I said, I will miss her." He leaned forward and drew a file folder from a neat stack on the corner of his desk. Apart from the telephone and computer monitor, the folders were the only things that marred its smooth steel and faux-wood surface. "I'm afraid I don't have much more I can tell you."

The words and the action were clear: *we're done here.* Christy moved, ready to rise from the uncomfortable metal chair. Quinn stayed put.

"It's November. Won't you have difficulty recruiting someone to take her place?" He sounded curious, even sympathetic.

Peiling frowned. "There is no doubt that her death will set the program back somewhat. However, I have an excellent team and I know they will put in the extra hours that will now be necessary. The real problem," he said, his voice filled with the disgust of an academic for the administration, "is filling her teaching assistant position. Until she is replaced I will have to run the lab as well as do the lectures."

Quinn pounced on that. His eyes brightened and a hopeful expression dawned on his face. "Brittany was a TA? Did she share an office?"

Peiling's frown deepened and he said, "Well, yes, but…"

"Great. We can talk to the other TAs then. Where did you say the office was?"

"On the third floor, but…"

Christy stood up. "Thank you, Dr. Peiling. It was very good of you to see us today. I know you have a busy schedule." She eased away as Quinn shoved out his hand and shook Peiling's. They escaped from the office before the professor thought to forbid them to visit Brittany's former office.

"What did you think?" Christy asked as they moved off down the hall.

"He doesn't strike me as being capable of the kind of stealth used by the person who broke into Ellen's apartment. Nor do I think he would be able to convince Brittany to come along on a break-and-enter so he could kill her on the terrace."

"Put that way, it's unlikely *anyone* would be guilty."

They reached a stairwell. Quinn paused, his hand on the door. His expression was compassionate as he looked at her. "It's a possibility we have to consider."

"I can't believe Ellen might be guilty of murder," Christy said. Her voice hitched and she sighed. "She not a nice woman, but murder?" She shook her head.

Quinn bent to brush a quick kiss along her lips. "Come on, let's go talk to the office mates. Maybe they'll give us more information than Peiling was prepared to offer."

CHAPTER 5

The third-floor hallway was a long, straight corridor that ran the length of the building. On either side of the linoleum-covered floor were office doors, some open, some closed, all painted a depressing dove gray. The dismal decor carried through to the walls, which sported an ivory shade that had faded to a yellowing cream. The numbers for each office were inscribed on small black plaques, which were affixed to the wall on the handle side of each doorjamb. Below the number sign was the name of the occupant and a small corkboard, apparently used to indicate office hours, or occasionally a change in office hours.

Most of the doors Christy and Quinn walked past were closed, even though the corkboard indicated that the professor lodged within should be available. Occasionally one was open, showing a busily working individual who didn't even look up as they passed.

When they reached their destination, room 317, the door was ajar. The nameplate indicated that the residents were Lorne Cossi, PhD candidate, Rochelle Dasovic, also a PhD candidate and Bradley Neale, a lowly MS student. The title of the program they were registered in was there as well. Brittany Day's name was nowhere to be seen.

Quinn took the lead, pushing open the grim gray door and walking boldly into the room. Christy followed in his wake, looking around curiously.

The room was about the size of her bedroom, perhaps sixteen by twenty feet. Four desks were crammed into the space. There were no partitions to separate the work areas and provide privacy. Everything that happened in this room was out in the open.

The desks were standard office style: double pedestal, steel-frame construction, a gunmetal gray that was a couple of shades darker than the door. They looked as if they had perhaps once been issued to secretaries or other support staff but had been discarded, considered too battered to use any longer. Now they were hand-me-downs suitable only for the lowest of the low—students.

Opposite the door, the exterior wall was mainly windows. There was little view to speak of, but lots of light. A dark-haired woman sat at a desk pushed into the corner made by an inside and exterior wall. She was hunched over a laptop and didn't look up as Quinn and Christy entered.

Kitty-cornered from the woman, at a desk just inside the door, a young man was seated. He straightened and said politely, "Can I help you?"

Quinn nodded crisply, his tone no-nonsense. "We're friends of Brittany Day. Dr. Peiling told us she worked out of this office."

The young man's friendly expression closed. He nodded, pointing to the desk across from him. "She sat there."

The woman looked up, her attention caught. She shifted in her seat to view them without craning her neck.

Quinn's gaze flicked to the desk, took in its blank, empty look, then returned to his scrutiny of the young man. "I'm sorry. I didn't introduce myself. I'm Quinn Armstrong, and this is Christy." He left off her last name. They were searching for information about a woman who had provided an alibi related to Frank Jamieson's death. Christy figured Quinn didn't want either of Brittany's office mates to hold back because of her relationship to a murdered man.

"Bradley Neale—Brad," the young man said. "I'm one of the chemistry students working on Dr. Peiling's project." He pointed to the woman. "That's Rochelle Dasovic."

Quinn nodded acknowledgement. Christy said, "If you have a few minutes, we'd like to ask you some questions."

Rochelle stood up. She was tall and heavy-boned. The jeans and cable-knit sweater she wore gave her body a bulky look. "Sorry. No time. I have a lab that starts in fifteen minutes and it's clear across campus. Maybe Brad will help."

"Glad to," Bradley said. He shot Rochelle a disapproving look.

"Will you have time later in the day? Or tomorrow?" Quinn asked Rochelle.

She hesitated, then shrugged. "I have office hours at four o'clock this afternoon. You could come back then."

It was on the tip of Christy's tongue to say four wasn't possible, but Quinn smiled that gorgeous smile of his and said, "That's great. We'll talk to Bradley now and I'll come back to see you at four."

Rochelle's eyes widened, then she swallowed and nodded. She pushed her laptop into a bag and followed it with a collection of books, then slung the strap over her shoulder. "Okay. See you later." She blew past Christy and Quinn, shooting Quinn an appreciative glance as she went. Then she was gone, leaving them alone with the young man.

Bradley Neale had thin dark hair, gray eyes all but hidden behind thick lenses in metal-rimmed glasses, and a straggly beard that gave his face a surprising boost of interest. Christy thought he looked like an open, honest person. She hoped they'd have better luck extracting information about Brittany from him than they had from Dr. Peiling.

Quinn gestured toward the empty desk. "I didn't think Brittany was such a neat freak. Her desk looks like it's been cleared out."

The gloomy expression on Brad's face deepened. "Peiling had Lorne clear it out as soon as he heard about

Brittany's death. He said it was because he needed to send her things to her parents, but I think he wants to have it ready for whoever replaces her in the project."

"That's harsh," Quinn said.

Neale nodded. "I don't think Dr. Peiling meant to be hurtful, but Brittany was a real asset to our group. We all miss her like crazy."

Quinn smiled as he raised his eyebrows, inviting further confidences. "That says positive things about Brittany, considering the small size of this office space."

Brad snorted. "It's an easy place to get on each other's nerves, all right. I can't tell you how many times Brittany had to step in and ask Lorne to tone it down."

"Lorne likes to bitch about stuff?"

"Lorne finds fault with a sunny day," Brad said.

There was an edge of bitterness in his voice and Christy wondered why. Had the apparently cranky Lorne Cossi bullied his younger colleague? Or was Neale just an envious sort who clashed with those further up the ladder than he?

"Lorne had a thing for Brittany," Brad continued. His hand tightened on the pen he was holding. "She made use of it to keep him in line." He shrugged, but there was nothing indifferent in the rest of his body language.

It looked to Christy as if Brad had forced himself to make the casual gesture, but she couldn't be sure.

"How about the other person, the woman who just left— Rochelle, wasn't it?" Quinn asked. "How did she get along with Brittany?"

"She was jealous of Brittany's looks. Rochelle is good at her work, but she's not that attractive," Brad said, with the supreme indifference of a male who wasn't interested. "She thought Brittany focused too much on appearance and not enough on math equations."

"Sounds like a relationship with a lot of potential problems," Christy said. She smiled at Brad, inviting more confidences, even though she thought that Rochelle might have good reason for her dislike of the beautiful Brittany.

She must have succeeded, because Brad was nodding emphatically. All he said, though, was, "Brittany and I spend the most time here. The other two come and go. Between us we made it work."

Brad sounded like a man bragging about a relationship that wasn't. There was a wistful look in his eyes that said he wished he'd been more to Brittany than a co-worker who shared an office, particularly now, when deepening the relationship would never be possible. Christy knew she could work with both of those emotions. She pushed admiration into her voice and said, "I guess you know a lot about Brittany's comings and goings."

She wasn't surprised when Brad preened. "We were close. When Brittany needed help, she came to me."

Quinn, who was leaning against Rochelle's desk, said, "What kind of help did Brittany need?" His relaxed stance and position on the other side of the room was meant to be open and invite confidences. It worked.

Brad, whose focus had been on the much closer Christy, glanced at him. He straightened and thrust out his chest. "She'd ask me to fill in for her from time to time. I was happy to do it."

Brad's focus was chemistry. Brittany's had been math. How could Brad act as her stand-in in the rarified atmosphere of an academic community when they were not even in the same discipline? The skeptical question hovered on the tip of Christy's tongue, but she didn't voice it. She sensed that there was still more relevant information to be got from Neale and it would never come in a critical atmosphere.

"Did she do that a lot?" Quinn asked in that same casual, interested tone.

"Often enough. She had a busy life." Bradley shrugged. "I didn't mind helping her. She was generous and appreciative."

Quinn's brows rose. Christy guessed that he was thinking about Brittany as she had been at the IHTF Gala. Bitchy. Mean. Snarky. Generous she was not.

"Did you help her out the night Frank Jamieson died?" Quinn asked.

Silence fell after he asked the question. Neale stared at him, the open, grieving expression gone from his face, replaced by a cautious calculation. "Why do you ask?"

Quinn straightened and moved a few steps closer to Brad's desk. "Because Brittany Day provided Aaron DeBolt with an alibi for that night and I think that's why she was killed." Quinn's gaze bored into the other man's face. Brad didn't flinch. "I think the alibi was a lie and she was really here, working or teaching."

Brad began shaking his head before Quinn had finished speaking. "You're wrong. She was supposed to supervise the project lab that night. It's open twenty-four seven and there's always one of us there. We take turns and it was hers that night. She told me she wasn't feeling well and asked if I could cover for her. Of course, I said yes." He looked momentarily downcast as he realized he'd been played. Brittany hadn't been unwell. Her affidavit said she'd been having wild drug-fueled sex with Aaron DeBolt.

The door slammed open, hitting the wall with a bang, before it bounced back. They all jumped and Brad's expression swiftly turned from downcast to apprehensive to carefully blank as a tall, beautifully proportioned man sauntered into the room. He was wearing a leather jacket, open to show a tight T-shirt over toned abs and snug jeans that emphasized his lean hips. He moved to the desk beside Bradley's, one of the two by the windows, and tossed the backpack he carried on one shoulder onto it. Dark blue eyes under arched black brows scrutinized Quinn for a moment, then moved on to Christy.

When he smiled at her the smile was devastating. Wide, generous, friendly, it shone out of a handsome face that was as beautifully proportioned as his body. "I'm Lorne Cossi. Are you Brad's students?"

Christy was the one who replied. She took the lead because the gorgeous Lorne Cossi was staring right at her.

His look was appreciative and all male and she figured he'd respond better to questions from her than from Quinn. "No, we're friends of Brittany Day's. We're here to find out about her EBU experience."

Bradley closed his laptop with a snap and shoved it into a backpack. "I'm going to the lab," he said, not looking at anyone.

"See you," Lorne said. His tone was dismissive, though the charming smile never wavered.

Christy looked from Lorne to Brad. Something was definitely going on between the two men. Brad couldn't wait to escape from the office and, although Lorne's expression was friendly, his eyes were cold as he tracked Brad's movements. She cocked a brow at Quinn, wondering if he was seeing the same bad blood between the two that she was. There was an opportunity here to mine the animosity, but she thought to do so they would have to separate.

Quinn's mouth tightened as he caught her look and interpreted it, then she saw him deliberately relax. He'd got her message and he'd play along, but he didn't like leaving her alone with Cossi. Still, he was prepared to do it.

He looked at Brad. "Why don't I walk over to the lab with you?" he said. "I've got a couple more questions and I'd like to see the lab setup."

Bradley nodded abruptly. "Sure." He slung the backpack over his shoulder, then, head down, he hustled out the door.

Quinn followed, leaving Christy alone with the outrageously handsome Lorne Cossi.

"So you're a friend of Brit's," Lorne Cossi said. He looked her over, from the top of her head to her feet. His gaze lingered too long on her breasts and then— disconcertingly—on her groin for her comfort and when his gaze drifted back to her face there was something unnerving in the depths of his dark blue eyes. "Frankly, you don't seem her type."

Christy flushed. She'd met guys like Cossi before. Arrogant, self-absorbed jerks who assumed every female in sight was a sexual plaything there for a man's enjoyment. "And what was her 'type'?"

Cossi smiled slowly. It wasn't a nice smile. "Silly women who'll do anything for a lay. Especially if they can get high at the same time." He cocked his head. "You now, you look disturbingly sober."

Christy figured he'd meant that as an insult. She thought it was actually a compliment, given who it came from. Resisting the urge to cross her arms over her breasts, she leaned back against Bradley Neale's desk and stared Lorne Cossi in the eyes. "If you bothered to listen, you'd find that people act out of 'type' all the time."

Cossi raised his brows. There was a contemptuous curl to his upper lip that said he didn't like backtalk from uppity women.

Christy allowed herself a small smile. "Take Brittany, for example. Here she was, EBU grad student, privileged daughter of a wealthy Calgary family, and a party girl with the likes of Aaron DeBolt, a man whose reputation doesn't bear scrutiny. Now tell me, Mr. Cossi, what exactly was Brittany's 'type'?"

His eyes lit with temper for a moment, then he too leaned back against a desk. He shoved his hands in his pockets before he said mildly, "Brittany Day was a nasty little tease who came on to every man she met."

"Including you?"

"Including me."

"Did you take her up on her offer?" Christy could hardly believe she'd asked that, but she thought that if she didn't it would tell Lorne Cossi that she was afraid of him and then who knew what would happen? As long as he believed she was immune to him, she figured she was safe. If he knew she was vulnerable, she was quite sure he would pounce.

His mouth quirked up into a very real smile and he laughed. "What do you think?"

"I think you did." *Deep breath, Christy. Deep breath.*

"And you'd be right." He straightened. Took a step forward.

Christy didn't move. But she wanted to. Oh, how much she wanted to.

"If a sexy piece like Brittany Day offers me her body, who am I to refuse?"

Another step. At this rate he'd cross the small space in another couple of moments and he'd be right in front of her. In her space. Intimidating her. Maybe even taking it further. The desire to flee was strong.

She glared at him. But she straightened too, sending him a message. "That's pretty cold."

He shrugged, but he stopped. "There was something dark in Brit and she pulled it out in other people too. She liked Ecstasy and Meth. She tried to get me hooked on the stuff."

"Did she?"

This time he shook his head. "No. No way am I polluting my brain with that kind of junk."

The answer sounded honest to Christy's ears. Lorne Cossi was a PhD student. He probably had aspirations of entering the academic world as a professor. Frying his brain wouldn't help him achieve his goal.

"Have you shared this office space with Brittany since she started at EBU?"

The question didn't fit with the previous ones. Cossi eyed her thoughtfully and paused to think before he answered. Why? It wasn't a hard question. It was a yes or no answer.

"Yes," he said, finally. "Rochelle and I set up the office the year we both began. Brad came next, then Brittany."

"It's a small space. An easy place for everyday habits to become irritating. Tempers tend to flare when people have to share limited resources."

His expression hardened and anger glinted in his eyes. "Are you accusing me of Brit's murder?"

Was she? Until he reacted with such heat she hadn't actually thought of it. She shrugged, but didn't confirm or deny.

Lorne Cossi chose to take her shrug as acknowledgement. His temper flared hotter. "Brittany Day was a lazy bitch who used her body and her family connections to smooth her path. She was entitled and manipulative. Worse, from my point of view, she wasn't even all that good as a mathematician."

"Then why was she here?" Christy wasn't sure she believed Cossi, though he sounded genuinely annoyed.

He flung himself away, turning toward the window. "Jesus Christ! Don't you get it?" he said. "She was sleeping with our fearless leader, the good Dr. Peiling. Why else?"

CHAPTER 6

"He gave me the creeps," Christy said as Quinn was chauffeuring her from the EBU campus to the closest Skytrain station. He'd wanted to drive her back to Burnaby, then return to meet with Rochelle Dasovic, but Christy had told him she was fine using public transit. The walk from the nearest station to the townhouse would do her good and give her time to think.

His hands tightened on the steering wheel as she told him more about Lorne Cossi. "I shouldn't have left you alone with him."

Christy shook her head. "How could you know? He looked so non-threatening when he came into the office."

He had looked like a damned smug male on the prowl. Quinn gritted his teeth and tried to remember that Christy valued her independence. "Bradley Neale doesn't like him. I got an earful while we walked over to the lab."

"I'm not surprised. I bet Cossi bullies him. Bradley is probably putting up with it because he has to, and because he knows that Cossi will leave eventually."

"Stupid way to live."

"I suppose," Christy said.

Out of the corner of his eye, Quinn saw her shrug. He glanced over at her, risking a quick look despite the bumper-to-bumper traffic. She was staring straight ahead, her expression that blank mask he'd seen her use when dealing with the Jamieson trustees. He didn't consider the way Bradley Neale dealt with Lorne Cossi the same as how Christy had handled her life as the wife of the Jamieson heir, but maybe she did. Which meant that he'd hurt her. Inadvertently, sure, but that didn't mean his words hadn't stung.

He reached over and covered her hand with his. He squeezed gently and she turned her hand so she could clasp his. The action told him she was okay, that she understood what he'd meant, even if his delivery stank. The gesture was so quiet, so intimate, that his heart did a little flip. A red light halted the heavy Broadway traffic. He turned his head so he could see her face, then he smiled at her. She smiled back. The expression lit up her eyes and eased the tension from her face. Suddenly all was right with his world.

The light changed and they crawled forward again. "Do you think Cossi was sleeping with Brittany?" he asked.

"Oh, yeah," Christy said. "He had that whole conceited predator thing going. Yeah, he was sleeping with her, but I don't think she was the one who did the seducing."

"He came on to her."

"Absolutely. I'm not sure what to think about his accusation that she was also sleeping with Peiling, though. When we talked to Peiling, I got the impression that there was something more than he was telling us, but that Brittany was his mistress? I'm not sure that was it."

"I agree. Peiling was covering up something," Quinn said.

The Skytrain station loomed one set of lights ahead. Christy flipped off her seatbelt, leaned over and kissed his cheek. "Drop me at the corner. I'll cross with the lights."

He nodded.

"See you at home." The light turned red. Quinn stopped. Christy hopped out of the car and onto the sidewalk. Then she sprinted across the street to the station. He drove around the block and headed back to EBU.

His first stop was the third-floor TA office where he hoped to find Lorne Cossi still at his desk. The door was locked and Cossi nowhere in evidence, which annoyed him. He'd wanted to let Cossi know that Christy was not only off limits, but also not without allies.

He had an hour and a half to kill before he met with Rochelle Dasovic, so he headed to the campus library and settled down in front of a computer to do some research on Dr. Jacob Peiling. He was particularly interested in the man's scientific publications, so he dug into the university's scholarly databases to see what he could find.

It was a profitable interlude. He discovered that Peiling had worked hard to gain status and respect, publishing paper after paper in his first few years at the university. His work had been well received, and although he was not in the forefront of his field, he was considered capable enough to be offered tenure. Once his academic position was secure, the flood of academic literature stopped. He continued to publish, but now he usually loaned his name to papers written by the students working under him, rather than producing his own work.

Quinn also discovered that Peiling was married, had three children and was on the boards of several local charities. Putting all the data together, his research pointed to a man who had worked hard to further his career. Once he'd reached a position he was satisfied with, though, Peiling had stopped pushing, and instead had chosen to make the best of what he'd already achieved. Would a man like that risk everything by having an affair with one of his students? Quinn's gut told him no, but it also told him that Peiling had been keeping something back. If not an extra-marital affair, then what?

He considered this as he walked across campus, but he came to no conclusion. The TA office was locked when he reached it, so he propped up the wall with his shoulder and worked his smartphone. Creative waiting was a skill he'd mastered long ago.

It was four thirty when Rochelle Dasovic breezed down the hallway. Her steps hesitated when she saw him waiting there, but that momentary pause was the only indication she had reservations about the meeting. As he straightened, she lifted her chin and, head high, marched forward. She unlocked the door, pushing it wide, and Quinn followed her in.

"Thanks for seeing me," he said, as she set her shoulder bag onto her desk.

She nodded jerkily. "You wanted to talk about Brittany." She bent over her bag, removing her laptop. Her long dark hair flowed forward, hiding her features.

"We knew her through Aaron DeBolt," Quinn said. He let the simple statement hang, wondering what kind of reaction DeBolt's name would generate in this world so very different from his own.

"Oh, Aaron!" Rochelle tossed back her hair so it flowed over her shoulders.

It was a coquettish movement, at odds with her no-nonsense style and clothing choices. Quinn had a sense of a woman who wished she was alluring to a wealthy playboy like DeBolt, but knew she wasn't. Pity stirred. Then he reminded himself that she was better off well away from DeBolt and everything he was.

"Brittany loved Aaron, but he just used her." Rochelle said. Her lip rose in a sneer. "She freely gave him what everyone else had to pay for."

Shock shivered through Quinn. There was jealousy in Rochelle's voice, and a meanness in her words he had not expected. He frowned at her, but she paid no attention as she unloaded her bag. Her heavy fall of hair slipped back over her shoulder to hide her features and disguise her expression.

"Are you saying that Brittany sold…er…sex?" He couldn't quite disguise the dubious note in his voice. There was nothing in her background to indicate that she had ever had the need or desire to resort to taking payment for sex.

Rochelle looked up impatiently. Her lips were pursed, her jaw tight. "Yes."

Quinn scrutinized her. There was anger in her expression now and it put him on firmer ground. There was something between the two women. He just had to find out what. "That's a pretty heavy accusation. Do you have any facts to support it?"

"What are you, the police?"

"No." He watched her redden, her skin stained pink from her collarbone all the way up to her cheekbones. Embarrassment? But why? Because she'd identified a colleague as a hooker, or at best a call girl? Or because she'd fabricated the allegation and had no information to back it up?

She looked away, letting her gaze drift around the room as she gestured with one hand. "Look at this place. It's tiny. We each can hear whatever the others say. There are no secrets here."

Possibly true, but…"So what did you hear that made you think Brittany was selling her body?"

Rochelle shrugged. She was still flushed and she couldn't meet his gaze. "It was late one afternoon. There were only the two of us here. Brittany's phone rang and I saw her glance my way, then turn so her back was to me."

Quinn could visualize the scene as she described it. The beautiful Brittany hunching over her phone, speaking softly as she tried to keep her conversation private, while Rochelle, full of irrational resentment, listened avidly.

"She thought I had my earbuds in, but I didn't. I'd taken them out a few minutes before because they were hurting my ears. I heard her say that she wouldn't go to his place. That he had to come to her, because she didn't like waking up in a man's bed." Rochelle's face was now scarlet. "Then she said, 'It will cost you. Yes, that's the price.'" Shuddering, Rochelle added, "I was shocked. I didn't expect it of Brittany."

"Why?"

"Because she was gorgeous." The words were a simple statement of fact. Quinn guessed that Brittany had the looks Rochelle always wanted, and to Rochelle's mind, Brittany had misused them. "And because she was rich. She didn't need the money and she certainly didn't need to worry about finding men."

Quinn knew all about the heirs of very wealthy people who had no money to speak of. Frank Jamieson had been one and he'd gone to extreme measures to get his hands on ready cash. Aaron DeBolt was another. Perhaps Brittany Day suffered from the same complaint. "DeBolt did a lot of drugs. Maybe Brittany was into them too and needed more cash than she could lay her hands on in order to keep up with him."

Rochelle's shoulders shifted again and she stared out the window past the parking lot to the gleam of ocean beyond. "Maybe. Lorne thought so. And he should know."

An interesting way to phrase that thought. Quinn said nothing and waited for her to elaborate.

Rochelle sat down at her desk. She flipped open her laptop, hesitated, then turned in her seat to face Quinn. "I don't like to admit this, but she went to the bathroom one day and left her phone here. A text came in while she was gone and, well, I read it."

"What did it say?" Quinn asked. He kept his expression interested and his tone neutral. Rochelle Dasovic had been snooping and she was feeling guilty. He wanted to pry as much as he could out of her before she decided that she was doing more damage to herself than to Brittany by telling him what she'd found.

"It was part of a whole dirty conversation. I couldn't tell who the other person was, but he—I think it was a he—was telling her what he would do to her body the next time they were together. I think he liked rough sex. And from her replies, I think Brittany liked it too."

"What happened when she came back to the office?"

"She saw me paging through the conversation." Rochelle's lips thinned. "She got really mad and started shouting. She became so abusive I had to leave." She set her jaw, as if she was shutting a door. She clearly wasn't going any further on that subject.

"How was Brittany as a student?"

"If you mean, how much did she contribute to the program, not much. She did her turn at the lab from time to time, but usually she got Brad to take her place. He's such a sap. He had the hots for her so bad he'd do anything she asked." She glanced at Quinn, then away. "Now, I'm sorry, I've got some calculations I need to work on."

"Thanks for your time," he said.

She nodded and settled in to her work. She didn't turn around as he left the office.

On his way back to his car, Quinn thought about Rochelle Dasovic. Unless he missed his mark she was envious of Brittany's looks, her money, and her way with men. That envy had hardened into a nasty jealousy that influenced her interactions with Brittany and colored her perception of the other woman to the point that they'd fought, at least verbally. The question was, had her jealousy gone from dislike and open hostility to the kind of passionate anger that lead to violence?

CHAPTER 7

Christy made it back to Burnaby with time enough time to stop in at the townhouse and drop off her purse before she had to pick Noelle up from school. Unfortunately she'd forgotten that Natalie DeBolt was lunching with Ellen.

At her house. In her kitchen. In her space.

She was rudely reminded of Natalie's continued presence as she climbed the steps to the front door.

She's still in there.

Crouched in a corner of the small porch was Stormy the Cat. His body was tense and his tail lashed. He looked ready to launch himself at anything that moved. She wondered aloud if Frank was goading the cat to attack Natalie when she finally emerged from the townhouse.

No, I'm not. Frank sounded testy. Irritated that she would even think such a thing of him.

Like the cat she hovered on the porch, debating whether or not to go inside. She didn't have to drop her purse before picking up Noelle. She could just tromp back down the stairs and continue on to the school. She'd be a bit early, but that was okay. It would show Mrs. Morton, Noelle's prickly teacher—who still wasn't convinced that Christy was the proper person to have the care and responsibility of a child—that she was diligent and conscientious.

Yeah, she liked that idea. Flaunt her good behavior at the same time as she avoided an encounter with one of the people she liked least in the world. She turned to head back down the steps.

The cat bounded to its feet. *Where are you going, Chris? Never mind, it doesn't matter. I'll come with you.*

Not exactly what she had in mind, but…She knelt down, opened her large, hobo-style purse and said, "Hop in."

Stormy, who didn't like confined spaces, considered this for a moment. Then, apparently encouraged by Frank, he slowly, with picky deliberation, stepped into the bag.

It was their mutual downfall. Christy was straightening, the purse full of cat tucked under one arm, when the door opened and Natalie DeBolt emerged. She was wearing killer heels and a flirty dress with a tight bodice that boasted a plunging neckline that exposed the tops of her breasts. A short skirt hugged a firm butt and exposed long legs. It wasn't the kind of dress Christy would have chosen for an at-home lunch with a friend, but she and Natalie rarely agreed on any subject, so she told herself not to be judgmental. Ellen followed Natalie onto the porch. Her pantsuit was a miracle of tailored elegance, from the crisply pressed slacks to the slim-fitting jacket that mimicked the cut of a man's suit. Another example of an outfit Christy wouldn't have chosen.

Frank swore and the cat's head disappeared inside the purse. Natalie blinked, looking confused as if she wasn't sure she'd seen what she just saw.

Ellen's mouth tightened. "That cat!"

"Hello, Natalie," Christy said. She didn't add a polite *nice to see you again* because it wasn't. "Ellen, I was just on my way to pick up Noelle. I'll be back in about half an hour." She'd take Noelle and whatever friends she wanted to bring along to the park. Anything to avoid time spent with Natalie DeBolt.

"Darling!" Natalie said effusively, with unexpected delight. "We do not see enough of you!" She leaned toward Christy, at the last minute trading her usual air kiss for an actual embrace and kiss on Christy's cheek.

Christy stiffened and inside the purse, Stormy growled.

Natalie pulled away to perform the same hug and cheek kiss with Ellen. "I must run, darling. Thank you so much for lunch and showing me this quaint little house. So cute!"

Ellen embraced her back. "Are you sure you can't stay longer, Natalie? I feel adrift out here in the suburbs."

The fashionable sneer in Ellen's voice rubbed Christy the wrong way. "Don't worry, Ellen. Your condo will be cleaned soon, then you'll be able to return to it." She smiled the empty smile she'd perfected over the years as the wife of the Jamieson heir. Okay, she was being mean and shouldn't have said what she'd said, but she couldn't resist. If Ellen didn't like it here on Burnaby Mountain, she could always move out.

Ellen shot her a cool glance. "I will never live in that dwelling again. Besides," she added, almost as an afterthought, "I've been traumatized. I need family around me."

"Of course you do, darling! Have I told you how brave I think you are? Poor Brittany. Such a sweet thing. So refreshingly innocent."

Brittany Day? The grad student into drugs and wild sex with multiple partners she had been learning about at EBU today? "Are you talking about the Brittany Day who was Aaron's girlfriend, Natalie?" Christy asked.

Natalie's expression twisted into distress. She nodded. "Yes. She was with Aaron—thank God!—the day poor Frank…Well, anyway, she was able to reassure the police that Aaron was with her that night and not out harming Frank as he's been accused of. I don't know *what* will happen now. I am so afraid that Aaron will be wrongly convicted because she's gone."

In a minute the damned woman would start to cry. Revulsion flooded Christy and urged her to get going. Then the cat's head popped out of her bag. She could feel outrage in every tense muscle and clutched the purse more tightly. As she held the cat still, intent on keeping it from leaping out of the purse, Frank's fury vibrated through the animal's body.

Her bastard of a son helped murder me and she dares—DARES—to deny it in my house? In front of me? To my aunt? To my wife?!

The cat's legs began to churn and he hissed. Christy held on more tightly, afraid Stormy would burst from the bag and attack Natalie the way he'd attacked Aaron just a few weeks ago during her search to prove that Frank had been murdered.

Natalie stepped away, looking horrified. The cat's hiss turned into a yowl of rage. Christy moved to one side of the porch to let Natalie escape down the stairs.

As she passed, she shot Christy a look, much more like the ones Christy was used to receiving from her. When she reached the walk, she paused and said, "Aaron mentioned that your cat was rabid. I see that he didn't exaggerate." She minced off, hips swinging in a sashaying stride that was all woman, heading toward the visitor's parking on the far side of the complex.

"That display was inexcusable," Ellen said, watching her go, outrage in her voice.

Christy glanced at her watch. "And I'm going to be late if I don't hustle." She opened the bag and set it down. "Do you want to stay or come with me?"

Ellen took this question to be addressed to her. She sniffed. "Although it is hardly a *warm* invitation, I will come with you. I would like to see Noelle's school."

The cat shook himself all over and jumped out of the bag. *If she's coming, I'm not. Besides, Stormy is upset. He wants to hunt for mice. Or birds, but he never catches birds. Mice are dumb.*

"Right." Christy resisted the urge to add, *have fun*. Ellen wouldn't understand. So she simply said, "Let's go."

There was a little fuss while Ellen locked up, but they still reached the school before the kids were released for the day. *Bonus*, Christy thought, waiting for Noelle's classroom door to open. It always made a good impression on the teacher when the parents arrived early.

When the door opened a minute later and the kids piled out, Christy couldn't help a sinking feeling when she didn't see Noelle in the doorway. She waited for the torrent to ebb, then she motioned for Ellen. "Noelle must still be inside."

"Of course she is," Ellen said briskly. "She's a Jamieson. She wouldn't indulge in the kind of undisciplined behavior these little…"

A word hovered on her tongue, unspoken. Christy could almost hear it. *Savages. Barbarians. Peasants. Hooligans.* Any would do. She waited for Ellen to blurt it out.

"Children," Ellen said with a commendable show of restraint. "These little children are behaving rather wildly, don't you think?"

Christy shrugged. "No, I don't. They've been cooped up all afternoon. They just want to stretch their legs and let off some steam." She didn't wait for an answer or bother to see if Ellen followed her as she headed inside.

There she found Noelle sitting at her desk, a long-suffering look on her face. "Mommy. The social services lady came to visit again. And she told me I had to wait here for you. *Again.*"

Joan Shively, the child services worker, stepped forward from the desk at the head of the classroom where she had been talking to Mrs. Morton. She smiled thinly. "Good afternoon, Mrs. Jamieson."

Christy frowned at her. "I thought I'd cleared up the charges against me. They were bogus, laid by the very people who were embezzling my late husband's trust fund." She didn't look at Ellen. She hoped her ears were burning. Ellen had been part of that scam and she'd almost succeeded in tearing Christy and Noelle apart.

Shively sniffed. "You know we have to be careful, Mrs. Jamieson. The documents you provided were quite detailed—"

"They were conclusive!" Christy said, indignant.

"Perhaps." When Christy glared at her and opened her mouth to rebut, Shively said hastily, "Probably! But when children's lives are at stake, we have to be sure! I will be monitoring your family for at least several months. You need to be aware of that."

Mrs. Morton said, "I, for one, applaud the policy. You can never be too careful when it comes to children's happiness."

There wasn't much Christy could retort to that, so she merely nodded.

Ellen, who had been an observer of the conversation to this point, chose to intervene. "Happiness may be something we all wish for children, but it is not the school's duty to impart it. Schools are places of learning. And discipline." She fixed the teacher with a steely look. "The children I observed evacuating your classroom were not disciplined in any way. I see that as a failure. *Your* failure."

Christy saw Noelle's eyes widen and her mouth open in an "O" of fascinated approval. At the same time the teacher's expression turned to offended disbelief. Shively's mouth hardened and her eyes narrowed.

Time to get out of here while she still could. "Come on, kiddo," Christy said. "Is your backpack ready to go?" Noelle nodded, still wide-eyed. "Good." She held out her hand and Noelle took it. "Ellen?" she said with more than a hint of command in her voice.

"Who are you?" Shively said.

"I am Ellen Jamieson. Christy should have introduced me." She shot Christy a look of disapproval.

Christy ignored it. "Let's go, everyone."

"You're one of the trustees," Shively said. "You laid the claim against Mrs. Jamieson." She sounded excited, as if she'd just struck a mother lode of golden information.

Ellen must have heard that almost avaricious glee as well, for she raised her head a little higher and assumed the kind of look that usually made people quite aware that they were dirt under her feet. "I certainly did not. That was done by my co-trustees, Edward Bidwell and Gerry Fisher. I was not informed of the action."

"Ha!" said Shively.

Ellen's eyes narrowed. "You don't believe me."

"I do not."

Ellen raised a brow, curled her lip and looked down her nose at the unfortunate Joan Shively. "I am not surprised. You do not appear to be a perceptive woman. Or, indeed, an intelligent one. Christy! Is Noelle ready to leave yet?"

Already on her feet, Noelle said, "Yes, Aunt Ellen!" She was grinning hugely. Clearly this was the best entertainment she'd had all day.

Anxious to be gone before the battle worsened, Christy said, "Good-bye, Ms. Shively. I promise you, I am taking good care of Noelle. Goodnight, Mrs. Morton." She grabbed Noelle's hand and headed for the door without waiting to see if Ellen followed.

CHAPTER 8

R oy Armstrong clapped his old friend on the shoulder as the pair indulged in a manly hug in the small front hall of his townhouse. "Thanks for coming, Three."

Trevor Robinson McCullagh the Third, known only to Roy Armstrong as "Three," returned the hug and back slap. "My pleasure," he said. His voice was raspy, the casualty of years of courtroom dramatics, too many cigarettes, and an over-indulgence in strong liquors.

The greetings completed, they both stepped back. Roy took a moment to inspect his old friend. Trevor was looking healthier than he had in years. His hair was longer than it used to be. More silver than black now, it was still thick and there was a healthy sheen to it. His blue eyes were clear, his color good under the three-day-old stubble that was more a result of not bothering to shave than a fashion statement. He was dressed in faded blue jeans and a plaid shirt under a leather bomber jacket, an outfit that was similar to Roy's black jeans and dark blue shirt.

He looked, Roy thought, at peace. "Granola culture agrees with you," he said, grinning.

Trevor shot him a frowning look that said more than words. "Flakes can be amusing in small doses and when they're in conflict with suits, but *en masse?* They do good works and raise pigs."

Cancer had driven Trevor into an early retirement and the relative quiet of Salt Spring Island four years before. The rural life might have sent his illness into remission, but he evidently had never acclimatized to the alternative viewpoints of the other refugees from the city who populated his new island home.

"Pigs?" Roy proceeded up the half staircase that led into living room. "Bedroom's upstairs, but why don't you drop your bag here and we'll have a coffee?"

"Pigs," Trevor said firmly as he deposited his suitcase against the wall at the top of the stairs. "My next-door neighbor has a perfectly nice five-acre property that includes a beautifully renovated century home and a barn that was converted into a garage."

"Where do the pigs come in?" Roy asked as he entered in the kitchen; Trevor was a few steps behind.

"The madman converted the garage back to a barn and added pigs."

There was a story here, Roy thought, and it didn't deserve coffee. He went over to the counter area that housed a set of canisters his wife once used to store flour and other similar kitchen staples. They were pottery, whimsically designed in the shape of trees, the trunks providing the storage and the leafy branches the lids. They had been given to Vivien by a grateful tree hugger she'd defended back in their protect-the-rainforest days. He lifted the lid on the jar marked "Tea" and drew out the makings for a joint. He stashed his weed there because Quinn never drank tea. It was the perfect hiding place.

He turned and showed the items to Trevor, raising his brows in question.

"This is how you make coffee?" Trevor said.

He sounded incredulous. Affronted, even. Had life on Salt Spring changed him that much?

"I can make coffee…if that's what you want." Roy proceeded to roll a joint. He was going to indulge, even if

Trevor stuck to the straight and narrow.

"I quit when I went to Salt Spring," Trevor said, eying the joint Roy had rolled.

Roy nodded.

"I'm supposed to live clean. Healthy."

Roy nodded again.

"If I keep to a healthy lifestyle I'll live to a hundred." He sounded like he was repeating an oft-used mantra.

Personally, Roy thought that the odd joint should be a fundamental part of any healthy regimen, but to each his own. He nodded again and waited.

"Hell. Who wants forty years of virtuous boredom?" Trevor said, coming to a decision and looking pleased with himself.

Roy grinned. He pulled his ashtray out of the pottery tree then led the way back to the living room. The two men settled on the couch. Roy lit the joint, then handed it to Trevor. As he watched his friend indulge in his first glorious puff, he said, "So…pigs."

Trevor inhaled slowly before taking a second drag. He handed the joint to Roy before he slumped a little deeper into the couch. His gaze was not quite focused. "He's a stockbroker, you know. Made a pile and got out of the market before it tanked in '08. Came over to Salt Spring to live the good life." He snorted. "The good life. Do you know how much effort it takes to raise pigs?"

Roy shook his head. He'd never thought about raising any kind of farm animal. If he had, he'd be a vegetarian and he liked his steak too much to abandon it.

"It's all the idiot talks about. He has dinner parties and invites the other back-to-the-land types who had perfectly good jobs in Victoria or Vancouver and now think they've got to do penance just because they've been successful."

"Takes all kinds," Roy said. He handed the joint back to Trevor, who took another drag, savored it, then exhaled.

"Yeah. I suppose." They smoked in silence for a while, then Trevor said, "So tell me about this dead body of yours."

"Brittany Day, twenty-four, grad student at EBU, girlfriend to a nasty little twerp called Aaron DeBolt—"

Trevor sat up straight, suddenly alert. "Nathan DeBolt's kid?"

Roy raised an eyebrow. "You know him?"

"There's not a lawyer in Vancouver who doesn't. Kid's been trouble since he first started to walk."

"Have you ever defended him?"

Trevor's jaw hardened. "No."

"Good," Roy said. "Because Aaron is an accessory in the murder of Frank Jamieson and our dead body provided him with a false alibi."

Trevor held up his hand, lawyer coming to the fore. "Whoa! How do you know it was false?"

Roy took a drag, held it, then expelled the smoke slowly, keenly aware that Trevor watched narrow-eyed. He couldn't tell Trevor the truth—that Frank had told him— because his friend would never believe a cat could talk, even under the influence of prime stuff. "There's plenty of evidence. The point is…" He waved the joint for impact. "Brittany was killed on Ellen Jamieson's terrace. Ellen Jamieson is Frank Jamieson's aunt."

"I know who Ellen Jamieson is."

Was there a hint of disapproval in Trevor's voice? Just how well did Trevor know Ellen Jamieson? Roy watched his friend as he said, "The cops think Ellen offed Brittany because she wants to frame Aaron for Frank's murder."

"Did she?"

"She says not and I believe her," Roy said. "That's why we need your help."

Trevor accepted the joint Roy passed him as he considered this. Then he frowned as he said, "There's more to this, isn't there?"

Roy nodded. "Quinn and Christy—she's Frank Jamieson's widow—are out at EBU checking into the people Brittany knew there. We'll talk about what they found over dinner tonight." He'd invited everyone over to meet Trevor, including Stormy the Cat. He wondered if

Frank would communicate with Trevor the way he did with Christy, Noelle and him. He grinned. He couldn't help it. He hoped the cat made the effort. It would blow Trevor right off the straight and narrow and back onto a more familiar path.

"Will I get to meet Ellen Jamieson?"

Roy nodded, but he raised his brows. "I thought you said you knew her?"

Trevor shook his head. "Not me. I know *of* her, but we've never been introduced."

Roy laughed. "You may not like her much. She's pretty starchy."

Trevor took another drag of marijuana. He waved the joint around in a grandiose way as he said, "Not surprising. She's spent her life making up for her brother, the ice cream king's, sins."

Roy thought about the three trustees who had been Frank Jamieson senior's best friends. They were all men with flaws—big, deep-fissure flaws. It made sense that Frank senior would be as morally challenged as they were.

He eyed Trevor. Normally the man was pain-in-the-ass tight-lipped. Perhaps the weed had mellowed him. "Really? Like what?"

Amusement leapt into Trevor's eyes.

So not quite as mellow as all that.

He said, "This and that. Some of his decisions at Jamieson Ice Cream don't bear scrutiny. Thing is, he died young, and Ellen Jamieson has done a good job plastering over the cracks, so people have forgotten. I'm not going to bring them up again." He paused as he handed the now mostly burned down joint back to Roy. "Unless I have to."

Roy took a last drag and stubbed out his joint. "Let's hope you don't, then."

Quinn arrived home shortly after five. By that time Roy had a big pot of spaghetti sauce simmering, liberally endowed with hot peppers and garlic, except for the portion he'd set aside for the cat. Frank said garlic gave the cat indigestion and Stormy wouldn't even come near a bowl of human food that included hot peppers.

"Uncle Trevor!" Quinn said. His eyes lit up. "Good to see you." They shared a hug and back slap, then he turned to Roy. "Christy is coming over about five thirty. She's bringing Ellen and the cat. Noelle is having dinner over at the Petrofsky's."

"Why is she bringing her cat?" Trevor asked.

Quinn looked uncomfortable. Roy laughed. "It's a very sociable cat."

Quinn and Trevor shared a bit of get-together chitchat, but when the conversation began to veer into the murder, Quinn went off to clean up for dinner, promising to fill them in with the details of what he and Christy had learned once they were all together.

Christy arrived precisely at five thirty, carrying a couple of bottles of wine. She was followed by Ellen and the cat, who slithered around Ellen's ankles and bolted up the stairs to the living room where Roy and Trevor stood.

"That cat," Ellen said, brushing past Quinn who had let them in. He closed the door and headed up the stairs behind Christy and Ellen.

Nag, nag, nag, Frank said.

Christy sighed. Roy chuckled. Trevor stiffened. He looked around him, eyes narrowed.

I swear, she's done this to persecute me. Frank was on a roll, venting immediate and long-standing issues about his aunt and former guardian. *Anything to make my life miserable. Anything!*

By the time Frank had finished his rant, Trevor's complexion was pale and edging toward pasty. Probably thought he was hallucinating because of the joint they'd shared earlier, Roy thought. He shot the cat a warning look and said, "A bit over the top, isn't it?" Then he turned to Ellen. "Ellen Jamieson, my friend Trevor Robinson McCullagh the Third. Trevor is retired now, but he used to be one of the top criminal lawyers in Western Canada."

Ellen had looked at him strangely when he spoke to the cat, but at his introduction, she brightened and focused on

Trevor. "*The* Trevor McCullagh of McCullagh, McCullagh, and Johnson?"

Trevor recovered his aplomb and smiled winningly at her. He took her hand between both of his, as urbane and sophisticated as he'd ever been during his heyday. "The same, dear lady. I'm flattered that you know of me."

Look at her. She's eating it up.

Christy and Quinn had gone into the kitchen to stash the wine, and probably snatch a couple of private moments, but they were back in time to see Trevor whiten again. His eyes darted from one part of the room to the other, his expression wary. Christy picked up the cat and held him up so that they were eye to eye. "Behave." The cat meowed plaintively. She put him back on the ground, then turned to introduce herself. Trevor regained his equilibrium and order was restored. For the moment.

By the time they'd eaten the spaghetti and finished two bottles of wine, everyone was more relaxed. Quinn and Christy had filled Ellen, Roy, and Trevor in on what they'd learned at EBU and the conversation revolved around Brittany Day's murder.

"I don't understand why she was found on my terrace," Ellen said, not for the first time. "I don't know the woman. I've never even met her. How can the police imagine I would invite a stranger into my apartment? I don't indulge in risky behavior and I'm not such a fool."

"Are you sure you don't know her?" Trevor asked. He was deep in defense lawyer mode now and they were all focused on him. "That there's no connection at all, no matter how minor it is?"

"None," Ellen said firmly.

Trevor frowned. He rubbed the greying three-day stubble on his chin. "There has to be a connection," he said. "Bodies don't just turn up in someone's space for no reason. Our job is to discover what that reason is and make sure the police don't." When Ellen opened her mouth to protest, he held up his hand, stopping her before she started to speak. "We already know there's one connection.

Brittany Day is providing one of the people accused in Frank Jamieson's murder with an alibi. Are there any others? What about the people she works with or the fellow she studies under at EBU?"

"Her advisor, Dr. Jacob Peiling, looks pretty clean," Christy said.

"But he was holding something back," Quinn said. "He claimed he couldn't go into details because of the privacy laws that relate to students, but it may have been that he was having a sexual relationship with Brittany as Lorne Cossi suggested." He shook his head. "To me that seems like a long shot, though. I wouldn't put the advisor high on a suspect list, but I wouldn't rule him out either."

"How would he connect to Ellen?" Trevor said, zeroing in on the core issue.

"Until the embezzlement, the Jamieson Trust helped to fund his program," Ellen said.

Christy frowned at her. "I thought the Trust did an annual donation to EBU, then let the university decide how to distribute it. I didn't know they funded specific programs."

Ellen shrugged. "Normally we didn't. Then two years ago Natalie told me programs could be supported individually. She convinced me that Peiling's program was both ecologically and socially worthwhile. When I met with Jacob I was quite impressed. I convinced the other trustees to earmark our EBU donation to support his program."

"Interesting," said Trevor. "So Peiling knew you and I presume he knew Natalie."

"Yes, of course. He also knew Aaron's father. Nathan DeBolt is on his steering committee, along with Roger Day, Brittany's father."

"Yet another connection, but how would it relate to Brittany's murder?" Roy asked. He was feeding dishes into the dishwasher, but his focus was on the discussion.

Trevor shrugged. "He might have been having an affair with Brittany as this Cossi guy suggests."

Ellen narrowed her eyes. "Why would he bring her to my terrace to murder her?"

"I don't know," said Trevor. "Why don't you tell me?" He stared at her, his gaze level until Ellen's cheeks flooded with color and her eyes opened wide.

"Are you suggesting that Jacob is having an affair with me? At the same time as he was sleeping with one of his students?" She surged to her feet. "That is disgusting!"

I'm with Aunt Ellen. Having finished his spaghetti dinner, the cat jumped up on Christy's lap then sat so that his head was above the rim of the table and he could observe the people seated there. *Watch how you talk to my aunt, shyster.*

Christy looked down at Stormy, then over at Trevor, who was as red as Ellen. When she glanced at Roy, he nodded, confirming the assumption he saw in her eyes—yes, his old friend Trevor could also hear Frank speak.

Quinn had watched this interchange and now he said, "Really? Really, are you serious?" He'd clearly realized that yet another person had tuned into the cat's mental conversation.

"I am," Ellen said, the heat still in her face, though her tone was cold. "I will not remain here and be slandered."

So Ellen, like Quinn, was out of the loop. Time to smooth troubled waters, Roy thought.

Trevor beat him to it. "I am not a shyster. Nor am I trying to slander you or anyone else, Ms. Jamieson. I am merely attempting to identify the kind of connections the police are searching for at this very moment. Connections that lead to motive and are backed up by evidence. Connections that we will have to disprove, if the police arrest you for Brittany Day's murder."

"Why would they do that?" Ellen said, her tone now arctic. She was still standing, her body stiff, her hands clenched at her sides.

"Because she was killed on your terrace, in the pre-dawn hours of the morning. You admit to being in your apartment at the time, but claim that you did not hear anything untoward."

"I did hear what I thought was a scuffle. When I got up to investigate I noticed some of my furniture had been broken. That was when I left the apartment and came to Burnaby to stay with my niece-by-marriage."

Jeez, Aunt Ellen! Can't you just call Chris your niece, period? We were married for ten years!

Trevor's brow knit into a frown and he stared at Christy. She offered him a wan smile in return. The cat flicked his tail and looked smug.

Trevor returned his attention to Ellen. "Unfortunately, your explanation is unlikely to carry much weight. Because of where and when the murder took place, the cops will say that you killed Brittany, then came to Burnaby to provide yourself with an alibi. And if they can find a connection that provides motive, like a ménage-a-trois, they'll use it to arrest you."

"I will not listen to this any further!" Her face flaming, Ellen stomped out of the kitchen. Her footsteps receded, then the front door opened and banged shut.

There was a short silence, until Trevor said amicably, "Now, since Ellen appears to be the only one in this room who wasn't hearing phantom words in his or her..." he nodded at Christy, "head, just who the hell was doing the talking?"

CHAPTER 9

Quinn examined himself in the mirrored cupboard door that had been installed to make the small back bedroom appear larger. His faded jeans were fresh from the wash and snug on his body. The dark green sweater was an expensive wool-silk blend that hugged his torso, but was loose enough not to flaunt. He nodded at his image before he turned away. He didn't usually bother to check his everyday clothing choices, but today he was interviewing the kind of person who cared about appearance and style. To get the information he wanted, he had to make an impression. The right impression.

In the living room below he could hear the low rumble voices as his father and Trevor talked. It was good to see Trevor looking so healthy. It was even better to see his father's eyes sparkle with that subversive mischief he remembered so well from his youth, when his mother was still alive and the whole damn family was involved in one good cause or another. Battling The Man gave Roy Armstrong fodder for his novels and a world-wide reputation as an outspoken social critic. It also made him happy, something decidedly lacking since Vivien Armstrong's passing.

One voice said something, then Quinn recognized his father's laugh. He wondered if the cat was there, sitting with them and silently contributing to their conversation. He wasn't sure whether to be annoyed or amused that Uncle Trevor could also tune into Frank's mind-speak, while he, Quinn, could not.

Admitting that Frank's consciousness had taken up residence in Stormy the family cat after his death was difficult for Quinn. He was a man who dealt in facts and he never accepted what appeared to be true at a first glance. He questioned and he dug and he looked at the issue from every side he could think of. Once he had amassed a wealth of information, he made his conclusions. Sometimes they were the same as what appeared on the surface. Sometimes they were different. For Quinn it didn't matter, as long as he had a truth that was supported by facts.

While he helped Christy search for Frank and then for Frank's killer, he struggled with the idea that Frank's consciousness alive in the Jamiesons' cat. But Christy could talk to Frank and so could his father. Hell, Frank and Christy's kid could communicate with him.

Quinn had only known Christy few months, but those months had been intense. She was not the kind of woman who lived in a fantasy world only she could inhabit. She was grounded and practical, a down-to-earth person a man could rely on. His father, though eccentric, was as sharp as they came and he'd been the one who taught Quinn to question everything. If his father and Christy said Frank lived in the cat, then he did.

He turned away from the mirror. Everyone thought Quinn was the odd man out because he couldn't hear Frank, but he knew better. It wasn't Quinn who was the problem. It was Frank. Frank didn't want to talk to him because Frank was jealous of Christy's attraction to Quinn. Simple as that.

Quinn took a moment to contemplate his relationship with Christy while he dug through his closet for a jacket. They were both feeling their way through a maze of family obligations, old wounds and future opportunities. Christy's priority right now was Noelle. Keeping her daughter safe, minimizing the trauma of knowing her father had been murdered, and building a new life for them both was a big job. Quinn was prepared to give her time. To court her in an old-fashioned way that meant building respect before giving in to desire. This was new for him, since his past relationships had focused on the physical. They usually began with fiery sexual need, then simmered into liking before drifting into a lazier, easier sexual pleasure until they burned out completely.

His reaction to Christy was different. She inspired passion, yes, but even more he wanted to cherish her, care for her, ease the burdens that were too heavy for her to carry alone. And he wanted her to feel the same way about him.

He knew she was as attracted to him as he was to her, but he wasn't sure if she was ready yet to trust him with her heart and with her future.

Old wounds held her back. She'd given herself to Frank Jamieson when she was young and innocent, and he'd burned her badly. She had to learn to trust again before she'd be ready to commit. It was his job to help her along that path, which was why the damned cat wouldn't talk to him. Frank would do everything in his power to hang on to Christy and his daughter as long as he could.

Quinn found the leather jacket he wanted and pulled it out of the closet. He shrugged it on, then headed downstairs. He found his father and Trevor sitting together on the sofa in the living room. Between them, as he'd suspected, squatted the cat. Trevor was absently stroking its back while his father rubbed the spot just above its tail. Stormy's eyes were half-shut slits and his tail was arched. Quinn raised his brows. "The lap of luxury," he said.

Trevor laughed. Quinn wasn't sure if it was because of what he'd said, or if the cat had made some sarcastic comment. Trevor cocked a brow. "You look like you've dressed to impress. Going somewhere special tonight?"

Quinn put his hands in his pockets and leaned against the newel post. "I have an appointment to interview Cara LaLonde."

His father's brows snapped together into a frown. "Who's she?"

"One of Aaron DeBolt's babes." He remembered her vividly from the night of the IHTF gala when he'd let his temper push DeBolt against a wall because the bastard had insulted Christy. Cara LaLonde had been the dark-haired beauty who'd rubbed against him as she slithered past. She'd shot him a look promised sex and said she was ready when he was. He'd used that invitation to persuade her to meet him this afternoon. "I want to see what she remembers from the night Frank was killed."

Trevor's hand stilled. "Be careful with that, Quinn."

He pushed away from the post. "What do you mean?"

"We all know that Brittany Day gave false testimony when she provided Aaron DeBolt with an alibi."

Clearly Frank had been filling Trevor in on the details of his case. Great. "So what's wrong with proving that to the satisfaction of the police?"

"Because it will look like Brittany's death is directly related to Frank's murder and Aaron's alibi. That will focus police attention on Ellen Jamieson. She's already a suspect because of where Brittany's body was found. Tying Brittany's death to her nephew's murder will only make the cops suspect Ellen more strongly. Our best hope is to shed light on other parts of Brittany's life and show that Ellen wasn't the only one with a motive to kill her."

The purpose of a good defense lawyer wasn't to prove innocence, but to force the prosecution to establish guilt beyond a shadow of a doubt, Quinn thought. And Trevor McCullagh the Third had been one of the best. "Unfortunately, I'm not the only one who will be talking to Cara LaLonde about Brittany's alibi. I'm sure the cops are already on it." He shook his head as the cat rolled over on its back, all four feet in the air, begging to have its stomach rubbed. Roy chuckled at something Frank said and Trevor started to rub the cat's belly.

Quinn shrugged and went on his way to the front door. He'd been dismissed.

Cara LaLonde was as he remembered her: great body, long beautiful hair, sharp pretty features, eyes that were cold and calculating. He'd invited her to meet him for a drink at the bar of one of the better hotels; a public place he assumed would have the ambience to impress her.

He was right.

He arrived ten minutes before the arranged time and found a table with a view of the doors. She was late and made an entrance, pausing just inside the entry, apparently to look around for him, in reality to allow every male eye to observe her.

And they did. Quinn was amused to see two guys at the bar wearing business suits, ties loosened, slouching at the end of the day, straighten in an encouraging way the minute they saw her. Another group shifted to let Cara see the empty chair at their table.

Her gaze swept the room, flicked over the group at the table, lingered on the men at the bar, then came to rest on Quinn. She smiled a slow seductive smile that had the rest of her audience glaring at Quinn as she sashayed his way. She was on the hunt and he'd been singled out.

He stood as she neared and held a chair for her.

She smiled slowly. Approvingly. "Mr. Armstrong. Quinn. I can call you Quinn, can't I?"

"Sure."

Her smile warmed. Her voice was sultry. "Quinn. I'm glad you called." She observed him from beneath her thick, artificially enhanced, lashes. "You said you were working on an article about Aaron's part in Frank Jamieson's death."

He nodded. "You must miss him now that he's in jail awaiting trial."

She pouted. Prettily. "Poor Aaron! That awful Detective Patterson has been hounding me about him! First to find out if I knew what he was doing the night Frank Jamieson disappeared. Then she wants to know what poor Brittany Day was up to that night."

The waitress came to take their order. Quinn chose Scotch, neat. Brittany requested a crantini.

"I understand Brittany provided Aaron with an alibi for that evening," Quinn said. He grimaced, playing up to her assumptions. "If Aaron wasn't in that alley with Jamieson, I'm going to have to rework my whole piece."

"Poor you!" Cara said. She didn't sound sympathetic.

Quinn pretended she did and let her think she was snowing him. "I'm hoping you will be able to clarify what went on that night."

The drinks came, giving Cara time to construct her answer. As Quinn paid the tab, he watched her features from the corner of his eye and he thought she was considering exactly what she planned to say. He decided he should be ready for evasions and outright fabrications.

She sipped her cranberry martini, watching him over the edge of the glass, making play with her eyes. He smiled at her as if he was bowled over by a beautiful, sexy woman and when she put her glass back down, she leaned toward him, ever so slightly, implying intimacy but not really supplying it. "I met Brittany and Aaron at the club around nine o'clock. Aaron was supposed to meet Frank Jamieson about then, but Frank was late and Aaron was annoyed. He took Brittany off to a corner to have sex while he waited."

That wasn't what Quinn expected to hear. He raised his brows. "You saw them do it?"

Cara shot him a flirtatious look that was half pout, half amused. "Of course not! But I knew Brittany and I know Aaron. He gets off on doing it in risky places. I suspect he found some quiet corner where they were likely to be interrupted and teased her into letting him screw her."

Quinn frowned. "My editor has had me looking into Brittany's murder. I talked to her advisor out at EBU and to some of the students she worked with. She didn't come across as a mindless sex toy."

Cara sipped her drink. This time when she set it down, her look was knowing. "Once upon a time, Brittany Day was a sweet little girl from the ranchlands of Alberta with a bright future in the grad program she came to Vancouver to attend." Cara shrugged. "Then she met Aaron and everything changed."

Quinn drank some scotch. Her timing was right. From all they'd discovered so far, Brittany's grades had started to suffer about the same time she became one of Aaron's babes. "You aren't very complimentary."

Cara contemplated her rapidly dwindling drink, twirling the glass and watching the liquid slide up and down the sides. When she looked back at Quinn she said briskly, "Aaron seduced Brittany because I wouldn't play his games. I don't like sex in corners, not even with the enticement of free coke. He got Brittany hooked on drugs, then he convinced her that the only way he'd supply her was for sex. Anywhere. On demand." Her face twisted, showing contempt and compassion. "Poor stupid, silly little cowgirl. She had no idea what she was getting into when she met Aaron."

She raised the glass and downed the remainder of the martini. Quinn signaled their waiter for a refill. "I understand Brittany's father is a power in the oil industry. I'd have thought that she was prepared to handle rich playboys like Aaron DeBolt."

"She thought she was, but Aaron is in a class by himself."

The second martini arrived. Quinn paid for it, then looked thoughtfully at Cara LaLonde. "So Brittany disappears and you think that means she was with Aaron somewhere having sex."

She ate the dried cranberries that garnished the drink, sliding them off the cocktail spear with lips and teeth. Once the fruit was in her mouth she licked her top lip with the tip of her tongue. "Oh, yes." The words were little more than a low, sultry breath of sound.

Quinn watched, more amused than intrigued. She was playing him. But were the seductive techniques simply her regular behavior with an available male? Or was she trying to distract him, so he'd swallow her Brittany and Aaron story whole?

Call him cynical, but he'd put odds on the distraction motive.

He sat back in his chair, one hand on his drink, the other in his pocket. He smiled at Cara, waited until she smiled back, then pounced. "Frank Jamieson was murdered over six months ago. Why is it you remember that night so clearly?"

Cara frowned, her first unguarded look of the evening. "What do you mean?" She sounded wary.

He shrugged. "At the time there would have been nothing to fix the night in your mind. Frank went out to the alley, apparently to buy drugs, but that was nothing new. From what you said, Aaron taking Brittany off to a corner to have public sex was nothing new either. People remember incidents that are different, or important to them. What made that night stick in your mind so clearly?"

She had stiffened as he spoke. Now she relaxed and her sultry smile was in evidence again as she said, "It was Frank's disappearance, of course. The papers were full of how he'd stolen a bundle and taken off to Mexico."

"That information didn't come out until later. The details about the night in the club are pretty specific. It's hard to believe that you'd remember one night of many so clearly."

Her mouth tightened and her eyes smoldered. "I do."

Quinn leaned forward. He put his elbows on the table and smiled at her. "Okay. Every minute of that night is etched in your memory. How long were Aaron and Brittany gone?"

"Gone?"

"Yeah, off into the corner having public sex."

She colored. "I don't know."

Quinn raised his brows. "Then it's possible that Aaron met Frank after having sex with Brittany, then took him out to the alley and pushed him into the trunk of the car that was used to transport him to his death."

"No!" Cara pushed back her chair and stood in one fluid, frightened movement. "Aaron was busy with Brittany that night. He couldn't have harmed Frank Jamieson."

Quinn rose too. "You've corroborated Brittany's alibi for Aaron, haven't you, Cara?"

"Of course I have, because it's true." She tossed her hair.

"That makes you party to Brittany's lies. She's dead now, but if Aaron goes to trial, you will have to testify. It will be you who is charged with perjury, not Brittany. Are you prepared to do some jail time?"

"It will never come to that," she said tightly. "Aaron is innocent." She turned away.

"How much are you being paid to do this?" he said to her retreating back.

Her steps faltered, but she didn't reply. Her back very straight, she slipped through the tables, ignoring the interested glances of the men drinking there.

Very un-Cara like, Quinn thought as he sat down again to finish his drink and consider what he'd learned.

Brittany Day had supplied Aaron DeBolt with an alibi for the night of Frank Jamieson's disappearance and death. Cara LaLonde was willing to corroborate Brittany's statement, adding substance and making it more likely that the police would drop the charges against him and release him from jail. Quinn knew that both Brittany's and Cara's statements were false. Was there anything Cara had said this afternoon that could be trusted?

Yes. Her statement that Aaron had started seeing Brittany to punish her for refusing him. Cara hadn't liked sharing Aaron, though. Now that Brittany was no longer around, she would have him all to herself once he was released. It was in her best interests to make sure Brittany's alibi stood and Aaron was freed.

His last question, accusing her of accepting a bribe to exonerate Aaron, had been a shot into the mist. He hadn't expected it to draw a reaction and he wasn't sure it had. Sure, she'd hesitated, but maybe she'd just wanted to defend herself against the slur. Or maybe she actually had been paid. If she had, then by who?

He didn't think Cara was involved in Frank's death, or in Brittany's. But she was covering for Aaron. Quinn knew that Aaron set up Frank in the alley that night. The trouble was, unless they proved Brittany had lied, Aaron would walk. And with Brittany dead and Cara LaLonde verifying the alibi Brittany had given Aaron, that wasn't going to be easy.

CHAPTER 10

"Homework in your backpack?" Christy said, running through the usual morning checklist with her daughter.

Noelle nodded.

"Any forms for me to sign that got missed last night?"

Noelle shook her head.

"Teeth brushed?"

Noelle's expression turned woebegone and she looked at her feet as she shook her head, no.

"Okay then," Christy said, "Do them quick before we go." As Noelle turned to scamper away, she added, "Oh, and tell Aunt Ellen that we'll be leaving in five minutes. If she wants to walk over with us she'll need to be ready."

Noelle took off, pounding up the stairs with a good deal of exuberant noise. As she loaded the dishwasher Christy heard the sound of water running in the bathroom.

The cat wandered into the kitchen and sat beside his bowl, his forelegs perfectly aligned in front of his body, his tail neatly curled around them. *What's for breakfast, babe? Oh, by the way, Ellen's not likely to walk over to the school this morning. She's still wearing that gauzy thing she calls a dressing gown.*

Christy opened a can of mystery meat cat food, then dumped it into the bowl. The cat stood up, inspected it with a disdainful sniff, then sat down again, his expression disapproving.

That's it?

"I have to go grocery shopping today. Those are our emergency rations. Take it or leave it."

"Are you talking to that cat again?" As Ellen drifted into the kitchen dressed in the peignoir set she had bought in Paris on her last trip there, her voice was as disapproving as the cat's expression.

Christy knew when and where the garments had been purchased because Ellen had taken great care to tell her. Not that she cared what Ellen wore as she wandered around the house in the morning. "Noelle told you we'd be leaving for school in a couple of minutes?" she said, carefully avoiding a discussion on the merits of talking to animals.

"Yes." Ellen sat down at the kitchen table and looked hopefully toward the coffeemaker. "I was awake half the night worrying. I don't have the energy to commit to any activities this morning."

It was a good thing Ellen wasn't a mother, then, Christy thought. Annoyance made her pivot sharply on her still-healing knee and it twinged, as if to remind her that moms didn't have luxury of moaning about a tough night or low energy. Or even about real health problems. They got on with life, which was what she was going to do right now. "Noelle! Time to go."

With one last, disappointed sniff, the cat turned away from his bowl, leaving his mystery meat untouched. *Maybe I'll walk over to the school with you.*

"I'm going to the grocery store after I drop off Noelle. I'll be another hour or so."

Ellen, assuming the comment was meant for her, sighed extravagantly. "Tell me again how to work that coffeemaker?"

"Easy," Christy said. She headed out, forcing Ellen to trail along behind to get the instructions. "Fill your cup with water then pour it into the top of the machine and put the empty cup on the heating pad. Place the coffee pod in the slot. Seal the compartment shut to punch a hole in the pod, then press the start button." Since she'd provided the same set of instructions for the last three days, she ran through them quickly as she went down the stairs to the front door.

She was slipping on her shoes when Ellen said in a defeated way, "I suppose I can manage it."

"Of course you can," Christy said heartily. She had eight years of mom training and she knew when she was being conned. Ellen was perfectly capable of brewing her own coffee. She just didn't want to.

Just like she wouldn't want to make her own breakfast.

Well, as far as Christy was concerned, Ellen could pick up a cereal box and shake the contents into a bowl, then pour in some milk all by herself. Like the cat, she might want something more exotic, but if she was starving the basics would do. "Noelle, hurry up! We're la—"

Noelle leapt down the stairs, taking them two at a time, and landed in a breathless leap on the landing. "I'm here, Mom!"

"Where's your backpack?"

That necessitated an energetic race up the stairs to retrieve the backpack from where it was stowed by the table in the kitchen, and another leaping descent to the front door. Ellen had disappeared into the kitchen to work the coffeemaker before she forgot the instructions, but Christy could still hear her *tsk-tsks* over Noelle's unladylike behavior. She hustled her daughter out of the house, holding the door open for the cat, and they were off to school.

She spent an hour in the grocery store, wandering up and down aisles containing goods she didn't want and would never consider buying. The store was almost empty and the quiet was bliss after the hustle to get Noelle going in the morning and the stress of Ellen's expectation that she should be waited on as long as she was staying in Burnaby.

Christy didn't want to go home and talk, but talk she would, because Ellen never seemed to stop. For a woman who lived alone, Ellen was very social.

And probably lonely, Christy thought, feeling guilty. She headed for the sole open cash desk. She shouldn't be so uncharitable.

Who was she kidding? She was thinking about Ellen Jamieson here, the aunt Frank had hated. The trustee who had never failed to criticize her behavior.

People change, Christy told herself, wanting to be positive. Ellen could change. Maybe she already had.

Ellen wouldn't make her own breakfast.

Christy paid for her groceries and headed home.

As she was unloading them from the trunk, Quinn came out of his front door. She left the grocery bags on the ground and went over to see him.

He greeted her with a kiss that had her twining her arms around his neck and pressing her body against his. "Good morning," he murmured, smiling as he raised his head after a long, delightful, couple of minutes.

She smiled back and made no attempt to pull away. "Good morning."

"You've been shopping." His voice was husky, charging the simple statement with potent sexual promise.

"Hmm," she agreed. His hands were around her ribcage, deliciously close to her breasts. She hoped he'd raise his thumbs and rub…Ahh, just like that. Her body warmed and she pressed against him until she could feel his response to her nearness.

"Minx," he said, amusement in his eyes.

"Hmm," she said again, keeping her gaze locked on his as she moved, ever so lightly, against him.

It was his turn to say, "Hmm," before he added, "Mrs. Wallace up the street just waved."

Christy would have leapt apart from him at that announcement except that Quinn still had his hands around her and his thumbs still fondled her breasts. Instead, she stiffened.

Amusement danced in his eyes. "I guess we'd better go sit on the steps, in case Mrs. Wallace decides to come and see what we're up to."

Christy laughed shakily. "Good idea." They settled onto the steps, close, but not touching, now the picture of propriety. "How did your interview with Cara LaLonde go yesterday?"

Quinn filled her in on the details. When he'd finished, Christy wrinkled her brow. "I don't get it. Was Brittany at the club that night? Did Aaron arrange to have her there to ensure he had an alibi? Or is Cara lying and part of a scam?"

"Aaron originally claimed to have been with Brianne Lymbourn. Her death meant he needed to find someone else to cover for him."

"Enter Brittany," Christy said.

Quinn nodded. "Cara told me Brittany was there that night, but I wonder?" He shrugged. "She could have been, I suppose, but she hadn't been seeing Aaron for very long before Frank was killed. Was she already so into him that she'd have public sex with him? Or did that come later?"

"Where Aaron DeBolt is concerned anything is possible," Christy said.

Quinn laughed and hugged her. She leaned into him and said with a sigh, "I guess I should put my groceries away."

"Do you have to?" he murmured.

It was her turn to laugh. "Yes." She glanced at her watch and saw it was past ten. "At least Ellen will have made herself breakfast by now. Hopefully she will have also put her dishes into the machine so I don't have to."

She stood as Quinn said, "Good luck with that."

He carried her grocery bags to her front door and was going to take them up to her kitchen, but Christy said, "Thanks, Quinn, but I'd better bring them in. The last time I saw her, Ellen was still in her nightclothes. She'd probably be mortified if you came in and she wasn't dressed yet."

He gave her a kiss, another lovely long kiss, on her front porch this time, then left her to manage her groceries by herself. She was humming as she unlocked the door and hauled the bags over the threshold. The cat raced up the porch stairs and dove through the doorway before she closed it. He must have been lurking in the bushes while she sat on the porch with Quinn.

And kissed him.

Twice.

Served Frank right if he got an eyeful, she thought as she slammed the door. He shouldn't be spying on her. If he didn't like what he was seeing, he ought to make himself known.

She picked up her collection of bags and trudged up the stairs. When she reached the living room she stopped and stared.

Ellen was sitting on the sofa, still dressed in her delicate peignoir from Paris. Right beside her sat Natalie DeBolt, her face scrubbed clean and absent of makeup, but wearing a body-hugging dress of Lycra and silk that was inappropriately sexy.

What the hell?

"I was just about to make Ellen breakfast," Natalie said, her eyes brightening as she noticed the grocery bags. "Are there eggs in there, by any chance?"

"Yes." Christy lugged the bags to the kitchen. Neither Natalie nor Ellen offered to help, though both trailed behind her into the room.

Christy put the bags on the counter, ready to be emptied, but Natalie forestalled her. She rummaged through the carriers, pushing the contents around but not unloading them, until she found the eggs, then she got to work to make the breakfast she'd promised Ellen. Christy thought uneasily that she appeared to be very familiar with the townhouse's kitchen.

Ellen sat down at the table on the far side of the large room, positioned so she was able to see Natalie at work at the stove. Her elbow on the table, her chin resting on the palm of hand, she watched. She didn't look at all disconcerted at being in her nightclothes while her friend cooked her breakfast.

"Ellen and I had a good talk while you were away," Natalie said to Christy in a chatty, make-conversation way as she melted butter into the frying pan. "She is very upset about poor Brittany."

"I am," Ellen said.

"I worry about her, you know." Natalie put whisked eggs into the pan and started to stir. "It's very hard to find a body on your terrace, especially for someone as sensitive as dear Ellen." She paused to send Ellen a speaking glance.

Ellen blinked, but didn't protest.

The cat prowled into the kitchen, looked at his dish—which still contained the despised mystery meat—then sniffed with disapproval.

Natalie tossed cheese over the scrambled eggs and waited a few seconds for it to begin to melt. She plated the eggs, added a piece of toast, which she carefully buttered, then took the plate and some cutlery over to Ellen, passing the cat on the way.

The cat sneezed as she passed. Reaching out a paw, claws extended, he swiped. The gesture was a near miss.

"Here you are, my dear. Eggs just the way you like them and your toast buttered too!" Natalie smiled, apparently unaware she'd almost had her ankle scratched by razor-sharp cat claws. She settled onto a chair near Ellen's.

"Thank you, Natalie. You're a doll," Ellen said before she dug in.

Drawn by the scent of cooked eggs—a favorite—the cat abandoned his dish, leapt up onto a chair, then onto the table. The result was immediate.

Natalie gasped and slammed her palm over her mouth in a shocked gesture as she pushed back her chair to get away.

The cat took a careful step to bring himself within snatching distance of the plate, then he sniffed appreciatively, his whiskers twitching.

Ellen screamed. "Get that beast off of the table! It's unsanitary!"

After Ellen's outburst, Natalie pried her hand away from her mouth and tossed her head. Her chin thrust out, she leveled a disdainful look at Christy. "What an abominable animal! So badly mannered."

Neither Ellen nor Natalie made any attempt to remove Stormy, so the cat took another careful step. He was now within striking distance of the eggs.

Natalie was more focused on Christy than on the cat. She added with a sniff and a sneer, "I would expect a normal person to be aware of how to control a beast like this one, Christy, but since I know you very well, I am not truly surprised that you allow the animal to act this way."

Bitch!

On the table, Stormy growled deep in his throat, perhaps in support of Frank's comment, or more likely because he wasn't getting access to the plate of eggs.

Ellen leapt up from her chair, almost knocking her plate onto the floor. "It's rabid," she cried, and backed away.

The doorbell rang.

Christy sighed and went over to the table. Picking up the still-growling cat, she tucked him under her arm, then went to answer the door.

CHAPTER 11

Christy opened the door with the now-wriggling cat still under one arm. Both she and the cat froze when they saw Detective Patterson standing on the stoop.

"Good morning, Mrs. Jamieson," Patterson said. She reached out to scratch Stormy's head, but snatched her hand back when the cat hissed.

Christy sighed. "Don't mind Stormy, Detective. He and Aunt Ellen just had a confrontation and he's still annoyed."

"Ms. Jamieson isn't fond of cats?"

Christy shook her head. She could have added that Ellen also wasn't fond of nieces by marriage and nephews she considered wastrels, but she didn't. Instead she waited for Patterson to explain why she was here.

"I'd like to speak to Ms. Jamieson, if she has a moment," the detective said politely, if implacably.

Christy wasn't surprised. On the one hand, she liked Detective Patterson, who had been helpful when Frank was missing and Christy was determined to find out what had happened to him. On the other, Patterson was trying to solve Brittany Day's murder and Ellen Jamieson was, if not the chief suspect, then certainly a person of interest.

"I'll ask her, Detective, but you'll have to give me a minute." She dumped Stormy onto the porch, pointed at

him and said, "Stay here." Ignoring Patterson's raised
brows, she closed the door, leaving Frank to deal with the
detective, and went upstairs to find Ellen.

She discovered her sitting on the sofa in the living room,
close to Natalie. Their heads were together, and Natalie
was whispering something in Ellen's ear. There was a
smile on her face and Ellen was chewing her bottom lip as
she listened.

What was going on? Christy knew this was the second or
third time Natalie had been out to Burnaby to visit Ellen,
but she tried to avoid Natalie, so she hadn't been home for
the other meetings. Since her relationship with Ellen had
always been strained, she had no way of knowing if the
intimacy she sensed was normal or new. She cleared her
throat and said, "Ellen, Detective Patterson wants to talk to
you."

Ellen's head shot up and Natalie eased away. "But I'm
not dressed!"

Christy said, "I'll tell her you want to have Mr.
McCullagh with you when you talk to her. Then I'll nip
over to Quinn's house and bring him back with me. Will
that give you enough time to get ready?"

"Trevor McCullagh the Third? The murder lawyer?"
Natalie asked. She looked horrified.

"That's right." Christy heard a belligerent snap in her
voice as she replied. She was trying to keep her tone even,
but there was something about Natalie DeBolt that always
rubbed her the wrong way.

Ellen looked from Christy to Natalie and back again. "I
suppose I can manage," she said slowly. "I don't really
have a choice, though, do I?"

"No, I don't think you do," Christy said.

Natalie patted Ellen's arm in a comforting way. "We'll
make it work, won't we, my dear?"

Natalie in the role of best pal—or something deeper—
was more than Christy could handle, so she nodded and left
them to get organized. She stepped out of the front door
onto the porch to find Patterson sitting on the top step, with

Stormy beside her, lying on his back and purring loudly as the detective rubbed his belly. "You've made a friend," she said lightly.

Patterson looked up and grinned at Christy. "He's not such a bad cat, after all."

Christy sat down beside Patterson, with the cat between them. "He has his moments." She tickled the cat's chin. The purring increased in volume, if that was possible. "Listen, Detective. Ellen will talk to you, but she wants to have her lawyer with her. He's staying with the Armstrongs, a couple of houses down. I'll get him now, but I'd like you to wait here until I get back."

Patterson said nothing for a minute. She stared silently at Christy—who met her gaze and held it—while she continued to stroke the cat's belly. Finally she shrugged and, like Ellen, said, "I suppose I can manage."

Feeling as if she had just faced down a herd of charging elephants, Christy nodded jerkily as she stood. "I'll be back as soon as I can."

Roy Armstrong answered the door when she rang the bell at Quinn's house. His eyes brightened when he saw her. "Christy! Quinn said he talked to you this morning and gave you all the latest data. I didn't expect to see you again so soon." But he opened the door wider to usher her in.

"Patterson's here and she wants to question Ellen," Christy said urgently, as soon as the door had closed behind her.

Roy's eyes widened, then narrowed, before he turned away to hustle up the stairs. "Three! Crisis! Listen up!"

Christy followed him. At the top of the stairs she saw Trevor and Quinn emerging from the kitchen. Both men looked cheerful and she thought they might have been sharing a joke. Trevor was fully dressed and street-ready in his faded jeans and a dark blue wool turtleneck sweater. That was a relief, she thought, though perhaps it would have been better if she had to wait half an hour for him to dress.

"What's up?" Quinn asked.

"Patterson's here," his father said. "She's planning to interrogate Ellen."

That wasn't exactly what Christy had said, but it worked like a cattle prod on Trevor. "Ellen should not speak to the police without council present," he said. The good cheer was gone from his face, replaced by a somber expression and tight lips.

"That was my thought," Christy said.

Trevor nodded. His tone brisk, he said, "Where is she?" as he headed down the stairs.

Christy put a hand on his shoulder. "Can you hold on a minute? Ellen isn't dressed yet and she wants some time to get ready before she faces Patterson."

Trevor hesitated, then nodded. As he turned back up the stairs, he said, "Where's Patterson?"

Christy grinned. "She's sitting on my porch stairs. Stormy is entertaining her."

Trevor's eyes opened wide and he glanced from Roy to Quinn. "You mean the cat can talk to her, too?"

Quinn grunted, but Christy and Roy laughed. Christy said, "No. At least, I don't think he can. No, right now all he's doing is purring." She chuckled. "I think Detective Patterson is a cat person from the dreamy expression I saw on her face when I found her rubbing Stormy's belly."

"I'm not surprised," Trevor said briskly. "Cats are very good at creeping around silently and turning up where you least expect them. From what I can make of her, Patterson is the same way."

A little harsh, but perhaps not far off the mark, Christy thought.

When they left the house ten minutes later, Patterson was still on Christy's porch and the cat was still purring as she stroked and rubbed where it most pleased him. She stood up when she saw Christy and Trevor.

The cat made a yip of protest, then rolled onto his stomach and stood up. Shaking himself he strutted into the bushes on the other side of the street. *My job here is done. The cat is hungry. We're going to look for mice.*

Inside the house, Christy was relieved to see that Ellen was dressed in a black pencil skirt, white silk blouse and a fluffy cashmere cardigan that was somewhere between a purple and a marine blue. She looked worried, though, which Christy didn't think boded well for the coming interview. Even worse, Natalie stood beside her, with Ellen's hand clutched between both of her own.

Not good. Not good at all.

"Thank you for speaking to me, Ms. Jamieson," Patterson said. She scanned the scene and her eyes lingered on those clasped hands.

"Not at all. Detective Patterson, please let me introduce you to my friend, Natalie DeBolt," Ellen said. "Natalie, Detective Patterson investigated Frank's disappearance and now she is attempting to discover who placed the body on my terrace." Apart from the reference to investigations and a dead body, Ellen made the introduction with polished grace. She could have been making two socially important friends known to each other, rather than a police detective and the mother of a man accused of being an accessory to murder.

Patterson's response was brisk. She clearly wanted to get down to business. "I've met Mrs. DeBolt, Ms. Jamieson, but thank you."

Ellen's chin jutted at that, but she sat down on the sofa. Natalie settled beside her, sitting very close. Too close, Christy thought, worried now.

Patterson remained standing. She surveyed the two women on the couch with observant eyes. "You must know Ms. Jamieson very well, Mrs. DeBolt."

Natalie smiled at Patterson, then looked back at Ellen, her expression gentle. "We've known each other for many years, but have become closer friends only recently."

Patterson's eyes narrowed. "That true, Ms. Jamieson?"

"Yes. I've known Natalie since we were at university. I introduced her to her husband, Nathan. We've served on many committees together. Recently, we realized how much we had in common and we've been—"

Louise Clark

"Where is this line of questioning headed, Detective?" Trevor said, an edge of frost in his tone. Like Patterson, he was standing. His feet wide apart, his hands in his pockets, he positioned himself to one side of the sofa, between the two women and Patterson. The spot allowed him to watch the faces of all involved.

Patterson said, "Just making small talk, Councilor."

"It's perfectly all right, Mr. McCullagh," Natalie said. Her expression was coy, her tone gushed. "I don't mind Ellen talking about our relationship. I think she's a very special person. Her friendship has sustained me recently. You see…my husband and I…Well, let's just say we don't get along anymore. Ellen has helped me deal with that."

"Really," Patterson said. She looked skeptical at this statement.

"Yes," Natalie said, eyes now suspiciously moist.

"Not another word!" Trevor said. The command came out as his courtroom bellow. Natalie and Ellen jumped. Patterson looked at him thoughtfully.

"Thanks for coming, Natalie," Christy said. She raised her arm, hand held out, a gesture clearly designed to usher Natalie to from the room. Natalie looked surprised at first, then she leaned over to give Ellen a quick peck on the cheek, before she rose, smiling graciously as she allowed Christy to sweep her out of the room and down the stairs.

When Christy returned from showing Natalie the door, Patterson was saying, "That's the information I have, Ms. Jamieson. I'd like you to confirm or deny it."

"I deny it, of course!" Ellen was scarlet, from the top of her cashmere sweater to the roots of her hair.

"Deny what?" Christy asked.

"This woman thinks I'm gay!" Ellen pointed accusingly at Patterson.

Since Christy had been wondering the very same thing ever since she'd seen Ellen and Natalie together in the kitchen, doubt flashed through her mind. It must have shown on her face, because Patterson raised her brows as she turned to Ellen.

"The information I obtained is that Brittany Day was bisexual. She usually preferred threesomes—with a male and another female—but she was open to solo relationships with another woman. My informant stated that in those cases she preferred older women."

Ellen was on her feet now, her hands balled into fists, her body wire-tight. "This is intolerable! I will not be judged this way!"

"Is it true, Ms. Jamieson? Were you having an affair with Brittany Day?"

"No, I was not!"

"She died on your terrace. There must have been some reason she was there. The post-mortem puts time of death at around six in the morning. You were in your apartment at that time, weren't you, Ms. Jamieson?"

"I'd already left and was on my way here!"

"The time is approximate. You were in your apartment when Brittany Day was killed, weren't you, Ms. Jamieson?"

"I heard sounds. I think. Certainly something…but I remained in my bedroom."

"There were drugs in Day's system when she was killed. Was she high? Stumbling around your apartment, stoned. Breaking things. Your beautiful, precious things? Did you decide you'd had enough, Ms. Jamieson?"

"Don't answer that," Trevor growled, stepping between Ellen and Patterson. "Ms. Jamieson has told you honestly and openly that she is not gay and that she was not having an affair with Ms. Day. She does not know how Ms. Day came to be on her terrace. This conversation is over."

As calm and collected as she had been while questioned—no interrogated—Ellen, Patterson said, "I will need to speak to you again, Ms. Jamieson."

"That's a threat," Trevor said crisply. "And I don't like threats. Please leave immediately."

Patterson waited a heartbeat and then another before she nodded and turned to the stairs.

Christy saw her out. As she closed the door, the sound of Ellen's sobs filled the house.

CHAPTER 12

"Did I tell you how glad I am that you agreed to come with me today?"

Quinn smiled at her and Christy's heart did a little flip. "Yes," she said, her voice low and husky with emotion she didn't bother to hide—from herself or from him. "And I'm happy that you convinced me to join you."

His smile turned into a pleased grin.

Every day she desired him more, she thought, as she watched him wrap his hands around the stark white mug that held after-lunch coffee. Desired him more and liked him better.

They were having lunch at a small, trendy restaurant that boasted no more than a dozen tables and featured an exotic mix of Spanish and North African cuisine. The menu items were share plates rather than individual entrées, so they had spent the first part of their lunch discussing the merits of each offering and what appealed and what did not. There was an intimacy about the process that Christy found almost seductive. As they ate, she was immersed in the moment, very aware of Quinn, her reaction to him and the pleasure she felt in his company.

And now he was smiling that lovely, reckless smile that transformed his handsome features into heart-stopping gorgeous ones. The warmth of his steady gaze told her he was completely focused on her, that her observations mattered to him. Heady stuff. Heady enough that she wished they were seated in a booth so she could slip in beside him and cuddle close.

Cuddling while at a restaurant was the stuff of fantasy, of course, but she suspected that if she did act on that lovely fantasy, Quinn would not be at all put out. He'd simply slip his arm around her waist and pull her against him.

"I had no idea I would like Moroccan food as much as I did. Or," she added with a teasing smile, "that you were into hot and spicy foods."

"Bland is not my thing," he said, the grin softening with a lazy sexuality that said he wasn't talking about food.

Christy blushed. "I was surprised at how much I like fiery foods, too."

His smile deepened and in his eyes she saw heat of a different kind. "Good to know. I'm going to enjoy finding the perfect place to tease your…taste buds."

Her eyes widened and the blush heated her whole body. At twenty, she'd never flirted with Frank when they dated at university. He'd been a senior, very cool, and his sexuality had overwhelmed her. They leapt into bed together with a straightforward desire to fulfill their needs. She fell for his earthiness, his charm, his fun. She'd been his from the moment he asked her out.

Quinn was different. She was attracted to him, certainly, and had been almost from the beginning. Their relationship had grown quickly, almost as quickly as had her passionate love for Frank, but this time she was more cautious. She was a mother, a widow who had been considering divorce before she discovered her husband was dead. She had responsibilities. And she had scars. She was falling in love with Quinn Armstrong, but slowly, savoring each step of the process. Flirting with this very attractive, very sexy man, was making her heart beat faster and helping her deal with the craziness that had become her everyday life.

The waitress came over to top up their coffee, saving Christy from finding a reply to Quinn's provocative comment. As she poured, she asked if either of them was interested in dessert.

Yes, Christy thought, she was interested, not in a calorie-laden confection, but in a romantic tryst in a room at the very nice hotel Quinn would be visiting after they'd finished their lovely lunch.

She blushed harder and grinned at Quinn's raised brow. "A naughty thought about dessert," she said after the waitress went away to finalize the bill.

That made Quinn's eyes widen, and Christy laughed.

"Lady," he said in a low voice that had a provocative roughness to it, "the things you say in public places. You realize you're cutting years off my life, don't you?"

She laughed again and shook her head. "I'm adding years, not taking them away. You'll see."

He smiled at her, his eyes intense. "I look forward to it."

His gaze, his voice, his smile, all added up to produce a tingle that warmed her from her heart to her center. If they didn't stop playing this sexy game, she was going to demand they get that room and to hell with Quinn's appointment with Brittany Day's father this afternoon. As that would never do, she drank some coffee to help her assume the cool manner of the Jamieson Ice Cream princess. Time to be a lady again.

Quinn raised his brows. He was very good at reading her moods and he knew when she was cloaking her emotions in the Jamieson persona. "What did I say?"

His words stripped away her camouflage. "Nothing! It was me." She looked down at her coffee cup, unable to meet his eyes. "I was thinking…" She bit her lip and dared to grab a glimpse of him through her lashes. "Naughty thoughts." He stilled and she rushed on. "I…today's not the right day and I…"

He caught her hand and turned it as he raised it to his lips to kiss the palm. "When it's the right day, you know I will be there."

His touch, his words, sent a warmth that was a potent combination of physical and emotional cascading through her. "Quinn, I…"

"You're right," he continued, moving up to her wrist and kissing the vein throbbing there. "Today isn't the right day." He looked up. His gaze was focused on her face, the expression in his eyes intense. "It will come, though."

"Yes," she whispered, caught in the moment. Excitement and desire pounded through her.

He smiled, then he looked down as he covered her hand with his other one. She watched him tamp down the potent sexual promise that flared between them until it was caught and contained—for now. Their hands still linked, he looked up and met her eyes. His smile was rueful now, and Christy's heart did a little flip. He had pulled back for her. His thoughtfulness had her melting inside.

When she smiled at him, something in her expression made Quinn sigh and say, "Much as I hate to do this, we should probably talk about the case and my interview with Roger Day. Are you sure you won't change your mind and come with me?"

Dr. Peiling, Brittany's EBU advisor, had called Quinn the previous day and told him that Brittany's father, Roger Day, was in Vancouver to deal with the police and to arrange for his daughter's body to be returned to Calgary for burial. Peiling thought it would be beneficial to Day to discuss the case. If Quinn was interested, Peiling promised to set up the meet. Quinn was interested and the arrangements were made for the next day.

Quinn wanted Christy to come with him, so he'd arranged for Noelle to be picked up at school, in case the early-afternoon interview ran late. The obvious person to collect Noelle if Christy wasn't available was Ellen, but Quinn knew Christy worried about Ellen's behavior, so he had arranged for his father and Trevor to accompany Ellen to the school. According to Roy, Quinn had given him strict instructions to keep Ellen in check. Since Ellen was still a committed fan, she was likely to listen to him.

At the last minute, Frank had confided that he would tag along as well. He liked the idea of an outing with two other guys and if Ellen misbehaved and got herself in trouble, well, that was just icing on the cake.

Though Christy had refused to participate in the interview, she did agree to a pre-interview lunch. Now she put her cup down. "I still think it's risky for me to come along. If Patterson has told him that his daughter was killed at Aunt Ellen's apartment, he'll recognize my name. I think he'll open up more if it's just you who see's him."

Quinn's gaze was steady on hers. "I'd like you there. You're good with people and you read them well. Day is grieving and he'll be hurting. He may want to lash out, but having a woman like you around will make him think twice. He may even open up more."

She sighed. Quinn might be right. However tenuous, she and Roger Day shared the experience of losing a loved one. Still, she shook her head. "If it were me, I'd refuse to do the interview." Quinn's mouth turned up in a fleeting smile. Refusing to talk to the press was her default behavior, and they both knew it. She shot him a rueful smile in response. "No, I'll use my rare afternoon off and do some Christmas shopping while you talk to Mr. Day." She sobered. "My afternoon will be far more pleasant than yours."

Quinn's face twisted as he released Christy's hand and straightened. He picked up his coffee cup. "Poor bastard. How much do you think he knew about Brittany's life here? For instance, her relationship with Aaron DeBolt?"

Christy shook her head as she picked up her own cup to sip. "He's not the kind of guy you brag about to your father." The mention of Aaron brought another thought to mind—Ellen and her apparent relationship with Natalie DeBolt. "Quinn, I'm worried about Ellen. She's acting strangely. Not getting dressed before Natalie arrives at the house and letting the woman make her breakfast. It's just not like her. If I hadn't seen it myself, I wouldn't believe she'd behave this way."

He drank some coffee, then stared down into his mug, pondering what she'd just said. When he looked up, he said, "If she's gay, does it matter?"

"No, of course not. But it does matter if she's in a relationship with Natalie."

A faint smile lifted the corner of Quinn's mouth. "I can see that."

It's okay to be upset, his expression said to her. *Don't sweat it.* "Quinn…"

He pushed the mug aside and reached over to take her hand. This time he held it in a comforting grasp. "From what Trevor told my dad, Patterson went at Ellen pretty hard the other day."

Christy nodded. "She held it together until Patterson left, then she fell apart. She spent the rest of the afternoon in her room. I think she's really scared." It had been a difficult time at the Jamieson house since Patterson's visit. Ellen had been moody and the unpleasant Natalie DeBolt had been forever underfoot.

"She should be," Quinn said. His expression hardened. "I don't know where Patterson got the information that Brittany was bisexual, and that she preferred older women, but if it's true, then it could go a long way to explaining why Brittany was on Ellen's terrace when she was killed."

"Natalie made it *look* as if she was more than casual friends with Ellen. I could see Patterson's brain ticking over as she watched. Trevor saw it too. Unfortunately when he bellowed at Natalie to stop talking, it only made it more obvious to all of us."

"Not Ellen, though."

Christy wrinkled her brow. "No. She denies it completely."

The waitress brought the bill, found out how Quinn wanted to pay, then went off to fetch the card reader with the promise she'd be back in a minute. Quinn reviewed the bill with a quick scan, then pulled out his wallet.

As he dropped his debit card on the table, Christy said, "Do you think it's possible that Brittany's death has nothing to do with the alibi she provided for Aaron? That she was killed simply because of her risky behavior?"

As good as her word, the waitress returned with the handheld card reader, interrupting their conversation. Quinn paid for the meal, but he waited until they were out of the restaurant before he answered Christy's worried question. "At this point, I think anything is possible. But my gut tells me that Natalie is tied up in this somehow."

They walked down the sidewalk, heading toward West Georgia Street where they would part—Quinn going to the landmark hotel where Roger Day was staying, while Christy went to the Pacific Centre to shop. "Then implicating Ellen is a diversion? But why Ellen? Quinn, it doesn't make any sense to me!"

Quinn took Christy's hand firmly in his. He held their linked hands in front of them both, then smiled down at Christy. Her heart gave a little flutter. *Together,* the gesture said. They were in this together. She smiled back.

"I know Ellen is a pain to live with," he began.

Christy rolled her eyes. "That's putting it mildly."

He laughed. "She needs lessons in houseguest manners, no question, but I think she cares for Noelle. She wouldn't deliberately do anything to harm her."

"She'd better not," Christy said. She'd risk everything to keep Noelle safe. She'd done it before, and she'd do it again. "Noelle is my first priority. If there's even a whiff of impropriety, Ellen's gone. I know that sounds harsh, but I won't give Joan Shively any ammunition to take Noelle away from me."

Quinn rubbed the back of her hand with his thumb. "My fierce tiger mom. Noelle's a pretty lucky kid to have you for a mother, you know that, Christy?"

His words warmed her, but it was the edge of a caress she heard in his voice and the affection in his eyes that had her beaming up at him like a besotted fool and feeling like the rainy afternoon was filled with sunshine.

* * *

Quinn met Roger Day in the lobby bar of the Hotel Vancouver where he was staying. A Vancouver landmark known for its luxury accommodations, his choice wasn't surprising. Nor was the tailored black suit that fit him perfectly even as it proclaimed his mourning status. Roger Day was a man of power who knew how to express it. And use it.

Quinn introduced himself and offered condolences as he held out his hand.

As he shook, Day said, "Mr. Armstrong, Jacob Peiling suggested I speak with you, but I am not sure how I can help you."

Quinn said, "I'm researching Aaron DeBolt and how he was involved in the murder of Frank Jamieson."

"Jamieson. That's the name of the woman who owned the apartment where Brittany was found." He gestured to a chair and they both sat down.

Quinn nodded. "Yes. Ellen Jamieson is Frank Jamieson's aunt. The police believe that Aaron DeBolt lured Frank Jamieson to his death, but your daughter claimed that at the time Aaron was supposed to be with Frank, he was actually with her."

A waitress, smiling broadly, sallied up, glad to have customers. In the early afternoon, the bar was almost empty. Day shook his head, though, and her face fell before she turned away.

"How much do you know of your daughter's life here in Vancouver and her relationship with Aaron DeBolt, Mr. Day?"

Frustration, quickly masked, showed on Day's face. "Not enough," he said. His expression hardened. "I trusted Jacob Peiling when he said that she was adapting well and that she was excelling at her grad work. I had no idea she was involved with a man who was accused of murder."

"She never said anything to you?"

Day shook his head. "Brittany told my wife and me about her successes, not her failures." He swallowed. "She took her bachelor's degree at the University of Calgary and lived at home. Moving to Vancouver for graduate school was her big adventure. I didn't want her to go. That's why I asked Jacob to keep an eye on her."

"Peiling was her academic advisor. Legally, since Brittany wasn't a minor, he couldn't talk to her parents unless he had her consent. Why did you expect him to report on her activities to you?"

Day shrugged. "Jacob and I go way back, to our university days. I asked him to look after my daughter as a favor to an old friend, not as part of his duties as her professor. He said he would." Day's mouth twisted. "I trusted him."

Emotion was very close to the surface. Quinn decided to lead the conversation in another direction. "Can you tell me a bit about Brittany?"

"She was a gifted student," Day said gruffly. "She worked hard and graduated at the top of her class at the U of C. She was popular in Calgary, and had a big circle of friends. She didn't go out during the week, though. She focused on her schoolwork. But she received lots of invitations for the weekends. So many she could pick and choose."

He was clearly a proud father, a man dealing with a pain he would never quite escape, but what fathers saw and what daughters actually did, didn't always match. "She lived at home, I think you said."

Day nodded. "She and her mother were close."

"Is it possible that Brittany confided in your wife and asked her to keep a secret, Mr. Day?" Quinn asked, careful to keep his tone neutral.

Day's hands, resting in his lap, clenched.

There was something here, Quinn thought. Something Roger Day didn't want to admit to.

"She called home a few days before her death," Day said slowly. "During the afternoon, which was unusual for her. I was at work, of course, so she talked to her mother. Lynn, that's my wife, spoke to her for almost an hour."

"What did they talk about, if you don't mind my asking?"

A muscle flexed in Roger Day's jaw. "Her program. She wasn't happy. She said that the other TAs she worked with had it out for her. She started talking about blackmail. Lynn said Brit began to cry and became incoherent."

"Blackmail!" Quinn couldn't mask the shock in his voice. "Mrs. Day must have been horrified."

Roger Day looked miserable. "She didn't know what to say or how to help Brittany. When Lynn tried to get particulars, Brittany said it was all tangled up. The university. Her friends. The donations. It was too complicated, she said, and her mom wouldn't understand. Lynn told me she was almost hysterical. She said something about being afraid, then said she had to go and slammed down the phone. Lynn was devastated and called her back, but she only got voicemail. By the time Brittany phoned again, she was calmer and said she'd overreacted."

"And your wife accepted that?"

Roger Day sighed. "Brittany was a smart kid, but she could be emotional under stress. Yeah, we accepted it. We thought she'd work out the problem and that it was just part of her growing up."

We failed her. The words hovered, silent, but no less deadly for not being spoken.

"You mentioned donations," Quinn said, not acknowledging the painful emotions in Day's voice. He sympathized, but the best way to help Roger Day deal with them, was to find out who killed his daughter.

Day nodded resolutely, responding to Quinn's professionalism, though his expression remained anguished. "The grad program she was enrolled in is an experimental one. The base funding is minimal and most of costs are covered by donations. She claimed that donations were drying up and Jacob was worried about whether he'd be able to keep all the grad students."

"Have you asked Dr. Peiling about that?" Quinn asked.

Day shook his head. "It doesn't matter now."

It might not matter to Roger Day, Quinn thought, but it would matter to the other students in the grad program, particularly if they feared the funding for their positions would be cut.

Roger Day looked down at his hands. "When the fall semester began, Brittany told her mother and me she wanted to dump her program and come back to Calgary. I talked her into staying." There was anguish in his voice. "I trusted Jacob. And he failed me."

CHAPTER 13

Christy and Quinn made it back to Burnaby in time for the triumphant return of Noelle and her guardians from school. Noelle was delighted. Apparently the parade of grandparent-aged adults had caused a stir amongst her fellow students, only surpassed by Stormy when he leapt up into her arms as she was leaving the classroom. The whole class of twenty-five students had crowded around wanting to pat him. Noelle, in her glory, had allowed them access and the cat, thankfully, had purred loudly.

By the time Noelle finished gleefully reciting her story, Stormy still in her arms, Christy was sitting on her front steps, shaking her head and laughing. Ellen was disapproving, but no one was paying any attention to her. Eventually she brushed past Christy without acknowledging her and entered the house. As the door closed with a snap, Christy stiffened, then went back to talking to Noelle and the others.

Over the next couple of days Quinn watched as tensions grew at the Jamieson house. Natalie DeBolt visited both days, arriving after Christy and Noelle left for school and while Ellen was still drifting around in her nightclothes. Quinn knew all about that, because Christy wouldn't stay in the house with Natalie and retreated both days to

Quinn's place. It was a situation ripe for disaster and Quinn thought that Natalie was at the core of it. He decided it was time to do some digging into her background.

He knew that she was married to Nathan DeBolt, the CEO of one of the province's wealthiest forestry conglomerates and a prominent member of Vancouver society. Nathan had a reputation of being a workaholic executive who used his recreational activities for networking rather than pleasure. Natalie, it appeared, had a similar philosophy. She had used her charitable work to enhance her profile and to provide her with a powerful position that built upon her husband's. Together they were a power couple.

Until their son was arrested as an accessory to murder.

That made Quinn wonder when Natalie and Ellen had become best buds. It also made him curious about how Natalie and Nathan DeBolt felt about their only son and his wayward ways.

Did Natalie have the kind of fierce protective feelings toward Aaron that Christy had for Noelle? How did Nathan feel as he watched his position and power erode because of a wastrel son who squandered the opportunities inherent in being the child of wealth and power and frittered away his time with drugs and wild sex?

Only one way to find out, Quinn thought, and that was to ask.

He secured an interview with Nathan DeBolt more easily than he'd expected. His reputation as an internationally known journalist was probably why the company communications director helped him out. Whatever the reason, he found himself in DeBolt's office at British Columbia Forest Industries at three on a Friday afternoon, sitting on one side of an oblong table with DeBolt on the other.

The BCFI offices were on the top twenty floors of a modern glass-and-steel tower on West Georgia Street. As was appropriate for the CEO of an international corporation with revenues in the billions, DeBolt's office was large and professionally decorated. Forestry products dominated the space. Gleaming hardwood paneling on one wall provided a surface for West Coast First Nations art.

Opposite the art wall was a bank of built-in shelves in the same dark, polished wood. These were home to more West Coast art; wood carvings this time. The shelves also housed a small bar, with appropriately expensive versions of manly drinks—single malt scotch, the best Canadian whisky, and the finest bourbon. Hidden in a cabinet below was a small fridge filled with that other manly drink—beer. Quinn knew about the fridge and its contents, because DeBolt had offered him his choice of the local microbrews stashed inside as he led Quinn to the dark wood table in the elegant meeting area in the back of the office.

"How may I help you?" DeBolt said, after Quinn had turned down his offer of a beer.

Quinn used the moment to study the man, allowing the silence to stretch out. Hopefully it would unnerve him, because DeBolt was already playing power games, as indicated by the offer of a beer, not a glass of one of the expensive and exquisite brands of hard liquor. Admittedly the selection of microbrews included the best of the best, but Quinn had a hunch that the sixty-year-old scotch was only offered to someone DeBolt considered an equal.

He was pretty sure DeBolt had offered the beer to put him in his place and to annoy him at the same time. Why? Did the man have something to hide? Maybe he did. Quinn decided he'd play along, let Nathan think he was uneasy in this luxurious office and not sure of himself or his position.

Perched on the edge of the comfortable leather swivel chair, he put his forearms on the gleaming surface of the table, then gestured with his hands, as if in supplication. "Thank you for seeing me, Mr. DeBolt. I know you are busy and have a large number of demands on your time."

DeBolt sat straight in his seat, his hands clasped before him and resting on the tabletop. He nodded, apparently open and ready to answer freely, when in fact the expression in his eyes was guarded.

"I'm writing an article, and a book, on the murder of Frank Jamieson. When I started the project it seemed pretty clear that your son was involved." Quinn spread his hands wider. His expression was earnest, a truth seeker looking for answers. "Now I understand Aaron has an alibi, provided by Brittany Day, who was recently the victim of murder."

DeBolt nodded. Cautiously. "That is correct."

"Have the police released him from custody?"

"I understand that the alibi must be confirmed before that can happen."

Quinn allowed himself to frown. "Is that possible, since Brittany Day is dead?"

"I believe she signed an affidavit."

Every statement the man made was careful, correct and cautious. He was clearly well trained in dealing with the media. Time to shake him up. "Ms. Day stated that she was with Aaron on the night in question. Do you know what they were doing?"

DeBolt's expression blanked. Quinn waited.

"I'm afraid I do not have those details."

Quinn allowed the corner of his mouth to kick up into a cynical half smile. He leaned forward. DeBolt shifted in his chair. "She claimed they were in a club, having sex," he said. "In public. According to one source I spoke to, that is a favorite pastime for your son."

DeBolt's hands flattened on the gleaming tabletop. Quinn pressed on.

"If Brittany were still alive, it's my guess that the media would have been all over her when the police released Aaron. Beautiful, smart, good family, she'd have made great copy. The details about what she and Aaron were up to on the night of Frank Jamieson's death would have created a sensation. But Brittany's dead and words on a page don't have the same impact. No visuals make for a harder sell. I think you lucked out. You may be able to bury what Aaron was up to and focus on Frank's best friend wrongly accused."

DeBolt's face was flushed. He looked as if he was holding on to control by the smallest thread. "Who is your source for my son's behavior?"

Quinn raised his brows. "You expect me to tell you?"

DeBolt narrowed his eyes. "My company is a major investor in the media network you work for."

"Wrong, Mr. DeBolt. I resigned two years ago. Now I'm an independent. I sell my stories to the highest bidder and I think I've got a gold mine here. Your son is rich, entitled, and spoiled. The only reason he may skate away from the Jamieson accusation is because one of his women was murdered. How do you think people will react when they find out that your precious son is morally corrupt and a sexual deviant besides?"

"I disowned him." The words came out in a rush. Nathan glared at Quinn as if he hated making the confession and blamed Quinn for forcing him to do it. "He's an addict. I arranged for him to go to a treatment center in the States where he could get clean and no one would know. He refused."

"When was this?"

"A year ago."

Now that the taps were open, the words were pouring out. "He said he didn't have a problem. I knew he did. I stopped his allowance and told him he had to survive on his own."

"That's when he started dealing drugs? Or had he been doing it before?"

DeBolt's face twisted. Quinn saw anger there, but he also saw the need to unload some of the anguish that must have been eating at him for a long time. Nathan DeBolt might be a powerful, well-connected businessman, but he was also a father whose son was destroying himself.

"He'd been doing it before." Nathan looked over Quinn's shoulder to the wall of First Nations originals. "My wife thought I was the cause of Aaron's downfall." He shook his head. "She couldn't see the darkness in him. She thought affection and cossetting would sort out his problems, when what he really needed was a spine."

Quinn thought that a personality transplant was what was actually required, but he didn't say it. He had Nathan talking and he wanted to keep the flow going. "Disagreeing over how best to help your son must have put a strain on your relationship with Mrs. DeBolt."

Nathan shrugged. "Natalie can be stubborn. When she wants to get her way, she doesn't care who she has to push aside."

Interesting. The answer was simple, but vividly expressive at the same time. Quinn decided to push a little and see what happened. "Was she having an affair?"

DeBolt's body stiffened. Quinn saw anger in his narrowed eyes. "What the devil are you suggesting?"

Quinn met his stare. "I have a source that claims your wife is having an affair with another woman."

Shock was followed by amazement on DeBolt's face and he burst out laughing. "Are you kidding me? Natalie? With a woman? I'd dump your source, Armstrong. If you told me she was having an affair with the pool boy I might have believed you. But a woman? My wife is many things, but I can guarantee you this. She lusts after men, not women."

"The husband is often the last to know," Roy Armstrong said. He was in the living room, presiding over a Saturday morning coffee klatch consisting of Quinn, Trevor, Christy and the cat. Rebecca Petrofsky had taken Noelle and Mary skating at the local community center rink and Ellen was out shopping with Natalie. Ellen and Natalie's relationship was the focus of the conversation.

"In novels," Quinn said. He accepted a mug of coffee from his father.

"In real life too," said Trevor. He finished doctoring the coffee Roy had given him a few minutes before. Two sugars, lots of cream. He cradled the mug between his hands, frowning.

Christy took the mug Roy handed her, but she put it on the coffee table in front of the sofa almost immediately. She and Quinn were sitting together, with Trevor in the easy chair at the end near her. The free chair near Quinn was where Roy would sit. The cat sat on the coffee table and eyeballed the cream, his whiskers twitching.

"I hope Nathan DeBolt is right," Christy said. "I've never been able to read anything more than malice in Natalie. She's power hungry and she's ruthless."

Power hungry? How? She doesn't do anything but run committees for charities.

"You never understood, Frank," Christy said, hostile. She knew she was bickering with him again, but she couldn't help it. In life, Frank had never understood the motivations of the DeBolts or the cruelty Natalie had dished out so effortlessly. "Those charitable boards she's on? The events she organizes? They make a difference in people's lives. The media thinks Natalie DeBolt is just this side of a living saint. Her good works give her the power to paint actions—hers or everyone else's—any way she wants."

The cat hunkered down, compacting his body into a crouch. Frank had never liked to lose an argument and death hadn't cured him of that flaw. She watched Roy put a saucer of cream on the table. There was pity in his eyes, but his action distracted Frank, because Stormy went right for the food.

"The detective seems to have bought into Natalie's storyline," Trevor said, gloomily watching the cat lap the cream. "Patterson admits that she knows about Aaron's threesomes. She even claims she wondered if Brittany had fabricated the alibi in a desperate attempt to focus Aaron's attention on her and only her. The cops are investigating the alibi and how it might relate to Brittany's death, but the evidence they have all points to Ellen. The murder happened in her apartment in the early hours of the morning when she claims she was alone. She has no one to confirm that. She's got motive. Brittany's alibi will get Aaron out of jail and in fact, will mean he never goes to trial. The cops will claim that Ellen believes Aaron took part in Frank's death, and that Brittany was lying. That's a pretty good motive to get rid of the only person who can put Aaron in the clear."

"You're talking about revenge as a motive," Roy said. Trevor nodded.

"If Ellen denies that, how can the police prove it?"

"They don't have to," Trevor said. "If they have a strong case built on physical evidence, they can suggest motive. A good prosecutor can sway a jury, particularly if the motive supports the evidence."

And Trevor McCullagh would know. With his record of acquittal after acquittal, he'd probably influenced a few juries himself. "Detective Patterson doesn't blindly accept the obvious," Christy said. "She was the one who thought Frank's disappearance was suspicious. She was the one who alerted me that Frank had apparently returned to Vancouver. It was her who helped us discover Frank's fate and set us on the trail to finding his killer."

"A good point," Roy said, settling deeper into his chair. "Gives us a clue as to how we should proceed."

"We need more information," Quinn said. He watched the cat lick the pads on one paw then rub the paw over its whiskers as it cleaned away the remains of the treat. "Why did Brittany provide a false alibi for Aaron in the first place?"

Maybe she loved him. Aaron always had babes falling over him.

"Maybe," Christy said doubtfully.

"He's good looking," Roy said. He sounded doubtful too.

"I've never met him. What makes him so special?" Trevor asked.

"Okay, so you're all talking about Aaron. What did the damned cat say?" Quinn sounded more resigned than miffed.

"You can't hear him?" The twinkle in Trevor's eyes indicated he found the Quinn's limitation interesting.

"He suggested that Brittany might have been in love with Aaron," Christy said, rushing in to change the subject. Quinn had gone a long way to accepting that he couldn't hear Frank's thoughts, but it had to be annoying when even the newly arrived Trevor did.

Quinn thought for a moment, then he shook his head. "Frank might be right, but I don't see her coming up with the alibi idea on her own. Everything we've learned about her says she was basically a decent kid who got lured into something she couldn't handle. I think someone put her up to it."

"Okay, but who?" Trevor asked.

Roy leaned forward. He waved his coffee cup in an enthusiastic way that had the beverage inside slopping up the sides dangerously. "Aaron's family, for starters. His father Nathan has a lot to lose, reputation wise. He's a pillar of the community. Having a son convicted of murder is a big blot on the family name."

"Natalie has always been besotted with Aaron. He's her only child and though she's cold to anyone she doesn't like," *like me,* Christy thought, "she can be a very affectionate to those she cares for."

"Then there's Aaron himself," Trevor said. "I'm sure he doesn't want to spend the next twenty years of his life in a prison cell."

"So everyone in the DeBolt family has a motive," Quinn said. "What about the blackmail that's been mentioned? Was it one of the DeBolts who was blackmailing Brittany? And if it was, what would they have on her?"

"Her lifestyle," Christy suggested. "She wouldn't want the sex-in-public stuff to become generally known. Her parents would be devastated. Nor would she want her drug habit to be public knowledge."

"That adds Cara LaLonde to our list," Quinn said. "She has a direct link with Aaron and she knows a lot about Brittany's relationship with Aaron. If Brittany is out of the way and Aaron is free, then Cara gets Aaron all to herself."

Who fed Brittany's habit after Aaron went to jail?

Roy, Christy and Trevor stared at the cat.

"What?" Quinn said.

"Frank suggested we follow the drugs," Roy said. He rubbed his chin thoughtfully. "It's a good point. If Brittany was hooked, she had to be getting her drugs from somewhere after Aaron was arrested. Where?"

Trevor shrugged. "Easily available on the street."

"Cara," Quinn suggested.

"Or someone Cara found. Cara had to find a new source too," Christy said.

"Let's find the new source, then," Quinn said. "Any more thoughts on the blackmail angle?"

"The girl TA—what was her name?" Christy said. She snapped her fingers. "Rochelle Dasovic, that was it. Maybe Rochelle had something on Brittany. We found out she snooped into Brittany's private stuff and we know she resented her."

"The university direction is a good one to go down," Trevor said with a nod. "It takes the attention away from Frank's death and focuses it on Brittany's life."

"But why would a TA from EBU murder Brittany in Ellen's apartment?" Christy asked.

Trevor shrugged. "To frame her?"

Roy drank his coffee and eyed his friend critically. "That's too easy. The question has to be repeated. *Why* would Rochelle Dasovic want to frame Ellen?"

Trevor tapped his bristly chin. "Ellen was the face of the Jamieson Trust's donations to EBU. When the Trust's funds dried up, the person who appeared to be stopping the donation was Ellen. Now, from what I understand, Ellen has money in her own right. Correct?"

She's loaded. My grandfather's will split his shares in Jamieson Ice Cream between my father and Aunt Ellen. The Trust was set up to control my father's share only.

Christy explained Frank's comment to Quinn. Trevor continued to speculate. "So an EBU TA, unaware of the details of the Jamieson family fortune could assume that there was plenty of money in Ellen Jamieson's pocket and Ellen was just being spiteful. If Rochelle, or one of the others, was afraid he or she was going to lose their grant, that person might be willing to kill the competition and get revenge against the person who put them in this position at the same time."

"Then let's assume Patterson is going to follow the direct path and look for evidence that implicates Ellen," Quinn said. "What we need to do is find links that focus the investigation elsewhere. We'll start with the EBU connection."

He looked around at the assembled company. They all nodded.

The cat jumped from the coffee table to Christy's lap and started to purr.

CHAPTER 14

Christy set the paring knife against the apple and expertly quartered it. The next step was to slice out the core and cut the quarters in half before she set the apple onto a plate. She worked swiftly and efficiently as she prepared Noelle's afternoon snack, but her mind drifted as she organized apple slices, cheese and crackers onto the plate.

On the other side of the room, seated at the table, Noelle was doing her homework with the help of Ellen. Noelle and Mary Petrofsky had arranged an afternoon of tag with some of the other kids in the neighborhood, but both Christy and Mrs. Petrofsky were adamant that homework had to be done first. Since the November evenings were closing in, Noelle was working diligently to get it done as quickly as possible. With Ellen helping her she was making admirable progress.

Ellen, while not an *asset* to the household, was beginning to find a place in it. Most afternoons she walked over to the school with Christy to pick up Noelle and she seemed to enjoy helping Noelle with her homework or being the adult supervising the children's play when they were outside. She couldn't hear Frank—which Christy considered a blessing, because Frank was often highly critical of what his aunt did—but she was getting along well with Noelle and she hadn't found fault with Christy for at least a couple of days.

She also seemed to have called a truce with Mrs. Morton, Noelle's teacher. She still raised her eyebrows when the kids were rambunctious and not chastised about it, but she no longer commented. Christy hoped that meant she was coming to terms with the reality of twenty-first century parenting and not that she was storing up choice comments for some future teacher takedown.

Now if only they could get this damned murder investigation sorted out. Christy didn't believe Ellen had killed Brittany. Or that Ellen was gay and that Brittany had been her lover. To her, both suppositions were malicious speculation. Together, they blackened Ellen's character, but they also diverted suspicion away from the individual who was the source of the gossip. The issue was to find the person who was targeting Ellen.

That was proving hard to do. In the meantime, she would believe the best about Ellen and—

The doorbell rang.

Noelle's head popped up, her attention hopelessly compromised. "Is that Mary, Mom? If it is, tell her I'm almost finished and I'll be out in a minute!"

"Focus," Ellen said, pointing at the assignment sheet beneath Noelle's pencil. "Do it right the first time and it gets done faster."

Christy headed down the stairs with Ellen's comment ringing in her ears. She was smiling as she opened the door, thinking about the diminutive Mary whose energy preceded her like a tidal wave. The smile faded when she saw who the caller was. "Ms. Shively."

"May I come in, Mrs. Jamieson?" Joan Shively asked. The expression on her face was serious.

Christy's heart sank. "Of course." She held the door wider and gestured for Shively to enter. "To what do we owe the pleasure?"

Shively blinked and looked confused.

"Why are you here, Ms. Shively?" Christy said gently.

The cat yawned in her mind and appeared at the top of the staircase, then settled there, its tail curled around its paws, body straight and stiff, like a feline bodyguard. *She's up to no good,* Frank said.

He was probably right, but Christy waited politely for Shively to state her reason for coming to the house.

"I'm here to see Noelle and evaluate her condition, of course," Shively said. She headed up the stairs. Christy followed. The cat sat its ground.

Noelle bounded into the living room, on the way to the stairs. "I'm finished!" she shouted. "Mary, I'll—" She skidded to a stop as she saw Joan Shively paused on the last riser, in a standoff with the cat. "Oh. You're not Mary."

"No. I'm Ms. Shively. You remember me, don't you, Noelle?"

All at once Noelle went from enthusiastic eight-year-old to a Jamieson. "Yes, of course," she said, drawing herself into a more ladylike pose. She advanced toward Shively, holding out her hand. "How are you, Ms. Shively?"

Ellen, following behind Noelle, narrowed her eyes at Shively, but said politely, "Good afternoon, Ms. Shively. How nice of you to visit. We were not expecting you."

"Exactly," said Shively. She stepped over the cat and advanced into the living room.

Christy breathed a sigh of relief when Frank did not allow Stormy to reach out and bat her leg, claws extended, but she had a sense that there was some kind of inner cat dialogue that went on and that Frank had only just retained control of the situation.

"I am here to inspect the home and ensure that Noelle is being well cared for," Shively said to no one in particular as she moved through the living room and into the kitchen. "Ah, what is this I see? Dinner preparations?"

"Snack," Christy said. "Noelle, back to the table and eat up before you go out."

"Surely it's rather late for the child to be playing outside?" Shively said.

"It's not dark and Ellen will be watching the kids," Christy said. She put the plate of apples and cheese onto the table. "You'll find that the bedrooms are tidy and clean, Ms. Shively. Please go ahead and do your inspection."

Noelle picked up an apple slice with her fingers and ate it daintily. "I have established order in my room, Ms. Shively," she said, very much the daughter of wealth and privilege. "With the help of my mother and aunt, of course. I would be happy to show you once I am finished my snack."

Well said, kiddo. The cat padded into the kitchen, blocky tiger's body tight with tense muscles ready to spring. *But don't get carried away. She's not used to kids with manners.*

Noelle munched another apple slice then inspected the plate and added cheese to a cracker. "Okay."

Christy froze. Shively frowned, and so did Ellen.

The doorbell rang.

Noelle immediately slipped from Jamieson heir back to eight-year-old. "Mom! That's Mary. Can I go out now?"

"Snack first," Christy said. Noelle immediately started stuffing the contents of the plate into her mouth until her cheeks looked like a chipmunk's. "Mary can have some too," Christy added hastily, fearful her child would choke herself.

But it wasn't Mary Petrofsky at the door, brimming with energy and enthusiasm. It was Detective Patterson, her expression grim. "Is Ellen Jamieson here, Mrs. Jamieson?"

Christy stared at the cop. Of all the moments Patterson could have chosen to come and question Ellen, this was probably one of the worst. "Yes, she is."

Patterson raised her brows. "May I speak to her, please?"

Once again Christy found herself opening her front door wide and inviting an unwelcome visitor in. The arrival scene repeated itself, with Noelle racing for the stairs and Ellen following. This time the cat had to dodge between human legs to assume his post at the top of the stairs and Shively was the one at the back end of the parade. When

Noelle and Ellen stopped short she crowded forward, peering over Ellen's shoulder to see who was there.

"Ms. Jamieson," said Detective Patterson, standing in the small foyer, just inside the door, her neck craned as she looked up the stairs. "I have some questions in the matter of Brittany Day's death. Is there somewhere we can speak privately?"

Shively pushed her way to the front. "What is going on here?"

This is not good. Frank's thought was a shout in Christy's mind, but it echoed concerns that had Christy had felt from the moment she saw Patterson in the doorway.

"And you are?" Patterson said, looking up at Shively with raised brows. Shively stiffened as Patterson raked her up and down in a thorough assessment that took in the sensible polyester slacks and jacket, synthetic white blouse and flat-heeled shoes constructed completely from man-made products. "Not one of the Jamiesons, I take it," she said at last.

A rush of color turned Shively's cheeks pink. She announced her name and position with child services like a badge of honor.

Patterson nodded briskly, but she shot Christy a sympathetic look.

Ellen looked at Christy too. Her gaze traveled to Noelle, then to Shively, before she focused on Patterson. "This townhouse is unpleasantly small, Detective, and it is currently full of people. I assume you have a location where we might talk privately. Allow me to get my purse and I'll go with you." She disappeared up the stairs without waiting for an answer.

Don't do this, Aunt Ellen! She'll take you down to the cop shop for questioning. Stop her, Chris!

Christy had a sick feeling in the pit of her stomach. Though Patterson had been willing to question Ellen here and not at the police station, the detective's formality was ominous. Ellen must be in deep trouble. She should talk to Trevor before she did anything and she should probably have a lawyer present when she talked to Patterson. Trevor was just up the street at Quinn's house, but calling and asking him to come would mean leaving Shively here at the top of the stairs, observing everything through those critical, damning eyes of hers. It would also force Patterson to be more specific about what she wanted to question Ellen about. And again, Shively would take it all in, then she'd use it to prove Noelle's living conditions were not acceptable.

Christy had already faced the danger of having child services take her daughter away from her. She'd fought and proved that the allegation against her was false and nothing more than a malicious threat. But once you were in the system, you stayed in the system and Shively took her job seriously.

"Mom," Noelle said. "Tell Aunt Ellen to stay here."

"We need Mr. McCullagh, the man who's staying with the Armstrongs," Christy said. She used her foot to prod the cat. She couldn't exactly say, "Go get him, Frank!" but it was what she meant.

"Ah, defense council," Patterson said. "I assume Ms. Jamieson will wish to have her lawyer present during our discussions."

"Why would she need a lawyer?" Shively asked, frowning.

"I believe that is between Ms. Jamieson and myself," Patterson said pleasantly.

The cat stood up, arched its back and hissed, then bounded down the stairs, slipping between Patterson's legs and out the door.

Patterson followed its departure with her eyes. "I see your cat is as, er, assertive as usual, Mrs. Jamieson."

Since the cat had been injured defending her against Frank's killer, and usually hissed at Patterson, except for that one morning on the porch, the detective's comment was reasonable. Christy suppressed the edginess that had rushed through her as Patterson watched the cat leave and said, "Stormy has the heart of a tiger, Detective. He just hasn't realized he doesn't have the stature of one."

Patterson's lips twitched and there was a gleam of amusement in her eyes, but she didn't laugh. Probably not allowed to when she was in cop mode and about to question a suspect.

Ellen came down from the bedroom level with her purse in hand and her head high. She paused to give Noelle a kiss on the head and to hug Christy. If there was a hint of a tremble in her embrace, she didn't acknowledge it. She ignored Shively as she glided down the last set of stairs to the foyer. "If you are ready, Detective?" She raised her brows, calm, elegant, in control. A Jamieson to the end.

Patterson immediately became all business. She nodded curtly and gestured Ellen out the door to the unmarked car that was parked—illegally—outside Christy's front door.

"Mom, do something!" Noelle's distressed voice drove Christy down the stairs and outside.

She hovered, uneasily aware of Shively behind her, gawking, and Noelle plastered against her side, dismay in every tense inch of her. "Ellen, hang on a minute. At least wait until Trevor gets here."

Ellen shook her head. "Christy, don't worry about me. Detective Patterson simply wants answers. I'll be fine. And I don't need the services of Mr. McCullagh. I've done nothing wrong."

Patterson had the door to the back seat of the car open and Ellen was preparing to enter it, when Trevor burst out of the Armstrongs' front door and bounded down the stairs from the front porch. "Wait just a damned minute."

"Mr. McCullagh!" Noelle squealed.

"Counselor," Patterson said, her hand on the top of the car door.

Ellen said, "This is not a good time, Trevor," in a low voice.

Trevor blinked and stopped, a puzzled frown on his face.

Roy, Quinn, and the cat had followed him out the door. They stood behind him, silent, but clearly friends who had his back.

Eyes on the men, Patterson said, "I am taking Ms. Jamieson to the station for questioning at her request, gentlemen."

"I'm fine, Trevor. Roy. I'm sure Detective Patterson merely seeks clarification on some of the minor details related to the case. She will ask me a few questions and that will be all."

"Not without me, she won't," Trevor said in his big, booming court voice.

"I'll get the car," Roy said, and disappeared into the carport.

Ellen bent to climb into the back seat of the detective's sedan.

"Stop!" Trevor said. "If you insist on interviewing Ms. Jamieson at headquarters, I will escort her there."

Patterson raised her brows.

Still positioned to enter the car, Ellen looked over at him and said, "Stop making a scene, Trevor. Detective Patterson, we are wasting time. Please proceed." She turned her back on Trevor and slid into the backseat. There she settled, elegant as always, her hands folded in her lap, her back straight. She looked more like a woman in a chauffeur-driven limo, than one being transported by the police.

A faint smile twitched the corner of Patterson's mouth, then she shut the car door, leaving Trevor standing with his hands bunched into fists at his sides. She walked around the front to the driver's side, then slipped inside and started the engine. Before she could pull away, Roy gunned his car out of his carport.

He paused long enough to throw open the passenger door and shout, "Hop in, Three. We'll beat her there!" before he roared off, the passenger door still closing as Trevor dove into the car and settled himself on the shotgun seat.

Patterson followed more sedately, leaving Christy, Noelle, and Shively standing outside Christy's front door, while Quinn and the cat advanced toward them.

"This is a most irregular family," Shively said, disapproval dripping from her tone.

Bitch. Frank didn't usually use derogative words like that. It showed the depth of his distress over Ellen's situation and his dislike of Shively and the power she held over the family he could no longer protect in a normal way.

Stormy hissed as Christy bent to pick him up, expressing some of the anger Christy could hear in Frank's voice. She rubbed behind the cat's ears in a soothing way. She really didn't want Frank putting ideas in Noelle's mind, ideas the child might blurt out at the wrong moment. She also didn't want Stormy to scratch or bite the irritating Shively. Who knew where that might lead?

Noelle sniffed. "What's going to happen to Aunt Ellen, Mom?"

"Like she said, the detective wants to ask her some questions," Christy replied.

"I believe I have seen enough," Shively said. She sent Christy a direct look meant to intimidate. "I will be speaking to you regarding the child's aunt and her legal situation, Mrs. Jamieson. I am not sure it is advisable for Noelle to be surrounded by persons under investigation by the police."

"No one said Ellen was guilty of anything, Ms. Shively," Quinn said pleasantly, coming up Christy's walk.

Shively turned a baleful look on him. "I have worked closely with the police many times during my career and I find they rarely act without cause. If they have determined that Ms. Jamieson is a suspect, there must be a reason for it."

Horrified, Christy said, "Ms. Shively, please understand—"

"The security of the child is paramount," Shively said briskly. "Ensuring the child is safe is my only priority."

"Yeah, right," said Quinn, who had a journalist's healthy skepticism of all levels of bureaucratic authority.

Shively glared at him, then turned and said curtly to Christy, "I will be in touch."

Christy watched her march up the road to the visitor's parking where she had quite properly left her vehicle.

"That woman is a pain in the ass," Quinn said.

Christy shook her head. "That woman is dangerous."

CHAPTER 15

Christy trudged along the sidewalk, on her way home after dropping Noelle off at school. The morning was cool, the air not yet warmed by the sun, but the cloudless blue sky promised that later in the day the temperature would rise. The beautiful fall day hardly made an impression on Christy though, for she stared down at the sidewalk as she walked.

Ellen didn't return from the police station last night and there'd been no message from her or Trevor with an update on her status. Quinn had called with the news that his father was back, but Trevor was not, and that was the last Christy had heard. She had a sinking feeling that Ellen had been arrested for the murder of Brittany Day.

She shoved her hands into the pockets of the jacket she was wearing and hunched her shoulders. It wasn't the cool temperature that made her shrink inside herself, but a fear of what the future would bring.

Noelle's morning had been blessedly normal. Mrs. Morton had greeted her at the classroom door the way she always did, and showed no evidence that Joan Shively had been on the telephone, telling her to grab Noelle and turn her over to child services. Noelle herself had been deep in conversation with Mary Petrofsky from the moment they met in the playground and she hardly noticed when Christy kissed her good-bye and left.

Now Christy was on her way home, desperately trying to figure out how to keep her daughter safe—and with her—and not in the custody of child services because the whole Jamieson clan had been designated as unsuitable adults.

She didn't see a lot of options. The best—and most obvious—would be for the police to admit that they had made a mistake and that Ellen was not implicated in Brittany's murder. Hopefully that would happen, but it didn't look likely to be anytime soon. The next option was to remove Noelle from the vicinity of the complex and scandalous Jamieson family.

She could do that, Christy thought. She could take Noelle home to Kingston, where they could stay with Christy's very respectable parents until this mess with Brittany Day's murder was all sorted out. Even the disapproving Joan Shively couldn't disparage a household that included two academics who taught at one of Canada's most prestigious universities.

Kingston was a long way from Vancouver, though. Across the Rocky Mountains and past the Great Plains. At the mouth of Lake Ontario, in fact, the most easterly of the Great Lakes.

She reached the bottom of her street and paused before heading up it. She and Noelle would be safe in Kingston, but they'd be biding their time, unless she decided to stay and rebuild their lives there. Did she want to make that change? Leave Vancouver behind and along with it all the good and bad that had defined her life here?

She started moving again and headed up the street. Her muscles protested as she tromped up the small rise, which was ridiculous. It was a little hill, not the Grouse Grind, a hiking trail to the top of one of the North Shore Mountains. But then, perhaps it was her thoughts that were making her footsteps drag, not the physical exertion.

She reached her townhouse and paused at the end of her front walk.

The cat was sitting at the top of her porch steps, tension visible in the bunching of his blocky muscles. *Don't bother coming up. We're going over to the Armstrongs.*

Christy resisted the urge to sigh. She wasn't sure she could handle seeing Quinn right at the moment, not when she was contemplating leaving him behind as she fled to Kingston for safety. "It's pretty early to be knocking on someone's door."

They're awake. I've already talked to Roy and Three.

"I need a coffee."

They have coffee. The voice was urgent. Impatient. *Look, Chris, I want to get this sorted out. Aunt Ellen is a prickly old broad, but she's not going to do well in jail. Not to mention prison.*

Christy stood her ground. "Frank…"

Stormy stood up, then bounded down the stairs with a tiger-like grace. The cat might have been any feline headed over to a human for pats and scratches, but for his tail, which lashed back and forth in an irritated way. *Three didn't get back until late last night and he was beat, so there was no time to plan. But we need to. Now.*

The cat brushed past Christy, rubbing the length of its body along her leg as it went. This time she did sigh as she turned and followed her dead husband and the cat he inhabited further up the street.

Quinn answered the door when she rang. There was a smile on his mouth and a welcoming warmth in his eyes. He was holding a coffee cup and morning stubble still covered his jaw. Christy's stomach did a little flip then settled into a warning cramp. If she went back to Kingston the promise in his gray eyes might never be anything more than a promise. Whatever might be between them would never come to pass.

He would be forbidden fruit. Perhaps he already was.

The cat prowled into the house, not waiting for an invitation. It hissed as it passed Quinn. His smile twisted into a rueful one and he handed Christy the coffee cup. "Come on in."

His voice was low, morning-rough. Awareness slithered through Christy and she had to clear her throat before she could say, "How did you know I needed a coffee?"

Quinn raised his brows as if to say, *You have to ask?* "My father told me to bring you a cup when I got the door."

She looked at the mug, then back at him and laughed. "Right. I should have figured. I told Frank I didn't want to come over until I'd had a cup."

"There you go," said Quinn. He glanced up the stairs. The cat's tail was disappearing around the corner as it headed for the kitchen. Quinn looked back at Christy, his gaze wicked. "Good morning," he said, his voice even huskier than before. Then he bent and kissed her.

Christy kissed him back. She loved the touch of his lips on hers and somehow the caress seemed to give her hope. Maybe there was a way out of this mess without going to the extreme of leaving town.

Anything was possible.

He broke the kiss all too soon. As she shifted back, he drew his knuckles down her cheek in a tender caress. There was a smile on his lips and in his eyes as he said, "Come upstairs."

The Armstrong kitchen was filled with edgy men and an upset cat when Christy and Quinn entered. Roy was at the stove, manning the frying pan, while Trevor sat at the table bleary-eyed, nursing his own mug of coffee. Stormy had taken up a position in the middle of the table and was sitting motionless, like a warm, furry statue. His stillness held its own kind of tension though, perhaps all the more anxious for it.

She's here now. Let's get to it.

"We haven't eaten," Roy said, flipping bacon. "Morning, Christy."

"Morning Roy, Trevor. Thanks for the coffee, Roy."

Roy looked over his shoulder. His smile was mischievous. "Thank Frank. He said it was the only way to get you over here. Would you like some bacon and eggs?"

She shook her head. "Thanks, but I've already eaten."

Roy nodded and went back to his cooking. Quinn dropped a couple of slices of bread into the toaster, then picked up a half-full coffee mug. "Have a seat," he said, gesturing toward the table.

"How was Aunt Ellen when you left last night?" she asked Trevor as she pulled out a chair.

"She was holding it together, but only by a thread, I think," Trevor said.

Of course she was. She's a Jamieson. She's not going to let some two-bit policeman break her.

Trevor's expression was so gloomy Christy's heart sank, despite Frank's bravado.

But what had she expected? Being booked for murder was a trauma Ellen wasn't going to get over for a very long time. "What can we do?"

Trevor shrugged. "An initial court date is set for this afternoon. When she appears before the judge, I'll ask that she be allowed to return home on her own recognizance. Because she's being indicted for first degree murder, the judge will probably demand that she posts a surety—bail, in other words—to ensure that she returns to stand trial. I'm hoping her good reputation in the community will mean that it's only a token amount, but it could be sizeable."

"It's murder. A messy, emotional murder that they're charging her with," Roy said from the stove. He put bacon to drain on a plate covered by a paper towel, then cracked an egg into the frying pan.

Christy stared into her coffee mug. What to do if Ellen was released from custody? She'd expect to return to the Burnaby townhouse, which would put Noelle square in Shively's disapproval sights. Could she put her daughter at risk for a woman who had never been her friend?

The egg sizzled. Roy cracked another and dropped it in. The toaster popped. Quinn pulled the bread out and dropped in two new slices. He put the toasted bread onto a place and buttered it, his knife scraping over the surface.

The sights and sounds of a normal morning meal. Christy drank her coffee and wondered if anything would ever be normal again.

Trevor rubbed a hand across his eyes in a weary gesture. "Yeah, and because the cops are painting it as a murder of passion, they may ask that Ellen be retained in custody."

Christy looked up, frowning. "You mean they may keep her in jail?"

Trevor nodded. "I'll do my damnedest to make sure that doesn't happen, but we have to consider it."

Why?

"Because the evidence is overwhelmingly against her," Trevor replied.

Quinn brought a plate with toast on it over to the table. "Don't mind me. Just pretend I can hear the damned cat like the rest of you."

Grates, doesn't it? There was a gleam of malice in the cat's green eyes.

"You," Quinn said, pointing at the cat. "Leave the food alone."

Stormy lowered his head to sniff at the plate. His whiskers twitched and his nose curled, then he studiously ignored the toast.

Quinn laughed.

He doesn't like toast. He wouldn't even take a bite, though I tried to convince him to. Frank sounded aggrieved. Christy wasn't sure whether he was mad at Stormy or Quinn.

"Emotions are running high," Roy said. He plated two eggs, then added another two to the pan to cook. "No need to bicker."

Quinn saluted the cat with a lift of his coffee mug and dropped more bread into the toaster. He picked up the coffee pot and brought it over to the table to refill the mugs. "What's the evidence against her?"

"Timing, to start with," Trevor said. "They can't believe she could be in her apartment and not be aware of Brittany's death. They found blood on the nightgown she was wearing that night. The blood type is the same as Brittany's and they expect that DNA testing will prove that it was Brittany's blood. And they found hairs the same color as Brittany's on the pillows of Ellen's bed. Those are being tested as well, but again the cops expect them to be proven to be Brittany's."

Roy handed around plates of eggs and bacon. "Sounds like they've painted Ellen into a pretty tight corner."

Quinn dropped cutlery at each place, then sat down. "Is Ellen still claiming that she wasn't in a relationship with Brittany?"

She wasn't in a relationship with Brittany or anyone else!

Christy picked up the cat and dropped him on her lap. "You can get back into the center of things later. For now, let the guys eat."

"Yes," Trevor said, apparently responding to Quinn's question rather than Christy's instructions to the cat. He popped a forkful of egg into his mouth. "The police don't believe her, though. The evidence is there and it's pretty clear. A woman's hair doesn't get on your pillow unless she's slept beside you and her blood wouldn't be on your clothes unless you were there when she was killed."

"Sure it would," Roy said. He dipped a piece of toast into an egg yolk and ate it. "I can think of a bunch of scenarios that would account for it and not implicate Ellen."

"You're a writer, Armstrong, and a damned good one. You snatch ideas out of the ether like they were fish in a pond. Most murderers aren't as smart as you. They don't have the imagination to successfully implicate someone else."

Good thing, since policemen wouldn't be smart enough to catch them if they did.

"Now, Frank," Roy said. "Think positive."

How can I? It took my wife and your son to prove I'd been murdered. The cops didn't even think I was dead!

"What's your scenario, Dad?" Quinn had obviously decided to ignore the rest of the dialogue, part of which he couldn't hear.

"Brittany wasn't dead when Ellen left the apartment."

While he calmly scooped up egg yolk with his toast, the rest of them stared at Roy.

"You're suggesting that the murderer and Brittany were in the apartment when Ellen woke up, packed her bag, and left?" Trevor said. "The cops have already ruled that out."

Roy shook his head. "No. I'm suggesting that the murderer came into the apartment, made noise that sounded like a scuffle, broke the mirror and table, then crept out again. When that person saw Ellen leave, he or she forced Brittany into the apartment, then took her out onto the terrace and killed her. He or she would know they had plenty of time since Ellen left with a suitcase. Once Brittany was dead it would be easy to soil the nightgown and put the hair strands onto the pillow. It would also be easy to slip away unseen before the housekeeper arrived."

"Ellen left the apartment about six thirty in the morning. The housekeeper usually arrives about noon. That's a pretty big window of opportunity," Quinn said. He looked intrigued. Clearly his brain was working along the same lines as his father's. "So how did he or she get in? I presume Ellen didn't sleep with her doors unlocked."

"I'm sorry to burst your bubble, Armstrong, but the police asked the same question," Trevor said. He sounded weary. "Ellen's lock is a standard Yale, but only the building superintendent and her housekeeper have keys. And she doesn't leave a key on the exterior of the residence, for instance on the lintel or under the carpet in the hallway."

Quinn studied him. "Let me guess. Both the housekeeper and building super have alibis for the time in question."

"They do."

"So Ellen is doomed?" Christy felt almost relieved as she said it.

"No, she's not. Keys can be copied." Quinn shot Christy a quick look. "Has she ever loaned her key to a friend to water her plants when she's away?"

Christy shook her head. "The super does the watering for all the tenants. It's part of the condo service."

"Left her keys on the table when a tradesman was in the apartment?"

What kind of tradesman?

"Does it matter?" Christy asked impatiently.

I'm just trying to get a clear picture, here. But actually, that's not the sort of thing Aunt Ellen would do. She's almost paranoid about watching service people when they're in her space. She trusts no one.

Quinn looked at Christy and the cat with a raised brow. She colored and said, "Frank says she would never be so careless."

"Then maybe the housekeeper murdered Brittany and planted the evidence," Roy suggested.

"And arranged for a falsified alibi? Not likely, Dad."

Roy shrugged. "The thing is, I don't think Ellen is guilty. I don't like the crime of passion as a motive. It's not in her characterization. I couldn't sell this to a bored reader, let alone to a hypercritical editor."

"I wish this was a novel, Roy," Christy said, surprising herself by how wistful she sounded. "But it's not. The cops think that the romance gone wrong motive is pretty good. They must. They're not even looking for other suspects."

"Then we'll have to do it," said Quinn. He stared across the table at the cat, raising his brow in a pointed challenge.

Still sitting in Christy's lap, the cat shivered in reaction. Frank might have conflicted feelings about his Aunt Ellen, but obligations to name and family ran strong in the Jamiesons. *Tell him he's on.* There was a moment of tense silence. *But he'll have to be the eyes and legs.*

CHAPTER 16

Christy cleared her throat nervously as she ignored her late husband's response to the challenge. "Frank and I might not be able to help."

Quinn frowned, but it was Trevor who spoke, his voice as sharp as his piercing gaze. "You don't believe Ellen is innocent?"

"No! No, it's not that. It's…I may be taking Noelle to Kingston, where my parents live, for safety. If I do, Stormy will come with us."

On her lap, the cat leapt to his feet, back arched, tail quivering. His extended claws bit into Christy's flesh and dug. *No! I won't go. I'll stay with the Armstrongs.*

"Ouch. Frank!"

I'm not going to abandon Aunt Ellen. The old broad might not be my favorite person, but she's family. I'm not going to let her be railroaded into prison without a fight. The cat wriggled out of Christy's hold and jumped down from her lap. He circled the table to where Roy sat, then jumped up into his lap where he positioned himself so that he could glare at Christy to the maximum effect. *I'm disappointed in you, Chris.*

"I'm not abandoning Ellen—"

"That's the way the police will see it," Trevor said.

"I can't help that," Christy said, her voice tight. "I have to do what is best for my daughter."

What's best for Noelle is for us to remain a family.

"Then come with us, Frank! You don't have to stay here."

If Ellen's here, I'm here.

"You're impossible!"

I'm trying to do what's best for my family, but you're not helping. If you run home to your mom and dad, you'll never come back to Vancouver. I told you I'd always look after you, but you aren't listening. You never listened.

She launched herself to her feet. "I hear plenty of talk, Frank, I just don't see any action."

That's because you don't believe. You never believed in me!

"This isn't about you, it's about Noelle. I'm going to talk to her after school, then I'll make the travel arrangements when we get home."

You're making a mistake, Chris!

"Maybe I am, but Joan Shively has power I can't defeat. I've already tried once, but she's still out there, after me. After us! I have to go if I want to keep Noelle safe."

Okay. Run. Turn away. It's what you do best.

Stung, she pushed back her chair and lunged to her feet. "I've heard enough. And I've had enough. I'm leaving."

Emotion and embarrassment had her keeping her head down to avoid Quinn's eyes and his outstretched hand as she hurried away from the table. She heard the scrape of his chair, but she didn't pause. Instead she ran down the stairs, anxious to be gone. She was out the door and halfway down the porch steps when his voice called her name. She stopped and turned slowly to face him.

He was standing in his open doorway, leaning against the doorframe, his hands in his pockets.

"I'm sorry," she said. "Listening in on a couples fight is uncomfortable. Only hearing one side must be torture."

His mouth quirked up in a half smile as he pushed away from the doorjamb and came toward her. "I don't care what the cat said. It's what you said that matters to me."

She watched him approach, not moving, her thoughts despairing.

When they were face-to-face, he reached out and gently tucked a stray lock of hair behind her ear. "I understand why you want to leave Vancouver. I don't think it will solve all your problems, but I do understand."

She swallowed the lump in her throat and sniffed back the tears that threatened. "Thank you."

His hand stroked down her cheek and came to rest on her shoulder. "There has to be a way to sort out the Shively problem without resorting to relocation to another province."

"I don't want to go, but it's the only option I can see."

"All I ask is that you don't rush away immediately. Give me a chance to work this out with you. Together we found out what happened to Frank, despite the odds against us. We can figure out what to do about Shively as well."

"Quinn, I—"

He brought his hand up again, and put his finger on her lips. "Shh. Come out to dinner with me tonight. We can talk it out quietly, without the damn cat interfering."

Despite herself, Christy laughed. It was little more than a chuckle, but it sounded good to her ears, although maybe it was Quinn's faith in her that lightened her mood. All she knew was that she wanted to be with him tonight. "All right. I'll come out with you and I won't make any arrangements until we've talked."

He rubbed his thumb over her cheekbone in a tender gesture. "I'll pick you up at six."

The afternoon was as beautiful as the morning had been. The air was clear, with just a hint of crispness, and the sky was a cloudless blue. In the woods surrounding the path, the sun shone through the stark, bare branches of the maple and cottonwood trees and made the dark needles of the evergreens gleam. It was a day to savor and enjoy, because the dull skies and raw drizzles of winter would soon be the norm. Vancouver's weather wouldn't matter, of course, if she relocated to Ontario, but Quinn's faith in their ability to solve this latest problem gave her at least a smidgeon of hope that she'd see another rainy BC winter rather than a snowy Ontario one.

"Let's go for a walk along the path before we head home," Christy said when picked up Noelle at the school.

"But Mary and I—" A glance at Christy's face made Noelle frown and swallowed the protest she was about to make. "Okay."

Christy bit her lip. She didn't want her daughter to fret, but she had to talk to her about their future and she thought it would be better to do it away from the house. She held out her hand and Noelle took it, then they walked together to the rear of the school grounds and out onto the path through the greenbelt.

When they had walked some distance from the school, Christy said, "Aunt Ellen was officially arrested today, sweetheart."

Noelle's eyes widened and she paled. "That sounds bad, Mom, but what does it really mean?"

"Aunt Ellen may have to spend some time in jail and then she will to go to court. It won't be nice for Aunt Ellen." Christy bit her lip. "Or for us."

Noelle kicked at the fallen leaves littering the path. "You mean like when Daddy disappeared and everyone thought he was a bad man?"

Christy sighed. "Yeah. People judge even though they don't know all the facts. It will be stressful."

Noelle was quiet while she processed this. She trudged down the path, her hand clutching Christy's. That she wasn't skipping along, full of exuberant energy, was evidence of the weight Ellen's arrest put on her. Christy's dark, troubled mood deepened. Finally Noelle said, "Do you think she did it, Mom? That she hurt that lady like the police said?"

Christy hesitated. Did she think Ellen was guilty of causing Brittany's death? Ellen Jamieson was a difficult woman and she could be cold, but murder? "There's a lot of evidence against Aunt Ellen. The murder happened in her condo, so naturally the police are suspicious."

"Yes, but do *you* think she did it?"

Yes or no. Christy had to jump down on one side or the other. She swallowed hard and stared at the lacy fronds of a distant cedar tree without really seeing them. "No, I think Aunt Ellen is innocent."

"Good," said Noelle, sounding more cheerful. "Because Daddy doesn't think she's guilty, and neither do I. I like Aunt Ellen. I'm glad she's come to live with us and I don't want her to go to jail."

Out of the mouths of babes. "Good point."

They walked on in silence for another few yards. Christy said cautiously, "What do you think about going to Kingston to visit Grandma and Grandpa?"

Noelle looked up at her, a big grin on her mouth. "Yeah! I love Grandma and Grandpa! When? For Christmas?"

"No. Sooner." *Tomorrow, so Joan Shively can't take you away from me.* But she remembered her promise to Quinn and said, "In a few days, perhaps."

Noelle frowned. "But what about school?"

"We could homeschool you while we were in Kingston. Or we could enroll you in a school there."

Noelle shook her head, a horrified expression on her face. "But Mom! My school is doing a Christmas concert just before the holidays. Every class has a project and mine is doing a play. I have one of the big parts. They can't do it without me!"

"Someone else will be given the part," Christy said.

"No! It's mine!" Noelle pulled her hand out of Christy's and stopped. "It's important, Mom. Mary and I are partners. We're going to practice together. We promised each other!"

"But Noelle—"

"Mary was scared and she didn't want to do the part, but I said I'd be in the play too and she said she'd try. I can't dump her and run away, Mom. She needs me!"

Noelle, the child of wealth and privilege, was used to being the focus of attention, hiding her moods and thoughts in front of others, acting on a stage that had nothing to do with a school play. She wanted to help her friend and now she had a way to do it.

"Noelle—"

"I love Mary, Mom. We are total BFFs. If I left, Mary would drop out of the play and then Mrs. Morton would be mad at her and she'd get into all kinds of trouble." She looked up at Christy, her eyes despairing. "How can I do that to her?"

Christy stared down at her daughter. Since Frank's disappearance Noelle's life had been one upheaval after another. Now she was putting down roots in this small neighborhood and at the local school. Christy should be relieved. Instead she was terrified. She no longer had the option of cutting and running.

She wasn't certain how she was going to make sure Noelle stayed in her care, but she knew one thing. She would fight to make damned sure Noelle had the opportunity to practice her lines with Mary Petrofsky for the next few weeks and that she would be on stage at the school's Christmas concert come December. She crouched down so that she was at eye level with her daughter. "Okay, kiddo. We'll visit Grandma and Grandpa some other time. We'll stay right here for now."

Noelle threw her arms around Christy with such enthusiasm that she almost knocked her over. Laughing, Christy hugged her back.

Now all she had to do was make sure Ellen didn't go to jail and to do that all she had to do was figure out who killed Brittany Day.

Simple.

Yeah, right.

CHAPTER 17

Quinn looked at the collection of ties on the tie rack in his cupboard and pondered which one he would wear tonight. He didn't have a lot of ties. Men with a lot of ties wore suits everyday to work and he didn't have to, thank God. He did have enough to make the choice of which one to wear tonight a bit of a decision, though. Then again, so far every one of his wardrobe choices had been a decision. Not surprising, he thought, when his future was hanging in the balance.

If Christy left Vancouver, it would probably mean the end of the very promising beginning of their relationship. He wasn't sure if, when, or how that relationship might end, but he was certain he didn't want it to end now. So tonight he had to convince Christy that if she stayed here in Vancouver, together they would they would be able to keep Noelle safe from the wicked witch of child services.

Clothes, it was said, made the man. Christy might not have been born a Jamieson, but she had lived as one for ten years. She knew the power that money and status brought, and she knew how men who wielded that power looked. They wore dark, expensive suits, power ties, and pressed white shirts. Their chins and cheeks were clean shaven and their hair was styled and combed.

Tonight he was wearing each and every one of the visual clues that said he had power and knew how to use it. He was taking Christy to a restaurant on Robeson that was not the most expensive place in town, but it was currently *the* spot for those in the know. Visiting movie stars making a film in Vancouver. Corporate executives who wanted to prove their discerning taste. Socialites who loved the new and unusual. He would take her there and he would show her that he could slide easily into this world, because he knew and understood power.

And then he would convince her to put her trust in him, stay in Vancouver, and explore the wondrous possibilities a relationship between them could bring.

He contemplated his tie collection. For what he planned tonight there were only three possibilities. One was a solid red silk that would contrast nicely with the navy blue fabric of his suit and stand out against his crisp white shirt. Red was a power color, another bonus, but it was also a favorite of Canadian politicians of a certain stripe. He moved on.

Option number two had a pattern of thin alternating stripes of blue and silver. The blue was a nice marine color and the silver had a bit of a shimmer to it. It too would work well with the suit. But how about his shirt? He held it up against one white sleeve. The silver washed out a bit, so the tie didn't have the punch the red one had. Still, he liked the combination. He put it aside for the moment.

The next choice was striped as well, but the stripes on this one were wide and the blue and red combination was eye-catching. The colors were also those of his alma mater. In fact, the tie was the official school tie.

He looked at the tie. Power was owned in many ways. Money and old wealth were the obvious ones, but networks made through friendships, shared experiences, allied interests, and personal outlooks were another. This tie represented such a network, one that was part of the new Vancouver, because the university was an upstart institution from academic expansion of the 1960s. Formed in the heady days of student protests, it began as an innovative school where the rebellious and radical congregated. Over the fifty years since, the student body had sobered up from that intoxicating beginning. The rebels of the sixties and seventies turned into the corporate CEOs of today and the upstart itself became one of the top educational institutions in Canada.

The red-and-blue striped tie said he was resourceful, inventive and creative. He might not have old money behind him, but he had something better—a link to some of the brightest minds and most successful entrepreneurs in the country.

He slipped the old school tie around his neck, flipped the shirt collar down around it, then knotted it.

After shrugging on the suit jacket, he fiddled with his shirt collar to make sure it lay flat, then moved the knot an infinitesimal bit to the left, just to be sure it was perfectly straight. A quick check of his chin, by rubbing his hand down his skin, to make sure he'd shaved closely enough, and he was ready.

As ready as he'd ever be when his future was on the line.

Christy's heart did a little flip when Quinn arrived to pick her up. She was attracted to him when he dressed in casual, everyday clothes and might or might not have shaved that morning, but tonight he'd clearly gone to some trouble for her. The suit he was wearing shaped to his body, the shirt perfectly pressed, and the tie an elegant understatement of good taste. He'd shaved and it looked like he'd had his hair cut that day. He'd done it all for her and the knowledge set butterflies free in her stomach and made her feel suddenly shy. She opened the door wider and said, "Hi. I'm almost ready. Come on in."

He smiled as he entered her small foyer. His gaze drifted over her, slow, sensual and yes, approving. "Take your time," he said, but the look in his eyes said she didn't need to do any more primping on his account.

She stood there for a moment, lost in that gaze, then she shook herself free and said, rather breathlessly, "I won't be long," and ran upstairs to put the finishing touches on her outfit.

She was wearing a dress that she'd bought a couple of years before, so it was hardly in the first stare of fashion, but she knew it looked good on her and she liked how the neckline dipped down in a vee toward her breasts and the way the teal-colored fabric hugged her body. Upstairs she checked her makeup, added some simple costume jewelry at her throat and on her ears and grabbed a pair of black pumps with spike heels that she knew made her legs look long and slender. She carried the shoes when she hurried back down the stairs; she didn't want to start the evening by twisting her ankle.

In the foyer she found Quinn sitting on the stairs talking to Noelle, who was going over to the Armstrong house for the evening. She was looking forward to her night out as much as Christy was. It was like, she'd confided earlier, having a Vancouver grandparent. Her eyes lit up when she saw her mother. "You look beautiful, Mom!"

Christy blushed, because her words had Quinn smiling that sexy smile again. "Thank you, sweetheart."

They walked over to Quinn's house. Noelle held her hand, chatting all the way and skipping every second step. Frank had made himself scarce, for which she was relieved. Tomorrow he'd probably say that Stormy wanted to roam the greenbelt looking for mice, but they both knew that seeing her prepping for a date and going on it with Quinn—another man—was hard for Frank to accept, even if his body was now that of a cat.

When Noelle was settled, Quinn took Christy's hand and led her out to the car. Noelle stood in the doorway with Roy behind her and waved energetically as they drove off. When they were out of sight, Quinn found a spot to park the car, then he'd leaned over, dug his fingers into her hair and kissed her thoroughly. When he eased away, he said, "I think you look beautiful, too," his voice low and sexily rough.

Christy looked into his eyes and saw the truth of what he'd just said in his gaze. Her heart did that little flutter again and she'd turned her face into his hand. "Thank you. I'm lucky to be going out for an evening with such a handsome man."

He grinned at that and whatever constraints might have existed were gone.

He took her to a restaurant she'd heard about, but never been to. It was a small space, very high end in ambiance and clientele, with secluded corners and muted lighting for privacy. The tables were covered with linen cloths, the cutlery was silver, and heavy in the hand, and the glassware was crystal. Despite the almost European look and feel to the place, the food was First Nations, with menu items that included West Coast salmon, plains bison, and eastern venison.

Quinn had reserved a table in a small alcove that gave them privacy to talk and enjoy the evening, but let Christy observe the action in the rest of the dining room. It also allowed other patrons to see her with Quinn, she thought with some amusement as they were seated. She cocked her head at him once they were settled. "This is an amazing place. Have you eaten here before?"

"No, but the restaurant critic at the paper claims it's a 'must visit' and he says that the food is some of the best in the city."

Since Vancouver had a reputation for top-notch, innovative cuisine, that was high praise indeed. Christy was about to say that, when she was distracted by the couple who just walked into the dining room.

She knew the woman through Vancouver Royal Academy, Noelle's former school. Her daughter had been in Noelle's class and she and Christy had been parent helpers on many of the children's field trips. The woman looked around the room with a casual glance. Christy knew when she'd been noticed. There was a quick hitch, almost a stutter, in the woman's glance, then she deliberately looked away.

Some things didn't change. Particularly when Ellen, formerly the most respectable of the Jamiesons, had been arrested for the murder of her lover.

Holding the drinks menu in one hand, Quinn frowned at her. "What just happened?"

She frowned back. "What do you mean?"

"Your expression blanked for a minute and you tilted you head up and your chin out. You only do that when you're being a Jamieson. What happened?"

Christy stared at him, the embarrassment of a moment ago dissipated by astonishment. He had her pat. She did push out her chin when she had to pretend to be one of the rich and unflappable Jamiesons. She also looked down her nose at the same time. Just the way Ellen did when she'd wanted to make Christy feel small.

She said, "You've been watching me." Her voice was low, almost throaty, and it sounded seductive, even to her ears.

What must Quinn be thinking?

"Always," he said. Something smoldered in his eyes, making them gleam.

In that moment, Christy had a very good idea of what he was thinking.

She blushed.

He smiled, slowly, and with a considerable amount of satisfaction.

The awkward moment passed. Quinn ordered a bottle of wine and they discussed appetizers and mains. Christy chose West Coast salmon, smoked Native-style and candied with fruit preserves for her appetizer, and wild duck roasted with salmonberries for her entrée. Quinn began with game soup and followed it with a ragout made from bison short ribs, flavored with wild berries, and served with wild rice. By the time they reached the dessert and coffee stage, Christy was much more relaxed.

"That was delicious," she said, putting down her fork and leaning back in her chair. Quinn had already finished his short rib stew and was drinking the last of his wine.

Their waitress appeared to clear the table. She smiled at them, in a friendly way. "Can I interest you in dessert and an after-dinner drink?" She was a pretty woman, with thick black hair that she wore in a single long braid, and wide dark eyes. She clearly had Native heritage in her ancestry.

Quinn cocked a brow at Christy. "Can you manage dessert?"

She laughed. "I shouldn't."

"We have a selection of fresh berry pies and tonight we are featuring bread pudding made with bannock instead of the traditional bread," the waitress said helpfully.

Quinn laughed at Christy's expression. "Your eyes just lit up." To the waitress he said, "We'll share a bannock bread pudding, please." He looked at Christy. "Would you like a brandy? Or a liqueur?"

She shook her head. "Just a coffee, please."

Quinn ordered two coffees and the waitress went away. He reached across the table to take Christy's hand. "I'm glad you enjoyed the food."

"I enjoyed everything!" She smiled at him. "Especially the company."

He smiled briefly at her, then sobered. "Christy, I know you're worried about Shively and what she can do to Noelle. But I want you to know that I won't let anything happen to her. To either of you."

Her heart did that little flip thing again, and she could feel tears gathering at the corners of her eyes. She didn't think that it was possible for one person to ever completely protect another. In that moment, though, she believed it could happen. Quinn was a man comfortable in himself and in his ability to create change when change was necessary. He could slip easily into the Jamieson world of elites, money, and power, or live quite happily in an everyday world. Tonight he wanted to convince her to stay in Vancouver. He deliberately chose clothes and a restaurant that would remind her that he could be successful in her world. He wanted her to know she wasn't on her own; he was there for her and she could depend on him.

She had already made her decision, but Quinn wasn't aware of that. Everything he had done tonight was deliberately staged to make her stay in Vancouver. To make her stay with him. His clothes, his choice of restaurant, his promise to protect her—Quinn might not realize it yet, but he had committed himself to her, and to Noelle, even if he wasn't able to express his feelings in words.

"I know," she said, smiling rather mistily at him.

He looked down at their entwined hands. His dark lashes swept down, covering his eyes. His expression was intent when he looked up again. Christy had a sense that he needed to reassure her. "You've been through a hell of a lot in these last few months and until September, you had to face it all on your own. You don't anymore."

"No," she said. "I have you, Quinn." Her voice was soft, little more than a whisper. His words were bringing her emotions so close to the surface it was impossible for her to speak in a normal way.

It took a moment for her words to penetrate, then he grinned widely. "Yeah, you do. And my dad. And it looks like Trevor is on your team as well."

She smiled. "Your dad is great, but it's you I trust." She sobered and sighed. "I need your help, Quinn. I talked to Noelle about a move to Kingston this afternoon and she told me she didn't want to go. In fact, she begged me to stay. I realized that she is putting down roots here, in Burnaby. She's making friends and she likes her new school. I promised her we'd stay. But I'm scared, Quinn. Shively is like a bulldog. She never gives up. And she has no imagination. She doesn't see that no matter how strange Noelle's family is, we love her and we'd never hurt her." She looked down at their joined hands as he had moments before. "Quinn, when I promised Noelle that we'd stay, I was thinking of you." A little sob escaped before she could catch it as she looked up and into his eyes. "Because I know I can count on you, no matter what."

He lifted their joined hands and kissed the knuckles of hers. "Shh. It's okay. We'll work it out."

She sniffed. "I know."

He laughed. There was a tender look in his eyes. "I'm a lucky guy."

She managed a watery laugh. "How do I answer that without sounding stuck on myself?"

He gave her a teasing smile. "Give it a try anyway."

She was saved by the arrival of their waitress carrying the bannock bread pudding and two spoons. A dark-colored sauce had been drizzled over the warm slice. Whipped cream was swirled to one side. A quick taste told her the sauce was whiskey-based. "Yum," she said, her mouth watering.

She scooped up a portion, then offered the spoon to Quinn. "You get first dibs, lucky guy," she said.

Something smoldered in his eyes as he opened his mouth and accepted her offering.

As his mouth closed over the spoon, Christy's imagination took flight, going to places that sent shivers of desire shooting through her.

Her body felt like it was on fire as he savored the morsel. Slowly.

Her eyes tracked his progress as he swallowed.

And while he savored, his eyes never left hers. "Delicious."

She drew a deep, unsteady breath, then moistened her lips.

He smiled as he spooned a portion of the pudding, added whipped cream, and sauce, then held it to her to taste.

She opened her mouth and let him in. The dessert's flavors exploded on her tongue, sweet and spicy at the same time. The pudding was satisfyingly solid, the whipped cream as light as air, the sauce sweet with just the hint of a bite. The perfect ending to a culinary feast.

The future blazed brightly in that moment. For her. For them.

"Thank you," she whispered when she'd consumed the pudding.

He smiled at her, an endearing half-smile that was pleased, though a little rueful. "Like I said, I'm a lucky guy."

"No. I'm the lucky one." And this time is was Christy who lifted their joined hands and kissed his.

CHAPTER 18

"Where's Uncle Trevor?" Quinn asked, when he found his father at the kitchen table with his laptop open. It was the day after his dinner with Christy. He'd been working in the basement rec room, which he'd converted into an office, for the last two hours. His research had been split between computer searches and telephone conversations. He'd come up to take a break and make some sense of the information he'd gathered.

Roy was peering at the screen, a frown on his face. "I hate Track Changes," he said. "Inserts right in my text and all these little balloons beside it. I wish the editor would just courier me a paper manuscript with good old-fashioned mark-up."

Used to this complaint, Quinn opened the fridge door and pulled out a jug of ice water. "It's faster this way." He poured himself a glass then offered his father one.

Roy nodded. "I'm going blind," he said. "What the hell does that mean? Is this guy nuts?" He hunched deeper into himself and began to mutter, "No, no, no," as he deleted proposed changes.

"Uncle Trevor, Dad. Is he around?"

Roy sighed, then sat back. He picked up the glass Quinn had placed on the table beside him and drank, still staring at the screen. Then he shook his head and ran his fingers through his hair, which was tied at his nape. The result was a rather wild lumpy look, with some locks bunching and others escaping to hang over his eyes. He shoved those back roughly, causing more damage. "No," he said. "He's gone out." He leaned forward, okayed or canceled another couple of changes, then dragged his gaze away from the screen. His eyes lit on Quinn's face and sharpened. "Down to the cop shop to see what he can do for Ellen. He left about nine this morning."

It was eleven now. Quinn made a noncommittal noise then drank the cold water.

Roy pointed at him. "You've been researching the university people. Did you find out anything interesting?"

Quinn rummaged around in the pantry cupboard, found a bag of jalapeño potato chips and brought them over to the table. He sat down opposite his father and said, "Lots."

Roy made a "give" motion with his hand, twitching his fingers toward himself. Quinn opened the bag of chips and offered it to him. Roy made a face, which caused Quinn to grin, but he took a handful and stared to munch.

Quinn delved into the bag and came up with a big round chip, heavily spiced. He bit off one side and chewed. "Turns out Dr. Jacob Peiling's research program is in deep financial trouble."

"You don't say." Roy dug into the bag for another handful.

Quinn nodded. "His funding for the program comes from a bunch of different places. The Jamieson Trust grant is only one of many and not particularly large at that. His major funding is from a government agency, the Science Council. The initial funding was for four years."

"And the four years are up?" Roy said, speculating.

Quinn nodded. "To get an extension, he had to write a results report and create a proposal for the next four years. He didn't get it in on time."

Roy raised his brows and raided the chip bag again. "Is he a perfectionist procrastinator who couldn't get his act together?"

"No." Quinn drew out the word, consuming one chip and digging in for another. He waved it at his father. "Not all of his grad students got their reports done and into him on time."

Roy sat up straight. "Brittany Day?"

Quinn nodded. "He used the excuse of Brittany's death and the resulting confusion to ask for an extension."

"Did he get it?"

"Apparently."

"Well, well, well." Roy leaned back in his chair and stared thoughtfully at his son. "That's very interesting. I'd say it gives Dr. Peiling plenty of reasons for being happy Brittany is dead, but does it provide him with enough of a motive to kill her?"

"Yeah, that's the question. A lot of his other funding is tied into the government grant, though, so it's important. If he loses it, he loses the others."

"Which ones?"

"The most important is a substantial grant from the university that comes out of their general funding. Then there's a provincial grant that is tied into the federal one. He also has sizeable grants from Roger Day's company and from Nathan DeBolt's company. Those are not reliant on the government funding, but they aren't enough to keep the program operating at the current level. If he doesn't secure the Science Council grant he'll lose at least two grad students, plus lab space."

Roy looked startled. "He only had four to start with. That would cut his program in half."

Quinn ate some more chips, then chugged half a glass of water. "Since the Science Council grant stretched over four years, the research is expected to produce significant results. The other grants are annual, but also achievement-based. He's got the Day and DeBolt grants for this year, but if he doesn't provide suitable outcomes, he could lose them next year."

"What happens to his grad students if he loses all his grants?"

Quinn shrugged. "The master's degree students like Brittany and Bradley Neale would have to look for a new program, possibly at another university, if they wanted to continue to the PhD level. I expect the PhD candidates would continue, but would have to find other funding. But they'd all be graduates of a failed program. Not much help if you're trying to build a career."

"So the TAs have good reason to be happy over Brittany's death, too. But like Dr. Peiling, is the funding issue enough to provide motive to kill her?"

"Probably not. There's also the problem of the location where Brittany was found."

"Ellen's apartment." Roy sighed and pushed the chip bag away. "How would Peiling get a key to her apartment to let himself in? And why would he kill Brittany there?"

"Spite over the cancellation of the Jamieson donation?" Quinn suggested. "The Trust provided the grant, but Ellen Jamieson was the trustee who networked with the university. Until the grant was discontinued, she was on Peiling's steering committee. We know the Trust had to cancel the grant because of the embezzlement, but maybe Peiling didn't. If he and Ellen had ever disagreed over committee issues, he might have imagined she had it in for him."

"And so he decided to get back at her in a way that would really stick it to her." Roy contemplated the idea as he sipped his water. "I like it. Makes Peiling seem just a little off-kilter. Gives him edge and makes us wonder what he might be up to next."

"This isn't a novel, Dad." There was amusement in Quinn's voice.

Roy managed to look indignant, but his eyes were alight with humor. "Is he a wimpy guy? Mild mannered and self-effacing?"

"I wouldn't call him a big personality," Quinn said, eying his father and eating more chips.

Roy pointed an emphatic finger. "Definitely an edge. Wimpy guys like him are unstable. They take it and take it and take it some more until they blow. What makes this guy tick?"

"His research," Quinn said without hesitation.

"There you have it." Roy raised his hand. "Threaten his program and you give him motive."

"Maybe," Quinn said, unconvinced. "I dug up another interesting fact, though."

Roy did his "give" motion again as Quinn, grinning, stretched out his announcement. "Nathan DeBolt is on Peiling's steering committee."

"Is he now?" Roy breathed out the statement. "That is very interesting. Brittany Day provides an alibi—a false alibi!—for Nathan's son, Aaron. Nathan's wife, Natalie, is a close friend of Ellen Jamieson, in whose apartment Brittany's body is found. Both Ellen and the DeBolts are involved with Jacob Peiling." He ticked off the points on his fingers as he itemized them, but by the time he was finished he was shaking his head. "There are links there, but I don't see how they connect."

Quinn shot his father a thoughtful look. "Maybe Peiling imagined he could settle a score and put the DeBolts into his debt at the same time, ensuring that the DeBolt funding would be guaranteed to continue. So he was the one who arranged for Brittany to make the false alibi statement. And when she decided to recant it, he realized that not only would DeBolt no longer be in his debt, but the man would be infuriated by the reversal. If that happened, DeBolt would ensure that Peiling lost the grant. So Peiling killed Brittany before she could make the change."

"And put her in Ellen's apartment to pay Ellen back."

Quinn nodded.

"I like it," Roy said, nodding. Then more enthusiastically, "I like it a lot!"

Quinn ate another chip. "There's still the problem of the key and getting into Ellen's apartment."

Roy waved his hand in dismissal. "Easy. All he has to do is filch a key from the super or the housekeeper, take it to a hardware store, and get a new key cut. He could do it in half an hour. The super or housekeeper would never know it was gone."

"Which would make the whole scenario very hard to prove."

"Yeah," said Roy, gloomy now in contrast to his enthusiasm from a moment before. "Still, Three says the defense doesn't have to prove who did the murder, it just has to throw enough doubt on the prosecution's case to convince the jury that the defendant isn't guilty."

Quinn nodded. "I'm going to continue to pick at the university connection and see if I can find any dirt on the TAs. The further we can push this away from Ellen, the better."

Roy nodded. "Good idea." He jiggled the laptop, shaking his head as the screen come alive. "I've had enough of this computer editing stuff for now." He saved the document, then clicked off the program and closed the computer. Then he beamed at his son. "What would you like for lunch?"

"Want to come out to EBU with me tomorrow?" Quinn was leaning against a tree in the wooded area above the townhouse complex. His hands were on Christy's waist and her hands were on his shoulders. They were standing very close together. So close he could feel the heat of her body.

So close his body was screaming out for hers.

She was smiling at him, her expression dreamy, her eyes not quite focused. He'd finished kissing her about thirty seconds ago and she was still locked in the pleasure of it.

He knew that because desire was thrumming through his body with an intensity that demanded more. Much more.

Hence the question. He needed to get his mind off the physical. Off the impossible and back onto something sensible.

Murder.

She blinked and looked confused, but she didn't pull away. "Do you have something specific in mind?"

She looked so gorgeous he wanted to kiss her again. Instead he reached up to stroke the hair at her temple. "I want to sweat the good Dr. Peiling."

She laughed and said, "Sweat him? That sounds ominous."

"It is for him," Quinn said. He could hear the lazy seduction in his voice. They might be talking about the murder investigation and a field trip to the other end of town, but his body—and certain parts of his brain—were still filled with desire for the woman he held in his arms.

And he didn't care. Hell of a thing, that. He was working on two levels, physical and intellectual, at the same time. He could still plan a cold-blooded interrogation of a reputable university professor who apparently had a lot to hide, while he contemplated the pleasure to be had kissing—and more—the woman in his arms.

Who seemed to be working on the same set of principles.

She nestled in a little closer and her smile deepened.

She had to feel his arousal. She had to know how much he wanted her. Maybe her movement meant she wanted him just as much. Now that was something to contemplate. The problem was, where did they go to take what they both wanted one step further?

"What did you find out?" she asked.

Her mouth was inches from his. The urge to close the distance, join with her and let nature take its course beat through him. The woods were thick here, relatively quiet at this time of the day. They could slip through the underbrush, find a private place—

A dog barked.

Maybe not. On this path, a barking dog meant a human walking it and at this time of day humans were likely to let their dogs off leash, even though technically it wasn't a no-leash zone. A dog off leash was likely to investigate interesting sounds and smells in the trees bordering the path.

He sighed, kissed the corner of Christy's mouth—chastely—and used both hands to ease her away from his body.

She laughed, her siren's eyes telling him that her thoughts were drifting in the same direction as his until the damned dog barked. "You were researching the people Brittany knew at the university. Any interesting connections?"

She stepped back and he took her hand in his. They resumed their walk down the path. The early December afternoon was chilly, with that crisp edge that signaled the damper, colder weather of winter was on its way.

"I told you about Peiling and the funding issues around his program. Bradley Neale, the TA who usually covered for Brittany, seems to be a straight-up guy dedicated to his studies. He's career-focused and has virtually no social life. He was smitten with Brittany, though."

"Smitten?"

Christy's brow wrinkled into a frown that did nothing to minimize her gorgeous looks. Man, he had it bad if he thought a frown was enticing.

"Neale asked her out a few times, managed to get her to go to dinner with him once. Then she took up with Aaron DeBolt and Bradley was sweet out of luck."

"A good reason for him to go after Aaron, not Brittany."

"That's what I thought. The other male TA, Lorne Cossi, is not very well liked by the female undergrads he supervises, but I couldn't get anything specific. It seems to boil down to he's curt sometimes, charming others."

"So he's moody. Not an easy guy to work for or with."

The dog they'd heard earlier came barreling around a curve in the path at a full gallop. Its tongue was hanging out, big ears flapping. It skidded to a stop in front of them and barked. Christy crouched down to eye level and shoved out her hand for the big golden dog to sniff.

Quinn reached for her. He wanted to grab her and pull her back behind him out of harm's way, even though there was no evidence that the dog was unfriendly or dangerous.

The dog inspected her hand, barked again and wagged a long, hairy tail. Christy laughed.

Quinn redirected his reaching hand to pat the dog. Christy bestowed a bright, approving glance at him. He scratched behind the dog's ears, his hand close enough to grab the animal's collar.

Just in case.

The owner trotted around the curve, huffing as she attempted to catch up to her unruly dog. "Bruiser!"

The dog barked and its tail wagged harder, setting the animal's whole hindquarters in motion. He licked Christy's hand and she laughed again.

When the owner came level, she clicked a leash on the dog's collar and apologized profusely. "Most people are at work at this time of day and the kids are in school, so Bruiser and I usually have the path to ourselves. He loves to run and, well, he's too fast for me to keep up. He's harmless, though, as you can see."

Christy said, "He's beautiful." She stood up. "Good-bye Bruiser. Nice to meet you."

The dog woofed. His mistress tugged at the leash and headed off in one direction while Christy and Quinn went in the other.

Christy laughed softly. "You never know who you'll meet on the path. Or when you'll meet them."

It was acknowledgement that their earlier, unvoiced, decision to put distance between themselves was the right thing to do. So her mind *was* working on the same level as his.

Interesting.

Reassuring. He tightened his hold on her hand and she squeezed back. Something—not sexual, but deeply intimate, nonetheless—flooded through him. He looked down at her and smiled. The laughter in her face deepened into tenderness. His heart began to pound.

He wanted to kiss her.

Again.

And take her into the woods.

And that would be as bad a decision now as it was ten minutes ago.

He dragged his gaze away from hers and drew a deep shaky breath. "Rochelle Dasovic is by far the most interesting of the TAs."

"Why?" Christy asked. Her voice sounded husky, as if she was thinking about the woods too. Well she would be, wouldn't she, if they were both on the same wavelength?

"Rochelle Dasovic is a fraud."

Christy stopped. Now fully engaged in the conversation, she stared at Quinn. "In what way?"

"She plagiarized her way into Peiling's program."

"Whoa! Are you sure?"

"Yeah. I found some Twitter chatter between Rochelle and another woman. The woman claimed she and Rochelle roomed together at the University of Victoria and that they were in some of the same classes there. In their third year, they worked together on a project that became the basis for the woman's fourth-year research project. She took the idea and ran with it, while Rochelle stuck to an easier path. When it came time to apply to grad school, Rochelle took the woman's fourth-year paper and submitted it to EBU with her name on it. It was the other woman's work that got Rochelle her place with Peiling."

"Was Peiling aware of the Twitter controversy?"

Quinn shrugged. "I don't know. That's why I want to go out to the university and grill him."

Christy looked thoughtful. They resumed their stroll, their feet making no sound on the layer of fallen leaves, already soggy with November rain. "If Peiling knew and didn't say anything, he could be in deep trouble. What if Brittany found out and the blackmailing she talked about was her blackmailing Peiling, not someone blackmailing her?"

"If Brittany threatened to expose him, his career could be on the line," Quinn said, agreeing. "It's a thread I think we need to pull."

"Absolutely," Christy said, nodding. "What time do you want to get out there?"

"I've got an appointment with him for mid-morning. Gives us time to get Noelle to school before we have to leave for EBU and time to have lunch together before Noelle has to be picked up."

Christy gave him a little bump with her hip that made him laugh, and said, "Sounds like a plan."

CHAPTER 19

D r. Jacob Peiling was a worried man. He tried not to show it, but his shoulders hunched and he refused to make eye contact when he greeted Quinn and Christy. That sparked a number of questions in Christy's mind and from the light that leapt into Quinn's eyes, he'd had a similar reaction. As they settled into chairs in front of Peiling's desk, Christy was careful to choose the one off to the side. She'd let Quinn do the questioning while she observed the professor's reactions.

"Thank you for taking the time to see us, Dr. Peiling," Quinn said after they all sat down.

Peiling nodded. "You would like to discuss Brittany's death further."

"Yes," Quinn said. "I talked to her father. He's understandably distressed, but the conversation raised more questions than it supplied answers."

Peiling nodded again. Had the worried expression on his face deepened? Or was he just dismayed by a violent, unexpected death?

"I understand from Mr. Day that you and he were at university together." Quinn smiled in an encouraging way and his tone was pleasant. Christy knew he was springing a trap, but Peiling seemed quite happy to hop into it.

"Yes. We roomed together as freshmen and later shared an apartment."

"So you were close friends."

"And continued to be after we graduated. Where is this leading, Mr. Armstrong?"

Quinn's smile widened into a self-depreciating grin as he shrugged. "Context and color, Dr. Peiling. I tend to dig deeper than most other journalists, but use less of what I discover in my finished articles. I need to get people and their backgrounds sorted out in my mind, you see, or what I write won't be coherent."

Peiling looked dubious, but he said, "Okay."

"Mr. Day told me that his company funded your research." Peiling nodded. "Did that funding have any influence on your decision to accept Brittany as a student?"

Eyes narrowed, Peiling said, "I don't like what you are insinuating, Mr. Armstrong. You say you don't plan to use the information you're after, but I don't believe you. You're digging dirt for an exposé and I don't intend to help you." He pushed back his chair, a clear indication that he planned to end the interview.

Christy said, "I don't blame you for feeling uncomfortable, Dr. Peiling." She leaned toward Quinn and put her hand on his arm. "Lighten up, Quinn! Dr. Peiling has recently lost both a gifted student and a friend of the family."

Quinn responded by raising a brow. Christy resisted the urge to wink, but she did let a little mischief seep into her smile. When she turned to Peiling she was serious once more. "It's just that Mr. Day came up will all kinds of allegations when Quinn talked to him. Personally, I think he was sounding off, but some of what he said was, well, inflammatory."

Peiling put his hands on his desk and leaned forward. "Like what?"

Christy smiled at him. She had intended to be more of an observer than an interviewer, but Peiling had taken her bait. It was up to her now to reel him in. "He said you've lost so much funding that your program is in jeopardy and you will have to cut some of your grad students. He also claimed that the grant made by his company is all that is keeping your program from being completely canceled."

"How dare he? That is not true!" Indignation added a snap to the professor's voice and he straightened.

Christy nodded encouragingly and smiled in a friendly way. "Then I suppose that you didn't agree to monitor Brittany while she was in Vancouver, both as a favor to him and to ensure he continued to fund the program?"

Peiling shifted uneasily, making his chair creak. "Roger did ask me to keep an eye on Brittany. Of course, I promised I would, but…" He hesitated, then said, "You have to understand, I'm a full professor. I have duties. Responsibilities to my faculty and to the university. I don't have time to shepherd a friend's daughter around. Or even to keep tabs on her. When Brittany came to Vancouver I took her on a tour of the city and told her what areas to avoid and where she shouldn't walk at night."

Quinn raised his eyebrows. "Wow. Shows a lot of caring." Evidently he had decided his role was to poke at Peiling until he lost his temper and admitted more than he planned. "You never told Day you weren't fulfilling your promise, did you?"

Peiling pursed his lips, but didn't reply. Quinn continued, mockery in his voice. "I don't think your casual definition of keeping on an eye on Brittany would have impressed her father. I bet he'd have pulled his funding if he found out. But then, you're a smart guy. You must have known that."

From the color in Peiling's cheeks it was clear that Quinn had touched a nerve. "You're wrong. Roger Day wouldn't have canceled the funding. He understands the importance of the work we're doing here. Besides, he's not the kind of man who would dodge his responsibilities just because I failed to monitor his daughter's social life."

"So you expect him to honor his promise, but you don't have to?"

Peiling set his jaw and didn't reply. Quinn curled his lip into a sneer and continued on. "Roger Day loved his daughter. Did you know that she wanted to drop out when school started in September?"

The shock on Peiling's face couldn't be manufactured. "No!"

Quinn nodded. "Yeah, her father talked her into continuing. He knew something was going on with her, but he trusted you. The end of the semester is coming up. Brittany would have headed home for Christmas and who knows, maybe when the winter semester started in January she wouldn't be back. Think her father would continue to fund your program then?"

His voice barely above a whisper, Peiling said, "That wouldn't happen."

"No? Think again, Dr. Peiling."

Peiling whitened.

"Do you know who introduced Brittany to Aaron DeBolt?" Christy asked, watching the professor carefully. She thought he might greet the question with relief after the grilling Quinn had given him, but he actually paled further.

"Aaron's father, Nathan DeBolt, is one of my most generous private donors. Nathan likes his company's name to be linked to science with a high public approval rating. The theories my program is working to prove squeak into his acceptable range, but the science is complex and difficult to explain to laymen. The media rarely features us for that reason, which is why the DeBolt funding is shaky." Peiling paused, then said with a rush, "I needed to give Nathan a good reason to continue to fund us this year."

"It was you who paired Brittany with Aaron?" Christy couldn't keep the disgusted amazement from her voice. "Did you know what kind of man Aaron is?"

Peiling was squirming now, shifting uneasily in his squeaky chair, his gaze resting anywhere but on Quinn or Christy. He cleared his throat. "Natalie DeBolt brought Aaron to one of the events I put on to allow the students to network with the donors and steering committee members. She asked for an introduction. What could I do?"

"Were you aware Aaron DeBolt supplied drugs to all of his girlfriends?"

"No." Peiling sounded defeated and his expression was bleak. "I swear I didn't. Look at it from my point of view! Natalie and Nathan DeBolt are reputable people. Why would I think that their son was not cut from the same cloth?"

Quinn eased the conversation into a new direction. "Did any of the other grad students in the program know that Brittany was the daughter of a man who both funded the program and was your personal friend?"

Coloring, Peiling snapped, "You make it sound as if I did something wrong."

Quinn leaned forward. "Somebody killed Brittany. On the surface, that somebody appears to be Ellen Jamieson. A simple, straightforward case, right? The more I learn about Brittany's life here in Vancouver, though, the less I like the straightforward answer." He stared at Peiling, his expression intense, and Christy could see that the professor's gaze was caught in Quinn's. For a minute they stared at each other, then Peiling looked away nervously.

Quinn continued as if the silent standoff had never happened. "I'm not judging you, Dr. Peiling. I'm trying to find answers and the more details we have about Brittany's life in Vancouver, the easier that will be."

Peiling cleared his throat. "Brittany was happy here. At least at first."

The words sounded stilted, as if he'd rehearsed them to be presented to anyone who would listen. Quinn nodded.

"She got along with everyone," Peiling continued. "I can't imagine that any of her colleagues here at the university would want to harm her."

Christy blinked. Who did Peiling think he was fooling? "The TAs Brittany shared an office with were pretty competitive when Quinn and I spoke to them. The only one who seemed to be at all friendly was Bradley Neale."

"Brad's a good fellow," Peiling said.

"Did you know he was filling in for Brittany at her lab classes?" Quinn asked.

"No!" Again, the surprise on Peiling's face looked real.

"He had a crush on her," Christy said. She leaned forward and smiled, turning the comment into friendly gossip, instead of a threatening revelation. "Unfortunately, Brittany wasn't in the least interested. I suppose that could have made him jealous."

Peiling drew a deep breath and said, "I have no idea. I don't interfere in my students' personal lives."

"Not even Brittany's?" Quinn said gently.

Peiling colored. "Look, I've had enough—"

"If you don't know about their personal lives, maybe you're better informed about their professional ones. Like the reason why Rochelle Dasovic passed off the research paper she used to get into your program as her own when it was written by someone else."

"Rochelle plagiarized?"

"You didn't know?" Quinn said the words, but they weren't really needed. The man's pale features were answer enough. Quinn's comment had caught him completely off guard.

Christy shook her head solemnly. "When I met the three TAs, I thought Bradley Neale and Rochelle were nicer than Lorne Cossi, so if they have secrets, Lorne must have some too. And I'll bet his are worse."

Peiling swallowed nervously. Christy had hit a nerve. "I'm not allowed to discuss my students with outsiders."

"Of course you're not. That's okay. I'll dig up the dirt on Lorne Cossi, just like I did on the other two," Quinn said cheerfully.

"Lorne is a sleazy sexual predator, but he's not a murderer!"

Quinn went very still. "Do you have proof?"

"Lorne has a…a need, I guess you'd say, to dominate women."

"Including Brittany?"

Peiling shrugged. "I don't know. But last year one of Lorne's female undergrad students accused him of forcing her to have sex with him. It was a difficult case, because the girl admitted to being attracted to Lorne, even though she said it was more of a fantasy crush than a real desire for a relationship. Other students testified that he made sexual remarks, but claimed he showed no interest in going any further than a light in-class flirtation. The one who leveled the accusation claimed he had a dark side and that he invited her to his apartment, where he threatened her until she agreed to have sex with him. He denied the allegation."

"What happened?" Christy asked.

"The case was thrown out because it couldn't be proved. It was the girl's word against Lorne's."

"Let's put this all together," Quinn said. He ticked the items off on his fingers as he spoke. "You, Dr. Peiling, were supposed to keep Brittany safe. You failed to do that and I think you feel at least a little guilty about it. Without Brittany in the program there is the question of whether or not Roger Day will continue to support it, especially when he finds out that you introduced Brittany to Aaron DeBolt and his unhealthy lifestyle." He raised a second finger. "You have a funding shortfall that could lead to the loss of one or more student positions. Brittany's position was seen as secure because her father is one of your key funders. That leaves three students looking over their shoulders, wondering if their grad degree is in jeopardy. That's an excellent motive for wanting Brittany—the one person who didn't have to worry—out of the way. Plus each of the TAs have the kind of personality flaws that could make them willing to turn envy into action." He paused, smiled and nodded with satisfaction. "I think I could make a good case that the cops should be looking to EBU for Brittany's killer."

"Then you'd be wrong." Peiling's lips were pinched and white, his eyes angry. "I think it's time for you to go. I have nothing more to say." This time when he pushed his chair back and stood up, he didn't back down.

Christy stood when Quinn did and followed him out of the office. "What do you think?" she asked.

Quinn slipped his arm around her waist. "I think Brittany deserved better than what she got."

Christy leaned against him as they wandered down the hallway. "Yeah. Her life here seems so barren. You know, until we started digging into Brittany's past, it never occurred to me that Aaron's girlfriends were anything but an extension of him."

"Probably because that's how he saw them."

Christy sighed. "So what now?"

"I believe the cause of Brittany's death is here, in Peiling's program. I'm not sure what it is yet, or how the details fit, but my gut tells me it's all tied together."

"Grad students, the professor, the donors, the steering committee. That's a lot of details."

Quinn squeezed her waist. She turned her head to look up at him and he smiled. "Guess we'd better get started."

CHAPTER 20

"Mrs. Jamieson."

The school door was still swinging closed behind her when Christy heard her name called. She identified the voice as coming from the parking lot and turned in that direction. She saw that Detective Patterson was striding toward her. Behind her, Christy saw the detective's familiar, unmarked car. Even as she wondered why the cop would seek her out at her daughter's school, she was straightening cautiously.

"Detective," she said as Patterson neared. "Is there an emergency of some kind?"

"No." Patterson hesitated, then said, "Is there somewhere we could talk? A café, for instance?"

Christy could have invited her to the townhouse and offered coffee, but she wasn't feeling particularly sympathetic toward the detective since Ellen's arrest. "This is a residential area. The closest coffee shop is over at the mall. We'd have to drive there."

Patterson raised her brows. Her car was in the lot nearby. Driving to the local mall wouldn't be a problem.

But Christy didn't want to get into Patterson's vehicle and drive anywhere with her. Patterson was dressed in her usual slacks, a sweater, and leather jacket, so she didn't officially look like a cop, but Christy knew what she was, and what her car represented. She would never willingly climb into Patterson's car, not here, near Noelle's school with all those potentially watching eyes. Not even at her townhouse, where there might be more watching eyes.

Nor did she want to hustle home, get her own car and follow the detective to a destination. She was upset about Ellen's arrest, and the stresses it had put on her and her family. The fears it had roused. The danger it embodied. She didn't intend to make anything easy for Detective Patterson.

She tilted her head, indicating the wooded area behind the school with a gesture. "There's a walking trail just over there. It's quiet and pretty much unused at this time of day. Would that be private enough for you?"

Patterson gazed at her for a moment, then she nodded. "Lead the way."

In this section of the path, trees grew thickly on either side of the trail. Salmonberry bushes edged it, growing profusely. At this time of year their raspberry-like fruits, a soft peach in color, were gone, but a few weeks ago the bushes had been loaded with berries and after school one day Noelle and Mary Petrofsky had come on a giggle-filled harvesting trip. This was her turf and here she felt ready to deal with whatever Patterson sent her way.

The detective waited until the trees surrounded them and the school was well behind before she told Christy why she'd sought her out. "Aaron DeBolt is being released today." Patterson stared straight ahead as she made the statement. Her expression was unreadable.

Christy's stomach knotted and her breathing hitched. "This can't be," she said, even as she accepted it was true. Ever since she'd heard about Brittany's alibi she'd known that it was only a matter of time before Aaron was freed.

Still…

"My God. He helped kill my husband! You can't just let him go!"

"He has an alibi for the night in question, Mrs. Jamieson." Patterson's voice was even. Her expression was still blank.

Christy rarely swore. Her upbringing and her years in the spotlight as the wife of the Jamieson heir had made her careful about her choice of words. But this was different. Outrage gripped her. Anger tripped off her tongue. "That's bullshit! Brittany was lying. Aaron lured Frank into that alley and then pushed him into the car that drove him to his death. Aaron is guilty as sin. Damn it, the judge wouldn't even grant him bail! And now he's going free?"

They walked on in silence. Christy struggled with her temper. Patterson gave her time to regain control.

Eventually the detective said, "For what it's worth—and right now that's not much—my gut tells me that you're right. Aaron DeBolt was an accessory in your husband's death. I haven't been able to shake the alibi Day gave him, though, and that's why I have to turn him loose."

Christy pursed her lips and stared anywhere except at Patterson. Ahead of her a chickadee danced in the thicket of low growing salmonberry. She recognized the bird's familiar call. Chickadees were abundant in the area and she heard their song every day. Usually she found the sound soothing. Now she was too upset to notice.

She couldn't think of anything to say to Patterson that wasn't ripe with frustration and anger. She got the picture. Brittany Day claimed Aaron had been with her on the night Frank was murdered. Brittany had also been murdered, and the person the police suspected had committed the crime was Ellen Jamieson, Frank's aunt. Why would Ellen kill Brittany? To keep her from testifying and to negate that damned alibi.

"Do you have *any* hard evidence I can use to prove that the alibi is false?" Patterson asked after a few minutes of silent walking.

Christy shook her head. "Quinn and I have been digging into her background, but we've found nothing that you could use in court." They'd been focused on finding other suspects to use in Ellen's defense, though, not disproving the alibi Brittany had given Aaron. Maybe it was time to change priorities.

Patterson shrugged. "Then there's nothing I can do."

"What would happen if I could prove that Brittany was lying?"

"It would have to be pretty good proof," Patterson said sharply. "Day swore an affidavit before she died and she's no longer here to defend herself. Evidence that she'd lied would have to be rock solid."

"And if it was?"

"Then I'd re-arrest Aaron DeBolt."

Christy nodded. "Okay. Thanks for the heads-up."

The purpose of the meeting achieved, they turned and headed back the way they came.

"With Aaron's release you need to stay away from the DeBolt family, Mrs. Jamieson. It doesn't look good, particularly now that your aunt has been granted bail. Nathan DeBolt is tight with a lot of powerful people and he knows how to manipulate the media. He won't hesitate to go after you, your friends, and your family if he thinks you are a danger to his son or his reputation."

Christy appreciated the warning, but the DeBolts' power and their wielding of it wasn't new to her. "Ellen won't be staying with me once she's released. Now that her condo is no longer an active crime scene, she's going to be going back there."

Patterson looked surprised. "She suggested that? Not something I would have expected of the woman."

"She's not going to like it, but I can't let her stay. I don't have the option. She has to go."

"Why?"

"Not because I think she's a cold-blooded killer. I don't. But the child care worker assigned to Noelle's case was horrified that Noelle might be residing in the same house with someone accused of murder. She all but told me she'd take Noelle away from me if I let Ellen stay. If I have to choose between my daughter and Ellen, my daughter wins hands-down."

They were almost at the parking lot as Patterson nodded. There was compassion in her eyes and a certain amount of frustration as well. "I understand. Please contact me if you find out anything new that might relate to the case, Mrs. Jamieson."

"Sure." A fine fall drizzle started as Christy watched the detective stride to her car.

Great. Now not only did she have to deal with the uneasy guilt that nagged at her conscience because she was banishing Ellen back to a crime scene, but she was walking home and she'd be soaked by the time she arrived.

She shoved her hands in her pockets, hunched her shoulders and started moving.

By the afternoon, Christy's bleak mood hadn't softened. On her way over to the school to pick up Noelle, she shut her front door with a snap and slid the key into the lock. Then, behind her, she heard the purr of an expensive engine as a car neared.

Uh-oh. Here comes trouble, Frank's voice said in her mind.

"What kind of trouble?" she asked, looking down at the cat to see he was staring intently at the car coming down the road. His tail swished back and forth, a cat clue that he was angry and prepared for anything. She threw the lock as quickly as she was able, then turned around to see for herself.

Frank was right. This was trouble with a capital T.

The car, a sleek Mercedes, belonged to Natalie DeBolt. It came to a quiet stop right in front of Christy's front walk. There were three people inside and they were all preparing to leave the vehicle.

Christy ran down the porch stairs and strode purposefully toward the car.

The cat stayed on the stoop now settled into his favorite position—seated on his haunches, back very straight, rear paws tucked under him, front legs straight and close to his body, tail curled around his feet.

"Don't get out," Christy said, as Ellen, seated in the front passenger seat, put one hand on the open door frame and angled a foot out of the car.

She frowned. "What are you talking about?"

By this time Natalie had emerged from the driver's side and the third person—Aaron DeBolt—was half out of the rear seat, passenger side.

Christy ignored Ellen and rounded on Aaron. "And you! I don't know how you dare to show your face here! All of you, away." She made swishing motions with her hands. "You're not welcome here."

Over the top, Chris. Ellen's family.

The voice, sounding nearby, was grudging. Christy looked down and saw that Stormy had left his post on the porch and was standing beside her. His back was arched, his fur stood on end and his eyes were narrow slits. As Christy watched, the cat crouched, ready to pounce.

Aaron on the other hand, is a good call. If he won't get back into the car, I'll help him along.

"Shit," said Aaron, looking down at the cat.

"Language," said his mother.

The cat growled, a low ominous rumble that promised danger.

"It's that crazy cat." Aaron flung himself back into the car and slammed the door.

"Aaron, what are you doing, darling? Ellen has invited us for tea," Natalie said. She ignored Christy and started round the car, clearly heading for the house.

Christy shot one look at Natalie, then focused on Ellen. "Did you talk to Trevor?"

"Yes," Ellen said, frowning. She was wearing the same clothes she had on when she left the house two days before. She looked rumpled and drained. Christy resisted the urge to give her sanctuary and let her come inside. "Then you know that your presence here puts Noelle's future in jeopardy. Trevor and Roy have been getting your place in order so that it would be ready for you when Trevor posted bail." She glanced at Natalie, now around the car and standing by Ellen's open door, then looked back at Ellen. "Why are you here with her, anyway?"

"Natalie looks after me," Ellen said. "Friends do that." She sniffed. "Family should too."

You have got to be kidding. There was disgust in the voice and some resignation too. It reminded Christy that Frank had spent much of his childhood being hassled and manipulated by Ellen Jamieson. Right now she understood what he was feeling. Ellen's refusal to see anything but good in the DeBolt mother and son made it easy to banish compassion and guilt.

"Uh-huh. And how did Natalie look after you?" Okay, her hostility was rude and maybe over the top, as Frank had said, but Christy couldn't help it. Aaron DeBolt, a man who had always treated her like unwanted trailer trash and who had helped to kill her husband, was sitting not three feet from her and Ellen was accusing *her* of behaving badly?

"She posted the bond to secure my release," Ellen said. Her voice was cold, but underneath there was a quaver. "She knew how desperately I wanted out of that place."

Christy could understand that desire. No one wants to stay in jail any longer than they have to. But to allow the mother of the man accused of killing your nephew to post bail? What was Ellen thinking?

Why is Aaron here?

Christy voiced Frank's question.

Natalie opened her eyes wide and her mouth curved into a delighted smile. "Aaron is free! Even though Brittany Day is no longer with us, her affidavit has been accepted by the justice system. Aaron is no longer charged in Frank's murder." The smile broadened, if that was possible. "I was at the police station picking Aaron up, and I asked about Ellen. When I learned that she was still incarcerated I couldn't let my dearest friend languish behind bars any longer. So I got her released too!"

The statement ended on a squeal that made Natalie sound like a brainless bimbo who had just maxed out her sugar daddy's credit card buying a new wardrobe. But Christy knew Natalie wasn't brainless. What was up? She narrowed her eyes as she said to Ellen, "Trevor arranged the bail money with your bank this morning. He planned to get you out today. In fact, he may even be down at the police station now."

Ellen, still seated in the car, now had both feet now on the pavement and her body angled out the door. "I knew his intentions," she said. "But Natalie was there and—"

Natalie reached down and grabbed her hand. "Come on. Let's go inside and celebrate!"

Aaron opened his door again. The cat growled, then hissed as he once rose into an angry pose, back arched and ears flattened.

Aaron shut the door with a snap.

Christy put her hand over Natalie's and said in a low voice that was her version of the cat's growl, "Celebrate somewhere else. I want you gone."

And if they didn't depart soon, she'd have to leave them behind, free to do whatever they wanted, because she had to be over at the school to pick up Noelle.

"I don't understand why you are being so hostile, Christy," Ellen said.

Christy looked down and sympathy tugged at her. Ellen's face was a frozen mask, but there was misery in her eyes. She was holding herself together, but at a tremendous cost. Christy sighed. "Do you remember Joan Shively, the child services worker?"

Ellen nodded.

"She's made it very clear that she will take Noelle into care if she is living in the same house with you. I have to decide between you and Noelle. There is no choice."

To her credit, Ellen nodded. At that point another car came down the street. This time it turned into the Armstrongs' driveway. Roy and Trevor were back.

Stormy bounded toward them. Evidently Frank intended to fill them in on the action. Good thing too, Christy thought. She could use the support. "Please get back in your car, Natalie," she said as politely as she could. "There will be no tea party this afternoon."

"Nonsense!" Natalie said. She smiled down at Ellen. "Ellen, tell her."

"Christy, Noelle isn't even at home yet. Natalie has done me a great service and I am so very grateful…"

Roy reached the Mercedes a few steps ahead of Trevor and the cat. "Ellen!" he said. "What are you doing here?"

"She's with me," Natalie said. She smiled.

Bared her teeth, more like, Christy thought, eying her. She looked at Roy and Trevor. "I have to go pick up Noelle. I don't want them here when I get back. Can you handle it?"

Roy nodded.

Trevor looked into the back seat. "So this is Aaron DeBolt."

Roy and Christy froze. Stormy hopped up onto the planter box beside the walk. Standing on the wooden frame he was just about eye level with the window in the car door. He hissed and arched his back in a threatening way.

Trevor was now bent over so he too was eye to eye with Aaron. "The cat doesn't seem to like you," Trevor said affably. "I wonder why?" He straightened, then stared at Natalie, assessing her. "Can't say I blame him."

Natalie's mouth tightened into a thin line. Temper flashed in her eyes.

On a roll, Trevor extended both hands to Ellen. "Come, fair lady. It's not a wise idea for you to be consorting with a DeBolt—"

"But we are such dear friends," Natalie said. The temper was gone and now her mouth was screwed up into a teasing pout.

"Really?" Roy said.

Ellen accepted Trevor's hands and eased out of the car until she stood in front of him. Trevor smiled approval.

"Come over to Roy's house. I need to talk to you about your case." He shot a cool look at the still pouting Natalie. "This needs to be a private consultation. I know you understand, Mrs. DeBolt."

Impulsively, Christy leaned over and kissed Trevor on the cheek. "Thanks!" She looked at him, then Roy, and finally Ellen. "I've got to go. I'll see you later."

Roy patted her on the shoulder. "Don't worry about anything. We'll be at my place when you get back."

Christy nodded. As she hurried down the hill to the main road, she heard Roy say cheerfully, "You're a sinking ship, Natalie. Better get out while you still can."

There was a moment of silence, then Natalie said, "I know when I'm not wanted," followed by the slam of a car door.

As the engine roared into life, Christy chuckled.

CHAPTER 21

With Christmas fast approaching, Christy decided that this weekend was the time to take Noelle shopping. She wanted to choose presents for her parents and mail them early enough to ensure they would be delivered in time for Christmas. It was important, too, that Noelle take part in searching for the gifts. With her grandparents living across the country, she saw them only occasionally. Any link Christy could foster to bring them closer was important.

The mall was festively decorated and in the central court, outside the venerable Hudson's Bay Company store, Santa Claus presided over a snowy compound staffed with photograph elves, organizing elves, and cashier elves. Noelle was entranced.

Jamiesons didn't visit shopping mall Santas. Mainly because Jamiesons didn't shop at the local mall, but also because Ellen Jamieson considered mall Santas tacky. Noelle's annual visit to Santa always took place at the Jamieson Ice Cream family Christmas party. There, in that clean and protected environment, she was the first child to sit on Santa's lap and tell him her secret wishes.

Surrounding the Santa enclosure was a miniature train ride. The cars were the perfect size to fit a small child, though the sturdy engine was able to haul the weight of adventurous adults as well. Sitting at the front of the train, on the cheerfully chugging engine, was the engineer. Dressed in traditional striped shirt and cap, he waved cheerfully to the children lined up to visit Santa. The regular toot of engine's horn added to the buzz of voices and the squeals of excited children.

Wide-eyed, Noelle watched the busy scene, her hand tightly clutched in Christy's. On Noelle's other side, Quinn also surveyed the scene. "This," he said, "is chaos."

Christy laughed. She was having a lovely time. Christmas shopping was usually a quiet business since she'd become a Jamieson, with visits to exclusive shops where the staff spoke deferentially and were never far away, or home visits by store managers who brought a representative selection of exquisite goods with them for Christy to review and choose. She'd forgotten how much fun the hubbub of a busy mall could be.

"Mom," said Noelle, "Can I ride on the little train?"

The awe in her voice made Christy laugh again. "Of course. Do you want me to go with you or will you be okay on your own?"

Noelle sucked in a deep breath, opened her mouth, then closed it again. Christy had a feeling she was about to ask that her mom accompany her, but when she tried again, she said, "On my own."

"Brave girl," Quinn said, rubbing her cheek with his knuckle and smiling at her. Noelle beamed and scampered ahead as they went to buy tickets. When Quinn had offered to come along today, Christy was delighted. It would be like a family outing and having Quinn suggest it made her say yes immediately.

The next time the train stopped to pick up passengers, Christy helped Noelle find a place midway along the parade of cars. Ahead of her was a father holding a bemused one-year-old, while behind sat one of the boys from her class. As soon as he recognized Noelle, he began to brag about the number of times he had ridden the train.

She sniffed and ignored him, holding her head high and assuming an air of unflappable boredom. In that instant she looked so much like Ellen that Christy uttered a soft cry.

"What?" Quinn said.

Christy shook her head. "Nothing bad. There was just a moment when I saw Ellen in Noelle's expression."

"And it reminded you of all the problems stacking up around you."

Christy nodded.

Quinn took her hand and squeezed it comfortingly. "Enjoy the moment, Christy. Look at Noelle. She's having a ball."

When Christy looked, she saw that Quinn was right. There was a huge grin on Noelle's lips, though she hung on to the side of the car with a death grip. As the train chugged slowly around the track, Noelle began to look around and her hold on the car eased.

"I bet once this ride is over she'll want another," Quinn said. He appeared to be watching the train with as much enjoyment as Noelle was having riding it.

Christy elbowed him. "You look like you're itching to have a go round yourself."

His face lit up and he laughed. "My parents used to take me to the park where the miniature train enthusiasts have a permanent setup. The place is huge and the tracks go through tunnels and up and down hills. It was an awesome way to spend an afternoon."

"Good memories," Christy said.

"Yeah." He looked down at her, the smile still on his mouth. "We'll take Noelle there when they open up in the summer. There's a picnic area on site. We can make a day of it and we'll all ride the trains."

"Sounds like a plan," Christy said. She found herself lost in his gaze and thought that this day would linger forever in her memory as special.

The train's whistle hooted as it neared the junction point. Catching sight of her mother, Noelle waved frantically, a huge grin on her mouth, her nerves forgotten. Christy waved back as the train rattled past for its second circuit. When the engine finally drew to a stop, Noelle bounded off her seat, excited, happy, and demanding—as Quinn had predicted—a second ride. There was a lineup though, so Christy suggested they do some shopping first, then come back to do the train once more and to visit Santa.

Noelle's eyes lit, then she frowned. "I'd like another ride, Mom, but can I visit Santa later?"

It was Christy's turn to frown. "Why? We're here now."

Noelle dipped her head and stared at her feet, not answering.

Christy looked at the milling crowd around them. The lineup for Santa visits snaked past the train tracks and wound around a corner toward an exit door. People were jostling others to make their way around the display and the train tracks to the big department store beyond. There was noise and action and so much going on. Noelle was probably frazzled. The train ride would be enough for today. Santa would be at the mall for a while yet. "Okay, kiddo. We'll come back later. Maybe one afternoon after school when the mall isn't so crowded and Santa has more time to visit with the kids who come to see him."

Reassured, Noelle looked up and beamed.

"Let's go shopping," Quinn said.

"Yeah!" Noelle said.

Quinn found Christy's hand and took it in his. She looked up at him as she felt his warm skin against hers. He smiled down, a question in his eyes. She grinned in return and eased a little closer to his body. Satisfaction gleamed in his gaze and he squeezed her hand. The moment of unspoken communication pushed her pleasure in the day a notch higher. The stresses of the past week seemed very far away as they set off on the hunt for the perfect gifts for Grandma and Grandpa Yeager.

At the bookstore, Noelle found a pretty bound book for her grandmother to write in and a few doors down, a fancy tie for her grandfather. Christy supplemented these gifts with a lovely set of jade earrings and a necklace carved in the form of a thunderbird for her mother and a beautifully carved cedar box designed to resemble a totem pole for her father. They wound up the afternoon with a stop for a snack at one of the small restaurants in the mall. Quinn treated Christy to a glass of wine, while Noelle had a milkshake and regained the energy that had been flagging at that point.

They headed home after a final visit to the miniature train. This time Noelle demanded Christy record the event by taking photographs with her phone as she rode around the track. Laughing, Christy agreed. She snapped some shots of the Santa enclosure at the same time. Just in case Noelle wanted to reassure herself a visit to Santa would be fun, not scary.

"I want to show Mr. Three and Roy my train ride, Mom!" she announced as they pulled into the Armstrongs' driveway. She had talked non-stop all the way home, filled with a sugar overload from the milkshake and an afternoon of fun.

"I'm not sure Mr. Three will be there, honey," Christy said. "And maybe Roy will be writing. We shouldn't disturb him if he is."

Quinn laughed as he cut the engine. "My dad will be delighted. Come on, moppet," he said to Noelle. "Let's go find him."

"Yeah! Can I have your phone, Mom?" Noelle was the first one out of the car and she was up the stairs and knocking on the front door, the cell phone clutched to her chest.

Christy and Quinn followed more slowly. Ahead of them the door remained firmly closed. Noelle raised her fist and hammered another impatient series of knocks with the flat of her hand.

"Noelle," Christy said sharply. "Manners. Give Roy time to answer before you knock again."

"But Mom!"

Christy frowned at her.

Noelle managed to look contrite. "Sorry—"

The door opened. Roy, his expression distracted, blinked at Quinn and Christy, then realized Noelle was the one who had been knocking. He looked down at her and raised his brows as she waved the cell at him. "Your mom bought you a new phone?"

"No! This is hers. It has pictures of me on the little train. Want to see them, Roy?" Noelle demanded, hopping from foot to foot.

Roy opened the door wider. "The miniature train from Confederation Park?"

"They were set up in the mall, by the Santa enclosure," Quinn said.

A dreamy look flashed over Roy's face, then he smiled at Noelle and ruffled her hair. "Sure. Come on up, little one. Three and your Aunt Ellen will want to look at them, too."

"Aunt Ellen is here? Yeah!" Noelle bolted into the house.

Roy remained behind. His smile faded as he looked from Quinn to Christy. "There's been an incident. We'll talk about it after Noelle has had a chance to show off."

A quick glance at Quinn showed Christy that he was feeling the same grim foreboding she was. "Is that why Ellen's here?"

Roy nodded before he turned to head up the stairs.

Christy swallowed hard. "How bad?"

Roy glanced over his shoulder. "Really bad."

Quinn caught her hand and squeezed it. His support helped steady Christy. They'd handle it. Somehow they would handle whatever was about to come their way.

Noelle's voice floated down from the living room where she was energetically describing the train, Santa's castle, and her snack, in no particular order. As Christy reached the top of the stairs she saw Ellen sitting on one end of the sofa. Trevor was beside her at the other end. She was leaning forward, doing her best to keep up with Noelle's excited rambling, but from the confused expression on her face she was losing the battle.

Trevor sat with one leg resting on the other knee and his elbow on the arm of the sofa. He looked bemused.

Evidently he wasn't even attempting to sort through the mountain of Noelle's details.

The cat was between them, seated in his usual tidy pose as he watched Noelle's performance.

When Roy reached the living room, Noelle scrutinized the apps on the cell phone and brought up the pictures Christy had taken. "Look. This is me on the little train. Isn't it awesome?"

She showed the pictures to Ellen, who jumped when the cat crawled up into her lap. Stormy was purring loudly and after a moment Ellen reached out to draw her hand from his head, along his back to his tail.

Noelle looked over her shoulder at Christy, a big grin on her face. Christy's heart melted. Despite the ominous news Roy mentioned, she wished she could capture this moment forever.

She heard the click of a camera and looked up to find that Quinn had his phone out. He smiled his crooked half smile and showed her the image. There was Noelle, delight on her face. Ellen smiling, her hand on the cat's back as she stared at the images on the phone Noelle was holding. Roy was beside Trevor and they were both looking at Ellen and the phone. There was a wistful expression on Roy's face, as if he was lost in memories. Trevor simply looked worried.

It was a moment Christy would keep in her heart forever and a photo she would cherish. She smiled up at Quinn. He worked the phone's keyboard, then said, "I e-mailed it to you."

"Thank you." The words were inadequate, but what she really wanted to do—put her hand up and drag his head down for a kiss—was inappropriate, so she had to hope that he'd understand from her expression and the inflection in her voice.

"You're welcome," he murmured. From his tone and the warmth in his eyes, he understood.

"Mom, can I show the pictures to Mary Petrofsky? Pleeease?"

"Yes, but only if you call first and make sure she's home, and that it's okay with her mom," Christy said.

Noelle plugged in the number, which she knew by heart, and retreated to the kitchen to talk to her friend. The adults in the living room chatted about the miniature train and Christmas shopping until Noelle returned a few minutes later.

Just inside the living room, she stopped, staged a pose with her arms flung wide and announced, "Mom! She's home and it's okay."

"Go," Christy said and smiled as her daughter bolted for the stairs. "Noelle, once you've showed the pictures to Mary, ask her mother to put my phone somewhere safe."

"Okay, Mom." She raced down the stairs. They heard the door slam. Noelle was on her way.

The echo of the closing door had hardly faded to silence when Roy said, without preamble, "Jacob Peiling was found dead in his office this morning."

CHAPTER 22

Christy stared at Roy. "How?" she asked.

"Anaphylactic shock. It appears to be an acute reaction to the peanut oil in the takeout dinner he'd been eating at his desk," Trevor said.

"Apparently Peiling had a very serious peanut allergy," Roy added.

"The cops are viewing it as an accidental death," Trevor said.

"How do you know?" Quinn asked. He was watching his father and Trevor, a frown between his eyes.

"It was on the morning news," Roy said. "Why?"

Quinn shrugged, but his frown didn't ease. "It's odd, that's all. A man dying from a reaction to a known allergy isn't news, it's a family tragedy. Are you sure the cops have called it accidental?"

Roy had settled into the armchair at Trevor's end of the sofa, so Christy picked up the cat and slipped between Ellen and Trevor, leaving Quinn the chair near Ellen. "Do you think Patterson planted the story, Quinn?" she asked. "That Dr. Peiling was actually murdered, but the cops don't want it to become common knowledge yet?"

"Could be," Quinn said.

Trevor brightened. "Well, if that's the plan, it's good news for us."

"Why?" Christy asked.

"Trevor stayed at my condo last night," Ellen said. She lowered her eyes demurely as she blushed a pleasing shade of pink.

Christy stared at her. The blush was provoking mental images she didn't want to visualize. She had a sudden realization that Ellen Jamieson, a person obsessed with following the rules of proper behavior and social etiquette, was also a woman who wanted to feel needed and appreciated.

"I was so upset. I couldn't use my bed, even though Trevor and Roy very kindly replaced the mattress and box spring for me. I knew I wouldn't sleep anyway, so when Trevor took me back to the apartment, I asked him to stay. We sat in the living room all night. Talking, for most of it."

"Ellen has an iron-clad alibi for Peiling's death," Trevor chimed in. There was satisfaction in his voice. "If the professor was murdered in his office, there's no way Ellen could have done it. And if she wasn't involved in Peiling's death, that makes it less likely that she was the one who murdered Brittany."

Why?

Apparently forgetting that Quinn couldn't hear Frank and Ellen didn't even know that Frank was rooming with Stormy in the cat's body, Trevor said enthusiastically, "It's obvious, of course! Roger Day asked Peiling to keep an eye on his kid. Somehow the man must have discovered something about Brittany that threw light on who killed her. The murderer then got wind of it and decided Peiling had to go. Since Ellen couldn't have murdered Peiling, it's unlikely she was the one who murdered Brittany."

Ellen listened to this with rapt attention. Apparently she assumed Trevor had just continued his thought process without interruption. She said eagerly, "So you think the police might withdraw the charges against me?"

Trevor put on his poker face. Christy had the impression he didn't want to disappoint Ellen, but he was a lawyer. He knew the police were not always quick to change. "If they find proof that implicates someone else as thoroughly as the evidence they have on you, then yes, they will charge that other person."

Ellen's mouth quivered, then hardened. She sat a little straighter. "In other words, no."

So. We figure it out. That was already the plan anyway.

Trevor glared at the cat. "Easier said than done."

I have faith in Chris. She came through for me when no one believed I was dead. It was Chris who figured out who killed me. She'll come through for Aunt Ellen.

Ellen was staring at Trevor, a confused expression on her face. Christy decided it was time to intervene before Trevor and Frank pushed them all into admitting to Ellen that they were in communication with her dead nephew. She'd never believe that, but it would be even worse if they had to admit that the consciousness of said nephew was residing in the cat presently sitting on Christy's lap.

"Quinn and I figured out who killed Frank. We'll do the same for this case." She looked around the room. "We need a plan of action. Let's start with what we know."

There were nods all around.

"Brittany Day was killed on my terrace, while I was in my bedroom mere yards away." There was a quaver in Ellen's voice but she cleared her throat and continued. "I did not do it, but whoever did could have killed me as well."

"Whoever killed Brittany chose your condo for a reason," Roy said. He cast Ellen a compassionate look. "You were targeted, though I don't think your life was ever in any danger. He or she wanted to frame you for the murder."

"Good point," Quinn said. "Let's look at motive. Why kill Brittany Day? What has she done recently that would make someone willing to end her life?"

"I don't think a sex scandal is enough cause," Roy said thoughtfully.

"There is no sex scandal. That is pure fabrication! I am not gay and Brittany Day was not my lover!"

Stormy's whiskers twitched. *Glad we got that one sorted out.* The voice was rueful and maybe a little relieved.

"So it must be the alibi for Aaron," Quinn said.

"We know she lied about what happened that night, so the alibi was false." Christy frowned. "That puts the DeBolt family in the forefront of our list of suspects. But there are others too. She had bad relationships with the TAs and she implied to her father that someone was blackmailing her. That suggests an EBU connection. Dr. Peiling's death also supports a university connection."

"Was Peiling's death a murder, though?" Trevor said. "The news report called it a tragic accident and the loss of a gifted researcher. Maybe we're completely wrong and Peiling simply didn't take enough care of his health."

"Jacob Peiling made no secret of his allergy. Indeed, he mentioned how severe it was every time he hosted a social evening that included appetizers. And they *always* included food of some kind," Ellen said. Her tone was tart, her expression disapproving. "He was exceedingly careful about what he ate. It wasn't enough that there were no peanuts or peanut products used in the cooking. He also refused to eat anything that might have been prepared with a utensil that had touched peanut products. He was so concerned about the allergy that he carried his EpiPen on him in the breast pocket of his suit jacket."

"He died in his office," Trevor said, "so he probably wasn't wearing a jacket."

"Then the pen would be nearby. On his desk, perhaps. Certainly somewhere in plain sight and within easy reach."

"An allergic reaction isn't like the impact of a bullet, or being hit by a car. The person has a few minutes to respond before shock sets in. Why didn't Peiling use his EpiPen and give himself a shot?" Quinn asked. "He sounds like he was almost paranoid about the issue. He'd know the symptoms. As soon as he felt them, he'd act."

Quinn's speculation had the rest glancing at each other and nodding. Christy said, "Maybe he couldn't find his pen."

"Then he'd call 9-1-1," Ellen said. "I saw him do that once at a party when he thought he'd eaten something toxic."

"So we need to find out if there was a 9-1-1 call and if the paramedics weren't able to get to him in time." Quinn looked thoughtfully at Ellen. "Do you have any idea who might know about his allergy?"

"Anyone who has ever eaten a meal with him, or who has ever been at one of his social events," she said promptly. Then she frowned. "Come to think of it, I don't think I've ever seen him eat a takeout meal. At least, not from a fast-food place."

"Two good points," Quinn said. "First, where did the food that killed him come from? If not from one of his preferred restaurants, then why did he choose this particular vendor? And secondly, which of our suspects have been with him at a social event where food was served? Or have shared a meal with him?"

"That could be a lot of people," Christy said. "All of the students. His advisory board. Those who donated to his program."

Quinn nodded. "It's a long list, but I don't see how Peiling's death can be an accident. He was murdered. So we go back to EBU and we talk to people, starting with Lorne Cossi, who has a bad rep with his female students."

"We should also look at Rochelle Dasovic," Christy said. "She plagiarized a friend's paper to get into Peiling's program. If Brittany found out, she might have been blackmailing Dasovic, causing Dasovic to snap. When Quinn and I talked to Dr. Peiling, we discovered that he didn't know what she'd done. He might have accosted her about it after our visit. If she'd already killed Brittany to keep her secret, she'd be capable of killing her advisor too."

"We also need to talk to Roger Day. He might be able to shed more light on who was blackmailing Brittany or who she was blackmailing."

"I think he's back in Calgary by now," Christy said.

Roy's eyes brightened. "Trevor and I can Skype him."

Ellen frowned. Evidently computers and video conferencing weren't her thing.

"We need to talk to Patterson too," Trevor said. "I can do that."

Quinn shook his head. "Not the best idea. Your relationship with her is confrontational. Christy should do it. Patterson respects her. She can be cagey, but she'll open up more to Christy than any of us."

Great. We've got a plan. The cat stood up and stretched. *Time to celebrate. Break open the tuna, old man, and let's eat.*

CHAPTER 23

"**D**on't you have a desk, Armstrong?" Trevor said as he frowned at the laptop on the kitchen table. He and Roy were searching out the best place to position the computer for the video conference call they were going to make to Roger Day. Their plan was to have Trevor make the call and be the one to interview Day. They both thought Roy should be able to see Day's expression and body language throughout the conversation, though, so they needed spot where Roy could view the screen, but not be in the picture. They'd decided the kitchen table had both, plus a good, large flat surface on which to place the laptop.

"Never used a desk," Roy said. "If you have a desk you have an office. If you have an office you have paper. If you have paper there's always clutter. If you have clutter you can never find what you want when you need it. I prefer the kitchen table. Nothing gets lost that way."

Trevor absorbed this as he looked around the room. It was spacious, well lit and tidy. But it was a kitchen. There was only one blank wall that would provide a plain backdrop for Trevor's image. Unfortunately the wall was a bright, pumpkin orange. He pointed to it. "The color clashes with my suit."

That was certainly true. The suit was a charcoal gray, the fabric a smooth, wool/silk blend. The tailoring was expert. It should have been at the price Trevor had paid for it.

"And my tie." He'd paired the suit with a crisp white shirt and a Mediterranean-blue silk tie. There was no possible way he could sit in front of an orange wall and look professional. "What about the Jamieson place?"

"Christy doesn't have an office either. Her kitchen wall is a nice yellow." Roy looked dubiously at the charcoal-gray suit. "I think it would be worse than my orange."

Trevor grimaced and raised his hand to run his fingers through his hair, but stopped before he made contact. He'd had his shaggy hair cut—styled, actually—at a salon rather than cut by a barber, to emphasize the power look he'd donned with the expensive suit. Running his fingers through it wasn't in the cards.

"What about McCullagh, McCullagh, and Johnson? Think they'd have a spare office?" Roy asked. "Or maybe they'd lend you a boardroom?"

Trevor's brightened. "Good idea! Technically they don't have to provide me with space since I'm retired, but I do consult with them on some of their high-profile cases from time to time." He punched numbers into his phone. "You know, I didn't really feel comfortable calling someone of Roger Day's status from a kitchen," he said over the sound of ringing. It stopped and was followed by the mumble of a voice. "Good morning. Trevor McCullagh here. I'm fine, thank you. Yes, I was wondering if…"

A few minutes later they had a conference room booked, a space with far more sophisticated video conferencing capabilities than Roy's laptop. Trevor had also arranged for a secretary to book a meeting time with Roger Day using the official McCullagh, McCullagh, and Johnson phone system.

"Very professional," Trevor said with satisfaction as they hurried out the door, heading for the carport.

"Frank," Roy yelled, as they descended the porch stairs. "Hustle up. We're calling Day from Trevor's office."

"We're bringing the cat?"

Roy nodded. "Frank likes the odd excursion. Christy usually puts him in a tote bag or a backpack, but I'll just carry him."

Stormy trotted up. He'd been sitting at the foot of the big oak that graced the bottom of the street, staring up at something he'd treed, his tail lashing. Climbing didn't come easily to him due to his size and heavy bone structure. The local wildlife had already figured out that the tops of trees were a much better refuge than going to ground.

Stormy is pissed. He wanted to outwait the squirrel he treed. I thought you were going to Skype from the kitchen?

"Change of plans," Roy said. He eyed the cat dubiously. "If Stormy is in a mood maybe I should get a backpack."

They reached the car. *I'll sit on Three's lap.*

"No way!" Trevor said. "The cat will shed."

"Backseat or backpack. Take your pick," Roy said, opening the car's rear door.

Fine. Stormy hopped into the back while Trevor and Roy got in the front.

McCullagh, McCullagh, and Johnson was on the eighteenth floor of a glass-and-steel tower on West Georgia Street. It was a power address for a firm that had a reputation of being tough in corporate law and rarely losing in the courtroom. Trevor fit right in with his expensive suit and pricey haircut. Roy, dressed in jeans, a sweater, and a leather jacket, his long hair tied into a tail at the back, and holding a large cat under one arm, did not.

Or maybe he did, Roy thought with inner amusement. McCullagh, McCullagh, and Johnson's clients came from all walks of life. All they needed was a bank account that stretched to lots of zeros and a problem that needed to be fixed. He grinned at the receptionist. She looked him up and down, her gaze lingering longest on the cat, though her polite, uncritical expression didn't change. Trevor never broke stride. He simply asked where Johnson had put him as he passed the reception desk. The girl had to leap to her feet, then race to keep up as she babbled directions. Roy slouched along behind, enjoying the show.

The conference room at McCullagh, McCullagh, and Johnson was tastefully decorated in creams and browns. The large oval table was a rich walnut, polished to a high gloss, the swivel chairs were upholstered in chocolate brown leather that was butter-soft to touch, and the carpet was a sandy brown that tied together the darker colors and the cream walls. Trevor sat down in the chair at the head of the table. Frank took the tabletop, while Roy settled in on one of the chairs a little way down from Trevor. The receptionist returned to her desk. She was replaced by a secretary, who brought coffee service for two, then set up the camera so that it focused on Trevor and not on Roy and Frank. To her credit she seemed not at all surprised to see that a cat had accompanied the two men.

"Mr. Day, thank you for taking my call. My condolences on the loss of your daughter," Trevor said as the connection to Calgary came up.

While the camera in the room focused on Trevor, Roger Day's image was projected onto a wall screen so that Frank and Roy were both able to see him.

Day nodded. His expression was bleak, his eyes tired, as if he wasn't sleeping. "I know of your reputation, Mr. McCullagh. I understand your firm will be providing the defense for Ellen Jamieson?"

"We will," Trevor said. "Although I am fairly confident the charges against her will be dropped."

Day raised his brows and for a moment curiosity lit his eyes. "When I left Vancouver, the police seemed pretty sure they had their culprit."

"The situation has changed. You knew Dr. Jacob Peiling as more than just your daughter's program advisor, I understand."

"I did. Look, what's this about, McCullagh?"

"Dr. Peiling's death."

"I thought the police had ruled Jacob's death accidental." Day frowned. "Are you saying that it was not?"

"It's a working theory," Trevor said. His expression was tightly controlled, giving nothing away.

Roger Day was not as cagey. His expression changed from grim acceptance to a frowning concentration. He leaned forward in his expensive leather executive's chair and put his elbows on the table in front of him. "Are you implying that Jacob's death is related to Brittany's?" There was urgency in the way he bit off his words, and in the tension in his body. Roy wondered why.

"I am," Trevor said.

Day remained still for a moment, then slowly he nodded. He sat back in his chair, not quite limp, but as if he'd been relieved of a burden and could now relax. "I think so too. Jacob phoned me on the afternoon he died. He said he had a lead on why Brittany was killed. He wouldn't tell me what he'd found out, though. He said it was big and ugly and he needed proof before he said anything."

"Have you told Detective Patterson this?"

The look Day shot the camera was derisive. "Of course."

Trevor thought for a moment, then he too leaned forward, clasping his hands together and placing his forearms on the tabletop. His expression and tone of voice were persuasive. "Can you think of a reason why Dr. Peiling would be so secretive?"

Day laughed. It was a hollow sound that held no amusement. "Jacob was always careful about what he said. He never made a definitive statement unless he had the facts to back it up. That's what made him such a good researcher. And why he always had trouble finding funding. He refused to speculate and he'd never lie for appearance's sake." Day shook his head and sighed. "When he called, Jacob was upset. No, he was dismayed, as if he couldn't quite bring himself to believe what he'd discovered. He said he'd know for certain that night and he'd call me with the details, probably in the morning if he ran late into the evening."

"And he never called."

Day shook his head.

Trevor pondered that for a moment, then he said, "Did you know Dr. Peiling had a food allergy?"

Day grimaced. "Sure. I shared a house with him and Nathan DeBolt when we were all at university. Before I met Jacob, peanut butter was one of my staple foods. After, I never touched the stuff."

Roy's eyes popped open at the mention of Nathan. He wrote furiously for a minute, then he held up the piece of paper so Trevor could see. *He roomed with DeBolt? How well does he know him?*

"You three were close then?" Trevor said mildly, looking interested, but not excited.

"Jacob and I were," Day said. "He was Brittany's godfather—which was why I asked him to keep an eye on her for me. Nathan was closer to Frank Jamieson and the pack he ran with."

My dad and the trustees. Who knew?

"Does Jacob's death relate to Ellen Jamieson and the case against her?" Day asked, unaware of Frank's comment.

"If Dr. Peiling was murdered, it does," Trevor said. "Ms. Jamieson has a rock-solid alibi for the time he died. If his death and your daughter's are linked, then Ms. Jamieson did not kill Brittany."

Roger Day sighed. "I can't believe Jacob would be so stupid as to eat food from an unknown source and not have his EpiPen nearby."

"You think someone laced the food with peanut oil?"

"Wouldn't take much," Day said. "Jacob was hypersensitive to it."

Trevor thanked Day, then broke the connection. He looked at Roy and the cat. "What do you think?"

"The murderer figured out Peiling knew something that would incriminate him, so he or she laced his food with peanut oil and kept him from using his EpiPen," Roy said. He shook his head. "Easy enough to do, but horrible to watch a man die a slow death in front of you."

"Who do you think did it?" Trevor asked.

Figure out what Peiling discovered and you know who the killer is.

"I'm with Frank," Roy said. "Peiling learned why Brittany was killed. And because he knew the *why,* he thought he knew the *who*."

Trevor rubbed his smoothly shaven chin thoughtfully. "He may have feared he'd be sued if he suggested the person as the killer, so he wanted to have iron-clad proof before he spoke."

Roy nodded. "But did the reason she was murdered relate to the alibi or something going on at the university?"

CHAPTER 24

The long hallway, loaded with little offices, most masked by closed doors, was the same as the last time Christy and Quinn had come to EBU. As they headed toward the office Brittany had shared with the other TAs, Christy could feel Stormy squirming in the tote bag she carried slung over her shoulder.

The cat wants out. He doesn't like closed zippers.

"Soon," Christy said.

Quinn looked at her, brows raised. "Frank's getting restless?"

"No. Stormy."

The cat has no sense of timing. He always rushes his moment. That's why he can't catch the squirrel that's driving him crazy.

Christy thought that Stormy wasn't the only one who was edgy. The three of them had come to EBU to re-interview Lorne Cossi as part of their quest to prove Jacob Peiling had been murdered and to link his death to Brittany Day's. Christy was taking the lead on this fact-finding mission. She figured Cossi would underestimate her because she was a woman and they would find out more than they would if Trevor or Quinn interviewed him.

There had been a lot of discussion about that and it had taken her some quick talking, but eventually she'd persuaded the men in her life to see it her way. Quinn insisted he needed to be nearby and Frank made a fuss too. In the end they both accompanied her to the university. Quinn would wait in the hallway, out of sight of the doorway but able to hear everything, while Frank went with her into the office, tucked safely in the tote carryall.

Quinn had insisted on another precaution as well. Before Christy went into the office, she set her phone to record, so that everything Cossi said was taped. Christy wasn't sure if the recording could be used in a court, but if it could be used as a deterrent if Cossi misbehaved and made Quinn's mind easier, that was enough for her.

Lorne Cossi had office hours in the afternoon, so Roy, Trevor, and Ellen were collecting Noelle from school. Then the four of them were all going Christmas tree shopping. Roy had a favorite cut-your-own lot out in Langley he was taking them too and he promised Noelle she could pick the tree. Christy wasn't sure what she was going to find when she eventually returned home. Noelle was used to giant trees, well suited to the great hall of a mansion, but not the living room of a townhouse.

Lorne Cossi was alone in the office when Christy knocked on the half-open door. He looked up as she shoved it wide and moved into the room. "Hi," she said, fixing a tentative smile on her face.

A frown appeared between his arched black brows and dark blue eyes. It did nothing to minimize the impact of the beautifully sculpted features. Lorne Cossi was flat-out gorgeous.

And he didn't remember her. She might be able to make use of that.

She moved deeper into the room, letting the smile morph into a pout. "You can't place me, can you?" When he raised his brows, she made play with her eyes, drawing him in.

His gaze assessed her. "Are you in one of my lectures?"

She laughed, making sure the sound was full of promise, throaty with allure.

Interest sparked in his eyes and he rose to her bait. "Tell me which class it is. I bet you're one of the top students. Ninety-fifth percentile, for sure."

Flirting with Cossi and pretending she was attracted to his authority wasn't how Christy had planned to start her questioning, but she thought she'd let it play out and see if it gave her any kind of an edge. Secured inside the tote bag, and trapped between her arm and her body, she could feel the cat move restlessly. Frank evidently didn't like her strategy. She wondered how Quinn was doing outside the door, hearing every word.

"I'm not," she said, pitching her voicc low. "But I…I'd heard that you were willing to provide…um…one-on-one tutoring."

Cossi's blindingly beautiful smile flashed. "Only for students I think are worthy of the help."

"Worthy?" She added a squeak to the word, which wasn't hard. Frank wanted out and Stormy was using powerful hind feet to set the tote-break in motion.

Cossi stood up. He headed toward her in all his tight abs, lean hips, and male beauty. He didn't walk when he moved, he sauntered, a sensual promise in every step. Christy figured that if she were truly an undergrad only looking for help, she'd be absolutely terrified right now. If she was an undergrad willing to barter a night of hot sex for top marks, well, she'd be meeting him halfway.

She stood her ground and watched him.

Cossi stopped inches from her. He looked down from his six-foot-plus height and the brilliant smile darkened into something demanding. "I don't carry undergrads," he said in a low, velvety voice. "I only help those who are willing to help themselves."

Christy looked up into his beautiful blue eyes, now smoldering with seductive heat, and said, "Really?"

He frowned.

"If you're going to proposition students you could at least be original about it."

His head jerked and the frown deepened. "Who the hell are you?"

She grinned at him. "I'm Christy Jamieson." She loosened the fastening on the tote and the cat's head popped out. "This is Stormy and Frank."

Stormy and Frank? Should be Frank and Stormy. Where are you priorities, Chris?

"Your cat has two names?" He reached out to pat the cat's head and Stormy flattened his ears, narrowed his eyes and hissed. Cossi pulled his hand away to avoid a scratch.

"He's something of a split personality," Christy said. "I didn't come to get my marks pumped up. I'm here to ask you some more questions about Brittany Day."

Cossi's eyes narrowed as recognition suddenly hit. "You were here a few days ago."

"That's right."

He shrugged and turned back to his desk. "Ask away. But if any of my students come in for a consult, you'll have to leave."

"Why?" Christy asked. "Do you have sex with them here?"

He whirled around to face her, feet set apart, hands knotted into fists, shoulders tense. "What are you talking about?"

Christy moved to Bradley Neale's desk by the door and perched on the edge. Quinn would be able to see her here and know she was all right, now that Cossi was starting to turn ugly.

He'd only get worse as she asked what she needed to know. "Before he died, Dr. Peiling told me that you'd been investigated for sexual harassment of your students."

He took a step toward her. "Those allegations were unsubstantiated. They were dropped."

She opened the tote a little wider. Stormy's shoulders appeared and he put his front paws onto the edge of the bag, but he didn't jump out.

"The afternoon before Dr. Peiling died, he talked to Brittany's dad. Did you know that?"

Cossi took another step. "No."

He's going to rush you, babe. He's going to jump you and rough you up, or worse.

"Nah. He's all bluff and no substance."

You're taunting him. I tell you, babe, he's dangerous.

"Who are you talking to?"

She scratched Stormy's chin and smiled at Cossi. "Who do you think?"

Cossi looked at the cat as if contemplating the possibility that a conversation was going on he wasn't in on, then his mouth tightened. "Are you wearing a wire?"

Clearly he wasn't the type to bond with animals. "No." True enough. She did have her phone on, though, so she needed to divert him before he guessed. "Good idea. I wish I'd thought of it." She shrugged as if it wasn't important, before she moved on. "Peiling told Roger Day that he'd discovered you were blackmailing Brittany. Is that true?"

Cossi visibly relaxed. "Why would I blackmail Brittany? And what could I possibly blackmail her about?"

"Peiling said it had something to do with the alibi Brittany supplied for Aaron DeBolt."

The color leeched out of Cossi's face, then rushed back up in a wash of blood that turned his cheeks red. "That's not true."

Yeah, right, Frank said, disgusted. *If ever a guy looked guilty, this one does.*

Christy laughed. "I think you were having sex with Brittany the night Aaron DeBolt helped to murder my husband, Frank. I think—"

"Frank?" Cossi stared at the cat.

That's right, moron. And if you don't lay off my wife, I'll make you sorry.

Christy ignored both of them. "I know Aaron is guilty and the alibi Brittany gave was false. I think Brittany changed her mind and decided to retract the statement she gave to the police. The thing I don't understand is why you killed her."

She smiled at Cossi, who looked both flabbergasted and irritated. "I didn't kill her. Why would I want to kill her? I wanted to have sex with her."

Too much information, jerk.

"But she didn't want to go to bed with you, did she, Lorne?" Christy said gently. "You had to blackmail her into it."

He flushed again, but didn't say anything.

"What did you have on her?" she asked.

He stared at her narrow-eyed, then after a moment he shrugged. "She stopped doing her job. She cut classes and let Brad Neale do her shifts at the lab. By the end of last March, we were getting complaints. I'm the senior TA, so I checked up on her."

"And you found out why."

He nodded.

"Let me guess," Christy said. "Aaron DeBolt."

Cossi raised his brows. "He had her hooked good and tight. Drugs, sex, who knows what else. He told her what to do and she did it."

Poor Brittany. "How did you find out about Aaron?"

He shrugged. "Once I knew she wasn't doing her shifts at the lab, I thought it would be useful to know why." He smiled thinly. The expression was a cruel mockery of his usual blinding smiles. "I thought it might be fun to make her squirm a little before I went to Peiling."

Nice guy.

Christy agreed with Frank's sarcastic comment. She had to resist the urge to walk away without asking any more questions. Lorne Cossi was a contemptible human being and she felt dirty just being in the same room with him. But she had come here to prove Peiling had been murdered and to find out how his death fit into Brittany's murder. So far all she'd learned was how despicable Lorne Cossi was. She needed more. "So you followed her."

"And watched her make out with Aaron." His smile widened into one that was smugly self-satisfied. "I knew I had her then. There was no way she would want to admit what she was up to. Not to Peiling. Not to her proper papa and uptight mom in Calgary."

A chill shivered down Christy's spine. "And the payment for your silence was sex with you."

Cossi nodded. He moved a little closer.

Christy eased the straps of the tote bag on her shoulder. "So your blackmail was successful. Brittany slept with you on the night my husband was killed."

"As it happened, yes."

"That's pretty specific. How can you be so sure of the date?"

"Because I only slept with her once." Cossi's lip curled. "She was a boring lay. She was so stoned she wouldn't even play."

"Play?" In the hallway Christy heard the rustle of movement.

Cossi did not. "I expected her to fight me. She'd already made it clear she didn't like me and wasn't interested. But that night she just lay there and let me do what I wanted."

Unable to say no, Brittany had drugged her senses so she would feel little and perhaps remember less from her night with Lorne Cossi. Filled with pity for a girl whose life should have been different, Christy said, "Oh, God! That's horrible. You're no better than Aaron."

"Aaron DeBolt is a drunk and a druggie who's nothing without Mom and Dad's money," Cossi said hotly. "He pranced into the parties Peiling gave for the donors and acted as if it was him who'd supplied the cash. I loathe him!"

Cossi's outburst gave Christy a chance to recover. "Why did you go to the parties, then?"

"I had to. We all had to! Peiling held at least one a semester. He said celebrations were the perfect way for the donors to get to know the program and the people in it." He snorted and his lip curled. "Yeah, sure. They all treated us like peons, but the DeBolts were the worst. They acted like we were a meat parade."

"I guess you didn't like Jacob Peiling much then either."

"Peiling was an idiot, but he knew his stuff."

"So you say. Was it you who laced his food with peanut oil?" Christy mentally crossed her fingers. She would be very happy if it turned out that Cossi was the one who murdered Jacob Peiling.

He stared at her, his eyes widened with surprise. "Peiling was murdered? I thought he was just being a hypocrite. He lectured us about bringing food into the office and eating at our desks. Constantly. Then there he is, doing exactly that and getting caught at it!" He shook his head and added, "And here I thought his death was just the universe being ironic."

That sounds like the truth, Frank said. Disappointment echoed in the voice, as if Frank, too, had hoped Cossi was guilty.

If it was the truth, she needed confirmation. "Where were you when Peiling died? And when Brittany was murdered, for that matter."

"Are you asking me if I have an alibi?" he asked, sounding incredulous. He took a step toward her.

Christy nodded. "That's exactly what I'm asking."

He took another step. "Why should I tell you?"

She slid the tote off her shoulder and set it on the desk, opening it wide. Stormy stepped out carefully. "I'm asking. You don't have to answer, but eventually you'll have to tell the police."

Another step. He was almost at the desk now. Christy wasn't sure why he'd suddenly turned hostile, but she didn't like his proximity.

He looked down at her and bestowed that devastatingly beautiful smile on her. "Maybe I've already told the police."

She looked into his marine-blue eyes. They were cold as polar ice. "I don't think so. If they had your testimony, they wouldn't have arrested my aunt for Brittany's murder."

He stepped closer, invading her space, crowding her against the desk. "I think you've got a real need to know what I was doing on those two nights. Tell you what. I'll give you what you want to know, but I want something in return." His voice lowered. Roughened.

Really? This guy is hitting on you for payment? Stormy hissed and sprang into action.

Christy caught him as he leapt toward Cossi. "Not a good idea, Lorne. My friend here doesn't like it. Just tell me where you were and we'll both get out of here." *Soon, I hope,* Christy thought.

"Too bad princess. No payment, no info." A sneer polluted the rough sensual voice, turning the potential of pleasure into the promise of mistreatment.

The cat hissed again, and his legs scrambled for purchase. Frank clearly wanted at Lorne Cossi. At that moment Quinn decided to intervene and walked into the office. The cat stilled and there was a moment when he and Quinn eyed each other and Christy could have sworn that they communicated.

Quinn's gaze swept from the cat to her. Christy felt her body respond with an undeniable rush as his eyes searched her for evidence that Cossi had harmed her. She smiled at him and shook her head. Quinn gave her an almost imperceptible nod, then he moved to within inches of Cossi. They were both similar heights and Quinn did nothing aggressive, except to push his way into Cossi's personal space, but the TA moved back a step, then another. "Tell the lady what she wants to know," Quinn said. "No strings attached."

Cossi looked from Quinn to Christy, then to Frank in Stormy, and back to Quinn. His face twisted. "The morning Brittany died I was shagging one of my undergrads. I like morning sex."

"And Dr. Peiling?"

"I was in the lab. I've got a dozen undergrads to prove it."

Quinn nodded. "I hope that's the truth, because I expect you'll be telling the police your story very soon." He reached out his hand. "Come on, Christy. Put Frank back in his carrier and let's go."

Looking grim, Cossi said, "Is the animal Frank or Stormy?" as he watched the cat step back into the tote.

Christy slung the bag on her shoulder and pushed away from the desk. She took Quinn's hand. He raised his brows and allowed his mouth to curl up in a tiny, superior smile. "Like the lady said—both."

CHAPTER 25

I wanted to scratch his eyes out. Better yet, I could have scarred his pretty face. The cat was practically vibrating with tension inside the tote bag on Christy's lap. *You should have let me, Chris. The jerk deserved it.*

"I don't like it when you put yourself in danger like that." Quinn's tone was grim, his body tight with strain as he guided the car away from the university, back toward the city center.

The two males were both upset. And because they were both vocalizing at the same time it was like being lectured in stereo. Though she wasn't frightened while she interviewed Cossi, his vile nature had given her the creeps, so Christy was edgy too. "Look, you were just outside the door, Quinn, and Frank was ready to mess up his face and make him suffer. I was never in any danger."

"Really?" Quinn grinned, apparently pleased by the thought of Lorne Cossi's handsome face marred by cat scratches. He kept his eyes on the road, though, so Christy couldn't be sure. It was rush hour and the street was packed with commuters, though fortunately the traffic heading downtown, as they were, was still moving freely between lights. On the other side of the yellow line, commuters on their way home after work were already in stop-and-go mode.

"Really. So both you guys stand down. I was fine."

The light ahead changed to yellow then red. Traffic slowed and stopped. Quinn looked over at Christy. His gaze was troubled. "I know I'm being overprotective, but it was only a few weeks ago that you were almost killed. You gave me a scare. I'm trying to deal with it, but…" The light changed and Quinn looked back at the road.

Think of me! I was worried too that day, but I couldn't do anything beyond trying to get this lug to figure out that you were in danger.

Traffic started to move again. Quinn's eyes were on the cars ahead as he added in a low voice, "Christy, please understand…"

He needs to open his mind and listen to me!

There was a charged silence. Christy understood the emotions motivating both males. Frank had loved her and failed her in life. She thought that was why he was still here, rooming with Stormy the Cat. He needed to deal with his human frailties before he could move on. Quinn's life as a conflict-zone journalist had shown him firsthand the devastation that violence brought. Both needed her support, but she couldn't answer one before the other, because the one she didn't comfort first would feel slighted.

Juggling two males sitting beside each other was more stressful than dealing with a sexual bully like Lorne Cossi. She swallowed hard and prepared to say what she hoped both would respond to.

She didn't get the chance.

"…I don't want to lose you," Quinn said. Emotion roughened his voice.

Inside the tote bag, the cat went absolutely still as Quinn's voice echoed through the car.

Hell. Open the bag, Chris. Stormy and I will go and sit in the backseat.

Christy sighed. She put one hand on Quinn's arm and hugged the tote more closely with the other. "Thank you. I understand your worries, I really do, but I was never in any danger. I walked into Cossi's office knowing I had backup.

I wouldn't have gone near the guy if you hadn't been there."

Under her hand, some of the tension eased from the muscles in Quinn's arm. She squeezed it briefly, then released him so that she could open the tote and give Frank the option of leaving her lap.

Stormy's green eyes looked up at her and he didn't move. Frank might want to lick his wounds in the relative privacy of the backseat, but Stormy preferred the comforts of a human lap. He butted her hand, demanding to be petted. She tickled him under his chin. When Stormy began to purr, Christy chuckled.

Quinn glanced over, brows raised in question, before returning his attention to the road.

"Frank is as upset with me as you are," Christy said. "He wants to go sit in the backseat and sulk. Stormy is resisting."

The cat's purr deepened with contentment and he sprawled on his side to give her access to his belly.

Quinn gave the utterly relaxed Stormy a quick, sidelong glance before he looked back at the road. A muscle jumped in his cheek as he stared at the traffic ahead of them. "Are you sure it's just the cat who doesn't want to leave?"

The purring stopped, then started up again, louder than before. *He's got a point. I am your husband, after all.*

Christy sighed, then deliberately changed the subject. "How long do you think it will take to reach the police station?"

When they left the university, they'd decided they needed to get the information they'd gleaned from Roger Day and Lorne Cossi to Detective Patterson without delay. A quick check had reassured Christy that Noelle was having a great time with Ellen, Roy, and Trevor. They were at the Christmas tree lot, walking through the stands of pine, searching for the perfect tree. The ground was soft, but not mushy, it wasn't raining and Noelle was out in the fresh air and having fun. During the call, Christy heard Ellen's voice in the background say, "That one is nice and bushy," followed by Noelle's shouted reply, "It's too small!" At that, both she and Roy had laughed and he told her not to worry and get back when she could.

"In this traffic? Probably another forty-five minutes."

Patterson had agreed to meet them at the coffee shop near the station. If Quinn was correct, and the traffic cooperated, they'd be right on time.

The small restaurant was much as Christy remembered it from her previous meetings with Detective Patterson, when Frank had been missing, and presumed to be the embezzler of the Jamieson Trust. The place was a favorite with the cops who worked out of the main police station and at any time of the day it was always packed. The décor was bare-bones—Formica-topped tables, vinyl-covered chairs, linoleum flooring, and walls in need of a paint job.

Patterson sat at a table situated so that she had a good visual of the entryway. There was a thick white coffee mug in front of her and she was turning it on the Formica tabletop as if her hands needed movement while her body remained still. When Christy and Quinn entered the room she didn't move, even though Christy was quite certain she'd seen them.

"Mrs. Jamieson, Mr. Armstrong," she said by way of a greeting as they reached her table and sat down.

A waitress appeared. Quinn ordered coffee. Christy shook her head.

When the waitress had gone, Patterson sat up a bit straighter, then leaned forward. "You have some information for me pertaining to the murder of Brittany Day?"

"Yes," Christy said.

Patterson raised her brows.

"My husband's aunt didn't kill Brittany."

Patterson sat back. The expression on her face was resigned. Or perhaps disappointed. Christy wasn't sure which.

"The evidence tells a different story."

It was Christy's turn to lean forward. "We have new evidence."

"I'm listening."

"Another murder and a false alibi."

The detective sighed. "You're talking about Dr. Peiling's death. We're treating that as an unfortunate accident."

"Are you?" Quinn asked.

Patterson turned narrowed eyes on him. "What are you insinuating?"

"Jacob Peiling's death was in the news and I can't help but wonder why? He was well-known in his field, but he wasn't a household name. He died as the result of an allergic reaction, which isn't a suspicious death, unless somebody fed him something he shouldn't have eaten. I don't think the media would be interested in Jacob Peiling's death unless someone asked someone else to run the story."

"You're smelling a conspiracy," Patterson said with a faint smile. "I'm not into them."

"My life is full of them," Christy said with a sigh.

That brought Patterson's gaze back onto her. "I guess it is," she said after a moment. "So you two think that Jacob Peiling was murdered." She made it a statement, not a question, and she raised her brows to invite comment.

"According to his friends and students, Jacob Peiling was paranoid about eating food containing peanut oil. He rarely dined out and when he did he only went to restaurants he trusted," Christy said. "He never ate takeout, yet there was a container of takeout food on his desk. Why?"

Patterson shrugged, though her eyes were watchful. "The food came from one of the restaurants he patronized. It wasn't ordinary takeout from a fast-food joint."

"He didn't eat at his desk. In fact, he had a standing order that none of his students eat at theirs, either. He thought it was a dirty habit and he wouldn't allow it. Why would he eat takeout food at his desk on the night he died? If the food came from a restaurant he used, why didn't he go to the restaurant to eat?"

Patterson drew a circle on the tabletop with the thick white mug. "Maybe he had a deadline to meet."

"Or maybe he had someone to see," Quinn said. "Someone involved in Brittany's death."

The mug stilled. "That's a stretch, Mr. Armstrong."

Quinn shook his head. "I don't think so. Roger Day told us that Peiling called him on the afternoon he died. He said he had news about Brittany's death, but he wouldn't reveal a name because he had to check his facts first. He was going to call Day that evening. He didn't."

"So you think that Jacob Peiling discovered who killed Brittany Day and he was meeting that person in his office later that day. And, when that person brought food to the meeting, he calmly ate it?"

There was a sneer in Patterson's voice as she ended the sentence. Christy flushed and rushed into speech. "No. We think he found out that the alibi Brittany provided for Aaron DeBolt was false. We also think that he figured out who asked Brittany to give Aaron the alibi and he was shocked. That's why he insisted on checking his facts. He found it difficult to believe the person he'd identified could have done it."

"So. The deaths of Brittany Day and Jacob Peiling are related."

"And the motives for both of them turn around the alibi Brittany gave Aaron for the night of Frank's murder."

Patterson rubbed the scar that ran down one side of her perfectly sculpted face. "Definitely a conspiracy," she said with a grimace.

"Did Aaron DeBolt have any visitors while he was in jail?" Quinn asked.

"Some," Patterson said. "Why?"

"Can you find out who and when?"

She frowned at Quinn. "Yes. Again, why?"

"Because I think that if you check, you'll find that Brittany Day was one of his visitors. And that she visited him after she produced the alibi and shortly before she died."

"And the significance of this is?" Patterson looked annoyed. She was sitting up straight again and the mug was still.

"Someone on the outside convinced Brittany to give Aaron the alibi he needed in order to have the charges against him dropped. But then Brittany had second thoughts. She went to Aaron to apologize. Or perhaps to warn him that she was changing her statement. That's why she was killed. So she didn't have a chance to retract."

"We've thought of that," Patterson said slowly. "I checked the visitor list, but I couldn't find any correlation. As far as we're concerned, Brittany Day's affidavit stands."

"Then you'll need to talk to a rather nasty grad student at EBU by the name of Lorne Cossi," Christy said. "Brittany couldn't have been with Aaron DeBolt on the night Frank was killed, because she was having sex with Cossi across town."

CHAPTER 26

Busting Brittany's credibility with the revelation that she was with Lorne Cossi at the time she claimed to have been with Aaron got Patterson's attention in a big way. It took a bit of effort, but Quinn managed to convince the detective to share the names of Aaron's visitors while he was in the holding facility and when the visits had taken place.

The information was startling.

Natalie was a daily visitor—no surprise there. Christy had long known that Natalie was a devoted mother—but the day before Brittany had come forward with the alibi for the night of Frank's murder, she visited Aaron. Furthermore, she hadn't gone to the prison alone. She'd accompanied Natalie on one of her regular visits and had waited until after Natalie and Aaron met, to have her own visit. When her time was up, the two women left the facility together.

Brittany made a subsequent visit to Aaron two days before she was murdered. According to notes made at the time of the visit, she appeared distressed when she left.

Cara LaLonde had also visited Aaron while he was incarcerated. She began by visiting regularly, but by the time Brittany was concocting the alibi, Cara's visits had dwindled to only the odd time here and there. One of those visits occurred the day before Brittany's first visit. Another was the day before Brittany died.

The rest of Aaron's crowd seemed to have abandoned him as soon as he was charged in Frank's death. The only other visitor of importance was Nathan DeBolt who saw his son on the eve of Brittany's murder.

Christy and Quinn speculated on what this meant as they drove back to Burnaby from the police station. "Brittany must have advised Aaron she wouldn't alibi him when she visited him the second time," Christy said. They were on East Hastings and had a straight run home, but the road was still packed with commuters, all headed in exactly the same direction they were.

"And Aaron must have told someone on the outside what she planned." Quinn braked hard when a car from the nearby lane abruptly swerved into his.

"So who?"

"Cara, Natalie, or Nathan DeBolt," Quinn said. "None of the TAs visited Aaron. And if the other two were like Lorne Cossi, they wouldn't be too willing to help Aaron out of this kind of fix anyway."

My money is on Nathan. They'd left Stormy in the car while they met with Patterson in the café. He'd been annoyed by that, but had to accept that taking a cat into a restaurant would have destroyed Christy's credibility with the detective. Now he was not going to be left out of the discussion. *Nathan has a reputation for being ruthless. Besides, he's pals with Gerry Fisher.*

Since Gerry Fisher had been the worst of Frank's Trustees it wasn't surprising Frank would vote for someone who was Gerry's friend. "Didn't Aaron start dealing drugs because his father cut him off financially, Frank?"

Yeah. He wanted Aaron to get a job. So he did. Nathan didn't approve of the kind of job he got though. That just made it better to Aaron. He liked pissing his father off.

"I assume the cat agreed?" Quinn said.

"He did. Cara LaLonde had a pretty good motive, too. I think she was in love with Aaron and she saw Brittany as a threat to her relationship with him."

"Given the number of times she visited him in jail, you may be right. But her visits had fallen off recently. I think she may have given up on him," Quinn said. He turned right on Boundary and headed south. "I'm going to try getting home using Holdom. If we stay on Hastings, we'll be here till midnight."

Traffic eased as they merged east onto the less-traveled street and their speed picked up. "That leaves Natalie," Christy said. "I can see her killing Brittany to ensure Aaron walked away from the charges against him, but why kill her in Ellen's apartment? Ellen is her friend and they've been chummy ever since I came to Vancouver with Frank ten years ago."

And they were pals long before that.

"Frank agrees," Christy said, translating for Quinn. "And says that their friendship is long-standing."

Besides, she's older than Brittany and not as big. It would be difficult for her to overpower Brittany, especially if Brittany was in fear for her life.

His eyes on the road ahead, Quinn said, "Let's consider Jacob Peiling's death. Someone brought him a dinner from one of the restaurants he usually frequented because he felt safe eating their food. He must have trusted that person because he was willing to eat the takeout meal he or she brought."

"And that person must have been very familiar with his habits as well, to have known what to add to the food and how to ensure that he couldn't reach his antidote in time," Christy said.

That leaves out Cara. She didn't know any of the university crowd.

Christy passed Frank's observation on to Quinn.

"But it does add Lorne Cossi and potentially the other TAs. They all knew about Peiling's allergy." Quinn said.

"Don't forget, Lorne had an alibi for the night Peiling died," Christy said.

"Right, so it could be the woman—Rochelle Dasovic—or the other man, Bradley Neale. We haven't checked on their alibis for the night of Peiling's death."

"But neither one of them could have killed Brittany, and I believe the two murders were connected," Christy said.

"Which leaves us with Nathan."

I'd like it to be DeBolt. He was never one of my favorite people. The voice was wistful.

Christy didn't bother to pass along Frank's observation. She said instead, "His firm supports Peiling's program, so he'd know the professor."

"Agreed, and Peiling would be comfortable with him." Quinn tapped his fingers on the steering wheel. "He'd also be shocked by the idea of Nathan as a murderer."

Christy nodded. "Frank says Nathan's ruthless. You'd have to be, I think to sit on one side of a desk and watch a man die of anaphylactic shock on the other."

"He's got the physical strength to have killed Brittany. He knows Ellen, but she is his wife's friend, so he doesn't have any emotional ties to her. He may also be angry that it's Frank, Ellen's nephew, Aaron is accused of killing. He may think it's fitting that Brittany's death is being blamed on a Jamieson. So, what's his motive for killing Brittany?"

"He's old money and a power in Vancouver society and politics," Christy said. "Having his only son go to prison as an accessory to murder would destroy everything he's worked for over a lifetime."

Quinn gunned the engine as the road began a steep climb up Burnaby Mountain. "The question is, how deeply does he value his family's reputation? Enough to kill?"

The re-arrest of Aaron DeBolt as an accessory in the murder of Frank Jamieson was all over the news the next morning and caused a sensation. Only days before, the media had been trumpeting Aaron's release and making a scandal of his false arrest. Now there was an even bigger scandal brewing, one of conspiracy and murder. There wasn't a media outlet in the Lower Mainland that wasn't focused on the arrest. Even the national news programs were picking up the story, since Brittany was from Calgary and her father was a power in the important oil and gas industry.

Aaron's arrest wasn't the only focus of the stories. The details of Frank's murder were dredged up, including a quick précis of his wild lifestyle with his socialite wife. Pictures of Frank and Christy partying were included, though the focus of the reports this time was the prominent DeBolt family. Secondary stories detailed Natalie DeBolt's rise from Cariboo country girl to the wife of the wealthy Nathan DeBolt and noted that they had been having marital difficulties for some years. Aaron's lifestyle and how it impacted his arrest were also featured. Questions were raised about Aaron's potential involvement in the death of Brittany Day and there was speculation her murder was somehow related to the false alibi she'd given.

Christy was alerted to the furor by Quinn, who called to warn her. He caught her before she set off to school with Noelle. She was able to warn Noelle that there might be questions about her dad and his death once again, from her classmates, their parents, and perhaps even some of the teachers.

"And Ms. Shively, too," Noelle had said, so matter-of-fact that she seemed nonchalant.

Christy agreed. The child services worker was very much on her mind.

They took the back way to school, using the path through the woods, just in case the press had figured out where Noelle went to school. Christy didn't think they had and she didn't think they would target the school since they hadn't camped out in front of her house, but she believed in taking precautions. Avoiding the building's front entrance was one of them.

When Christy dropped Noelle at her classroom, her teacher skewered Christy with a disapproving look and said, "The principal would like you to go to her office before you leave, Mrs. Jamieson."

Noelle opened her eyes wide and said, "Uh-oh, Mom. You're in trouble."

Christy looked down at her daughter and her heart did a little flip. Noelle's eyes were wide with dismay, but deep in them amusement lurked. She'd seen that look in Frank's eyes many, many times. That twinkle, hiding beneath the solemn expression, was one of the charming behaviors that had drawn her to Frank when she first met him, and which had kept her with him for a long time after their passionate love had been lost. It was the best of Frank, the real Frank beneath the Jamieson heir. And in that moment her daughter reminded Christy so much of her dead husband that she bent down and hugged her fiercely. "You're an imp," she whispered in Noelle's ear, careful that the teacher wouldn't hear.

Noelle hugged her back and giggled. "Go get her, Mom."

When Christy straightened both she and Noelle were Jamiesons, ready to deal with the people around them in a polite, composed way. Christy found the principal's office and was advised that the school would not allow the press to harass her daughter. Unlike Noelle's teacher, the principal was sympathetic. She understood that Christy couldn't control the media and that Christy simply wanted her daughter to have a normal school life. They parted on good terms, with the principal promising to phone Christy should any reporters happen to discover that Noelle was attending this particular institution.

Christy returned home via the wooded path. She spent her walk thinking about the murders, Aaron's re-arrest and what it all meant. By the time she was on her street and almost home, she was pretty sure she knew who had killed Brittany and also Jacob Peiling.

Quinn was sitting on her porch waiting for her. He smiled as she came up her walk and reached out to take her hands. "Are you still on for this morning?"

She leaned into him, bending to kiss him before she settled beside him. Yesterday, as they speculated on who was guilty of the two murders, they'd decided to seek out Nathan DeBolt this morning and ask him some of the questions that were still unanswered. "Do you think he'll be willing to talk to us? He must be inundated with reporters."

"I arranged an interview with him for eleven thirty this morning."

"Really? He agreed to talk to you? Why?"

"I got the impression that he was gutted by Aaron's re-arrest. He sounded…bewildered, like he couldn't take it all in. Right now he needs to unburden himself on someone."

"And that someone is you? Why?"

Quinn shot her an amused look laced with some cockiness. He slipped his arm around her waist to draw her snug against his body. "My reputation as a journalist who researches his material and is fair and unbiased." He sobered. "He opened up to me before. It may just be that I'm a name he knows."

"Where do we meet him?"

"His house."

"His house will be surrounded by the media."

"Yeah, and it's a mansion not far from your old place. It has gates and security guards who are there to ensure we get in and the other guys don't."

Christy thought about the media scrum that would be going on outside the DeBolt mansion. She remembered how trapped she'd felt when Frank had been labeled an embezzler and the news crews camped outside the Jamieson mansion for days on end. She thought too of the flash of cameras every time she had to cross that barrier, of reporters shoving microphones at her and shouting questions, even if she was safely ensconced in a car.

And she thought about Joan Shively believing the media reports, whether they were true or not. "I can't go to DeBolt's house."

Quinn drew away so he could look into her face. He frowned as he reached out to tuck an errant lock of hair behind her ear. "Too many memories?"

She swallowed and nodded. "But I'm worried that someone might recognize me and speculate that I'm somehow involved in the murders. Or they might just use a photo of us going into the compound and link me to the DeBolts."

He drew his hand down her cheek in a tender gesture. "It would only be speculation."

"It was speculation six months ago, when I was supposed to be the reason Frank embezzled from the Trust. Or years before that, when I was labeled a gold-digging, good-time girl who married Frank for his money." She sighed. "Once it's printed, speculation doesn't go away and lots of people think it's fact. Like Joan Shively, the child services woman."

"And you need to make sure Noelle is safe. I understand," Quinn said gently.

She leaned her head against his shoulder. "Thank you."

He hugged her tighter and kissed the top of her head.

She smiled. "I am so lucky I met you."

He laughed. "You tried hard enough to avoid me."

Christy's smile deepened. "So I made a mistake, then changed my mind. Lady's prerogative."

"Works for me," Quinn said.

They sat quietly for a few minutes after that, enjoying the closeness and each other, before Christy sat up with a sigh. "I should go in. I need to put the breakfast dishes into the dishwasher and get a laundry going. I'm sure Shively will show up sometime today on one of her unannounced visits. I want the house to be spotless."

"I'll come over when I get back from DeBolt's."

Christy nodded, then Quinn kissed her, a tender kiss that had her lifting her hand to cup his cheek before she slid her fingers into his hair. The kiss didn't demand, it evoked. It offered Quinn's understanding and soothed her own insecurities. It told her he was there for her whenever she needed him, and she responded by showing him how very deeply that moved her.

She wished the embrace would go on forever, but kisses had to end, especially kisses on a single mom's front porch.

Quinn rested his forehead on Christy's for a few moments after he pulled away. His voice had a rueful note as he said, "I don't want to leave you."

Christy made a sound that was half laugh, half sigh. "I don't want you to go, either."

"Someone's got to move," Quinn said.

"Yeah."

He laughed. "Guess it has to be me."

He rubbed his thumb over her mouth. His smile was tender. For a moment Christy thought he was going to kiss her again, but then he stood. He held out his hand to help her up. Then he was gone, loping down her walk, heading for his place.

She watched him go, then, with a little sigh, went up the steps and into her house.

CHAPTER 27

Quinn went from his meeting with Nathan DeBolt to visit the managing editor of Vancouver's evening newspaper. There he negotiated a deal for a series of articles on the DeBolt family. Before he left he wrote the first one, on his meeting with Nathan, so he didn't return to Burnaby until later in the afternoon. By that time Christy had picked up Noelle from school. She hadn't come in contact with any media and Noelle had had a normal day so she was able to breathe a sigh of relief once they were both home and back in their own space.

With Christmas fast approaching, preparations for the school play were becoming a focus for all of the children. When Noelle asked if Mary Petrofsky could come over so they could practice their parts together, Christy laughed and agreed, as long as it was okay with Mary's mother. It was, so the moment Mary arrived the two girls disappeared into the basement, leaving Christy to worry that Joan Shively hadn't shown up yet that day. She had been so certain she would, because Shively tended to do a home visit whenever the Jamieson name appeared in the press.

The afternoon seemed very quiet with Noelle and Mary off on their own. Outside a steady rain darkened the sky and added a nip to the air. Christy decided it was the perfect day to make a big batch of chili, so she set to work, humming to herself as she chopped onions and peppers and browned the meat in a large kettle.

When Quinn phoned at four thirty, the chili was simmering on the stove.

"Hi," he said. "I'm back. How was your day? Any problems? Did Shively drop by?"

Christy laughed. "I'm glad. Okay. No. And no."

There was a moment of silence on the other end of the connection. "I deserved that for shooting off a bunch of shotgun questions. If I got your answers right, your day has been quiet."

"Bingo. You win the prize." She stirred the chili. "How did your interview with DeBolt go?"

"He was surprisingly forthcoming. I don't think he was the one who killed Brittany and Peiling."

"No. I don't think so either."

There was another silence on Quinn's end. "You've figured out who the killer is?"

Christy stared out the kitchen window at the gloomy, wet afternoon. "If I've put it all together right, yeah, I think I have."

"Why don't you come over and we can discuss it."

"I can't. Mary Petrofsky is here and she and Noelle are playing downstairs. Plus I've got a batch of chili on the stove."

"Chili?"

She laughed. "Why don't you come over here? You can stay for dinner. Bring your dad and Trevor too, if he's around. I made a ton."

"I'll come. But…" There was a brief hesitation, then he said, "Trevor is here, but so is Ellen."

Christy thought about Joan Shively and her disapproval. It was unlikely the woman would show up this late. "Bring Ellen too, if she'll come. I'm sure Noelle would be happy to see her."

"What about you?"

Dear Quinn, she thought, worrying about her tangled and tentative relationship with Frank's aunt. "I'm fine. She should come."

"I'll try," he said. "When do you want us?"

"Whenever works for you." She laughed. "Thanks to my concern that Shively would come by today, my house is spotless. All I'll have to do is set the table, and I can do that just before we sit down to eat."

"Or I can do it for you. Okay, we'll be over in a bit."

She hung up the phone, then went to get a bottle of wine from the wine rack in the storage area under the staircase. While she was in the basement, she asked if Mary would like to stay for dinner. The invitation resulted in a spate of energetic activity as Noelle and Mary raced up the stairs so Mary could phone her mom, then, when the answer was positive, some gleeful jumping up and down, before the girls charged back down to the basement to continue their practicing.

The noise woke up Stormy, who had been snoozing on Noelle's bed. The cat padded into the kitchen, whiskers twitching as he took in the scent of stewing beef. *What's cooking, babe?*

"Chili." Christy stirred the pot.

Your mom's chili? There was a wistful note to the thought.

They'd had a chef at the mansion. In all the years she and Frank had been married, she'd never cooked him a dinner. When they'd met in university, though, he'd shared many meals with her family. Her mother's chili had been his favorite. He'd once told her that he'd never eaten anything better.

"Yup." She hesitated, then spooned some chunks of beef and a little sauce into a bowl. Chili might not be on a recommended cat diet, but she figured a little wouldn't do any harm. She set it aside to cool. Frank might prefer his portion of chili piping hot and right out of the pot, but that was probably more than Stormy's system would be able to handle. Since the cat had been remarkably accommodating for Frank, she wanted to make sure his needs were being looked after too.

Stormy had leapt up onto one of the kitchen chairs and was standing on his hind legs, front paws on the top of the backrest. He was watching her movements with a hungry intensity that made her laugh.

"Not yet." She pushed the bowl into a far corner.

Stormy eased back down onto the chair. He licked a paw just to prove he didn't care and he wasn't anxiously waiting for his supper.

Christy leaned her elbows on the counter and said, "Frank, I've invited the Armstrongs over for dinner so we can talk about the murders."

Don't let them eat all the chili. Save a little for tomorrow.

"Ellen's over at their house right now." She hesitated, then added, "I invited her too."

Stormy slowly lowered his paw. His green eyes stared intently at Christy. *I'm okay with that.*

"Ellen didn't kill Brittany Day or Jacob Peiling."

She had a sense of something she thought might be a mental snort, then Frank said, *Well, duh.*

"I think—" The doorbell rang. "That's probably them."

It was indeed everyone from the Armstrong house. Quinn entered first. He shot her a look that told her he'd like to kiss her, but was holding back in front of the others. He did give her hand a squeeze though. And she squeezed back. Roy followed, brandishing a bottle of wine. He gave her a kiss on the cheek and followed his son up the stairs.

Ellen was next. She had the Jamieson poker face on and said coolly, "It was kind of you to invite me, Christy," as she bestowed a reserved air kiss on first one and then the other of Christy's cheeks.

"I'm glad you agreed to join us," Christy said, and surprised herself by meaning it.

The last to arrive was Trevor. He was carrying a wine bottle too. "It's been hard on her," he said, and shoved the bottle into Christy's arms. Then he followed the rest up the stairs to the living room.

Except no one stopped in the living room. Christy, along with Noelle and Mary, who had bounded up from the basement when they heard the bell, found them all in the kitchen. Trevor and Ellen were already at the table, while Roy and Quinn were locating wineglasses and a corkscrew. The enticing aroma of chili provided a backdrop for the whole scene.

Noelle raced over to Ellen to hug her, then she picked up Stormy, who had taken up a position beside his food bowl, and put him into Ellen's lap. "You should be friends," she said, with great gusto.

There was a moment where all the other adults in the room stared, waiting to see how both Frank and Ellen would react.

"He's a nice cat," Mary said. Her voice was quiet, a little hesitant in the face of a kitchen crowded with adults.

"I'm sure he is," Ellen said gently. She stroked Stormy's head as she had the day before. The cat began to purr. Mary beamed and Noelle kissed both her aunt and the cat before she and Mary headed back to the basement.

"Well," Christy said. She was more shaken by that quiet family moment and what it meant to her daughter than she had expected.

Roy found the corkscrew and began to pour into the glasses Quinn had provided. Christy covered her emotional moment by stirring the chili, while the men passed around the wineglasses and settled at the table. Christy stayed on the cooking side of the counter and listened as Quinn began to talk.

"Nathan DeBolt may be many things, but I don't think a murderer is amongst them," he said. He put his elbows on the table and studied his wineglass as he made small circles on the maple surface with the base. "He was remarkably forthcoming. I think he wanted to talk."

"I am not surprised," Ellen said. "I have never thought Nathan anything but a very respectable man."

Respectable wasn't exactly how Christy would describe anyone in the DeBolt family, but she wasn't about to argue with Ellen, not at that moment. "Did he say why he visited Aaron just before Brittany's death?"

"He went to apologize for not believing in his son's innocence. At that point it looked like the alibi would stand and Aaron would be released. He decided his act of contrition would have more impact if he made it before Aaron was freed rather than once Aaron was out."

Wouldn't have made a difference. All Aaron cares about is money and his father isn't supplying it. The voice sounded sleepy, lazy, and contented. On Ellen's lap, the cat still purred.

Quinn continued on, unaware Frank had commented. "Aaron's reaction was not what Nathan hoped for. Instead of a reconciliation, Aaron sneered. They argued. When Aaron was released, it was Natalie who went to the jail to pick him up. Nathan stayed away."

"Did he see his son while Aaron was free?" Roy asked.

Quinn shook his head. "The first thing Aaron did after his release was to go out clubbing. He got drunk or high and made—in his father's words—a public spectacle of himself. Nathan was not impressed."

"Does Nathan have alibis for the two killings?" Trevor asked.

Quinn nodded. "Pretty strong ones, I think. On the morning Brittany was killed, he was catching an early flight. He was at the airport and already through the security check at the time of her death."

"And the night Peiling was killed?" Trevor asked.

"An emergency board meeting. He wouldn't go into details about why the meeting had been called, but it included all the senior executives in his company as well as a half a dozen outside board members, all men with impeccable reputations. The meeting didn't break up until after nine."

"And Peiling was dead by then. This is very interesting," Roy said with considerable relish. "So you think we can eliminate Nathan DeBolt as one of our suspects?"

"Nathan should never have been a suspect," Ellen said. "He is not the kind of man who would ever kill someone."

Quinn said quietly, "In normal circumstances Nathan DeBolt is capable of almost anything he sets his mind to, but right now he is a broken man." There was compassion in his voice. "He said that Natalie was at the police station with Aaron. I think Aaron's re-arrest has left him shocked and, well, almost devastated, as if he couldn't process it all."

"Surprising, considering his son was charged in Frank's murder before. Why would he be shocked?" Trevor frowned as he shook his head. "Disappointed, sure, but devastated? I can't see it."

Quinn shrugged. "That's how he seemed to me."

"Perhaps it's not just Aaron's re-arrest," Christy said. "I think he's more upset about—"

The doorbell rang. Roy glanced at his watch. "Who could that be? It's almost six o'clock."

"Oh hell," Christy said. Her eyes locked with Quinn's. There was a flutter in her stomach that had nothing to do with sexual attraction as she saw the startled dismay in his expression.

"Shively," they both said at the same moment.

CHAPTER 28

A houseful of people, most of whom were drinking wine and talking about murder. Two kids in the basement unsupervised by said adults. Was this enough for child services to remove a child from the care of her mother?

Christy drew a deep breath, gave herself a mental head slap, and told herself to get a spine. Shively could threaten. She could posture. But she couldn't take Noelle away just because the child was playing with a friend safely in her own home.

And, while the other adults in her kitchen were drinking wine, Christy had not yet touched a drop. She planned to, but Shively didn't know that.

The bell rang again. Three times in rapid succession.

Ms. Shively was getting antsy.

"Who is it, Mom?" Noelle shouted from the basement.

Christy reached the landing and looked down the stairs at Noelle, who was standing at the bottom. "I think it's Ms. Shively doing a checkup. Best manners now."

Noelle nodded. Christy drew herself up straighter and lifted her chin. Then she opened the door.

The person on the other side was indeed Joan Shively, standing with her finger on the bell, about to start another series of impatient jabs.

"Ms. Shively," Christy said. She made no effort to invite the woman in.

Shively pursed her lips and looked annoyed. "Mrs. Jamieson. I am here to do a home visit."

Christy raised her brows. "It's almost six o'clock. I was about to put dinner on the table."

Shively frowned. "Dinner at six o'clock? Surely it's rather late for that. I would have expected you would have ensured Noelle had eaten by now."

Was she kidding? Temper flared and put a snap in Christy's tone as she replied. "Have you fed your children, yet?"

Shively reddened. "I did not have your home scheduled for today, so I had to fit it in. Which is why I am running so late. I can assure you that normally I have my family's dinner on the table by five thirty at the latest."

Well, good for you, Christy thought. She was saved from blurting out that comment by Noelle who charged up the stairs to the landing, with Mary in tow.

Studiously polite, Noelle said, "Hello, Ms. Shively. Have you met my friend, Mary Petrofsky? She is in my class at school."

Shively dragged her gaze away from Christy and allowed a thin smile to replace her frown. "Hello, Noelle. It is nice to meet you, Mary."

"Mary is staying for dinner tonight," Noelle said. "I heard Mom say it's almost ready, so Mary and I are going upstairs to wash our hands."

Bless you, Noelle, Christy thought, as the two girls continued up the stairs. There was a powder room in the basement, fully stocked with soap and towels, which Noelle and Mary could have used. By heading upstairs to the main bathroom, and mentioning their purpose on her way there, Noelle had brought it to Shively's attention. The woman would have to give Christy full credit for teaching her daughter good hygiene habits. Hopefully, it would counter the late dinner disapproval.

"I not only have Noelle's friend, Mary, here, but also some other people," Christy said. She moved away from the door. Shively stepped inside.

"I will endeavor to intrude as little as possible."

Yeah, right, Christy thought. She gestured to the basement. "You may as well start at the bottom and move up. Please note that Noelle and Mary have been playing there for most of the afternoon. I ask Noelle to pick up after herself, and she respects that, but she's only eight. The room might not be perfectly tidy."

She left Shively to poke around in the basement and headed back upstairs. She found Noelle and Mary in the kitchen. Both kids were patting Stormy, who was still on Ellen's lap.

Mary was saying earnestly to Ellen, "I didn't like that lady. She has a scary face."

Ellen, still learning how to be a supportive adult in a child's life, looked taken aback at Mary's disclosure, but after a moment said, "She may look frightening, but that is just her way. She may not know how to be friendly to little girls."

Good one, Aunt Ellen. The cat stood up and stretched, arching his back and shooting his tail straight up so that it quivered. He jumped down and sauntered toward the living room. *I'll just go keep an eye on her.*

Noelle's face lit up. "So will I. Come on, Mary!"

"Where are we going?" Mary asked, even as she followed Noelle out of the kitchen.

"Where are they going?" Ellen asked as the two girls and the cat disappeared into the other room.

"They are scouting out the enemy," Roy said. He grinned. "I hope Shively isn't allergic to cats."

"I hope she is," Christy said, annoyed. "I hate it that she figures she can come in here and snoop around my house just because my name is in the news again. I've already proven to her that the allegations against me are false. What more does the damned woman want?"

"Good thing I'm here," Trevor said. He looked pleased by the idea of doing battle with child services and Joan Shively in particular.

There was the sound of footsteps coming up the stairs, then a thump, as if someone stumbled on one of the stairs.

"Stormy!" they heard Noelle say. "You need to be careful! I'm sorry, Ms. Shively. Our cat is very friendly. He likes people to pat him. That's why he was so close to your feet. He wants you to notice him."

Christy choked and put her hand over her mouth to stifle a laugh. Quinn chuckled quietly while Roy and Trevor each grinned. Ellen murmured, "That cat!"

They heard Shively say, "There, I've patted the animal. I hope that satisfies it."

"Him," Noelle said, chattily. "Stormy's a *him.* He's part of our family. Come on, Mary. Let's show Ms. Shively my room. I clean it up every day and I make my bed every morning. It's perfect!"

Light running footsteps sounded on the stairs going up, followed by slower, heavier adult ones.

Christy gave way to the giggles that had been consuming her. "Man, I love that kid," she said to no one in particular.

After a moment Ellen said, "She is very special."

It was amazing how very liberating laughter could be. As her giggles tailed off, Christy said, "And she likes having you here."

That made Ellen's features brighten with pleasure.

Children's footsteps, tearing down the stairs, sounded, again followed more slowly by adult ones. Noelle, accompanied by Mary, bounded into the kitchen. Mary's face was pink and she looked like she'd just had a taste of forbidden fruit. And liked it. Noelle's expression was sober, but there was that telltale twinkle in her eyes that told Christy that she was enjoying herself hugely. "Ms. Shively looked everywhere upstairs, Mom."

"Everywhere?"

Noelle nodded just as there was another thump on the stairs. This time they all heard Shively say, "Damn cat!"

Mary's eyes widened until they were as round as the "O" her mouth was making at Shively's use of a swear word.

Serves you right for poking through my wife's lingerie.

Noelle's eyes lit with amusement and she grinned. "Ms. Shively opened the drawers in the bathroom, Mom. And the ones in your bureau. She said she'd never seen so many socks. And Stormy sat in your underwear drawer when she said your stuff was totally in…inappropiate. What does inappropiate mean, Mom?"

"She looked in my panties drawer?" Christy's voice rose as outrage burned through her.

"Inappropriate underwear." That was Quinn and he sounded both amused and impressed.

Christy flushed red as Ellen said, "How dare she?!" and Shively stumbled into the kitchen. Herded there, it seemed, by the cat.

"You had no right to go through my things!" Christy said, fury making her body hot. She was so angry she wasn't even trying to be conciliatory.

"I was looking for drugs," Shively said. There was an edge of belligerence in her tone, but the expression in her eyes was wary.

Christy took a step back. "Drugs? I don't use drugs. I never have and I never will!"

The cat, who had been sitting on one of Shively's feet, now stood up on his hind legs and reached for her thigh. Stormy was a big cat, nearly twenty pounds and a good three feet long when stretched to his full length. His front paws reached nearly to Shively's pelvic area when he stood on his hind legs. In a lazy movement he dug his claws into the polyester of her pant leg and clung.

Shively freaked. "Get it off me!" she screamed as she backed up in a fruitless attempt to escape.

Stormy's claws were anchored tight. As Shively stumbled backward and the cat stayed put, there was an ominous tearing sound.

Christy dove for the cat. Angry as she was at Shively, she didn't want Stormy hurt. She knew that Frank meant only the best and that he was protecting her in the only way he could, but there were limits.

She scooped him up, disengaging his claws, as Shively started to babble. "He's a cat, Ms. Shively. He was only being friendly. How was Stormy to know you were afraid of cats?"

"That animal is a vicious beast! It needs to be put down."

Stormy wiggled in Christy's arms and she put him onto the floor where he sat, eyes on Shively.

"Don't be ridiculous," Ellen said. "You have been acting quite inappropriately—that is how you pronounce the word, Noelle, and it means unacceptable behavior—since you arrived in this house. My niece is a young woman who loves her child and will do anything to ensure she has a happy and safe life. I can see absolutely—and that is another very good word, Noelle, it means without restrictions—no reason for you to be pawing through her private drawers."

"Wow," Christy said.

Shively straightened and, torn trousers and all, launched herself into battle. "You!" She jabbed a finger at Ellen. "Have been accused of murdering a lovely young woman who was guilty of nothing but—"

"Being a drug addict and having sex in public places," Quinn finished for her.

Brought up short by his statement, Shively stared at him. "Excuse me?"

"The woman you were talking about," Quinn said mildly. "I was just filling you in on what kind of person she was. Don't get me wrong," he added as Shively opened her mouth to protest. "She didn't deserve to die. But I can't gloss over the reality of who she was when she was alive."

"A good point," Trevor said. "I have to add that I can make a good case for overzealous conduct on your part, Ms. Shively. You have no cause to go through anyone's drawers in this household. And you have no evidence, beyond unsubstantiated hearsay, that Mrs. Jamieson has ever indulged in narcotics or any other kind of mood-altering substance."

Roy, who was never one to let propriety get in the way, toasted Shively with his half-drunk glass of wine and said, "Time to go, Ms. Shively."

The cat brushed up against Shively's leg and she jumped. He looked up at her, green eyes gleaming.

"Yes," she said. "Perhaps you are right." She shot Christy a look that was hard to interpret. "I will be in touch."

Christy let her show herself out. She was still trembling with outrage and she didn't want to have to endure a private moment with the woman. She wasn't sure what she might say.

As the door slammed, Mary Petrofsky, still wide-eyed, said, "Wow, Noelle. Your family is really cool."

"I know," Noelle said, and beamed.

CHAPTER 29

As the sound of the door closing echoed through the house, Christy poured herself a large glass of wine.

"We're going back downstairs," Noelle said.

"Okay. I'll call you when dinner's on the table." Christy rounded the peninsula counter and sat down with the others. She took a slug of wine, then said with a sigh, "I'm going to have to wash everything in my dresser."

"Especially your lingerie," Ellen said. She shuddered dramatically, "Since the cat sat on it."

That was Stormy's idea. He likes open drawers. He just hopped in there before I could think of how to stop the old bi...witch, and stretched out. He hoped she'd rub his belly, but she didn't cooperate. She didn't have a chance to dig through that drawer, but she did do a pretty thorough search through your socks.

"Good for Stormy," Christy said as the cat jumped up onto her lap and circled, looking for a comfortable spot to curl up. "I'd rather have him sitting in my lingerie than Shively pawing through it." She scratched him behind his ears, then, when he was settled, gave him the belly rub Shively had denied him.

Stormy purred loudly. Christy drank more wine and turned to Ellen. "Thank you for defending me."

Ellen looked at her for a long moment, then she said, "We have had our differences, Christy, but you are a Jamieson. I regret some of the actions I have taken in the past. I can see now how devoted you are to Noelle." She smiled faintly. "And just how much energy you put into raising that child. You don't deserve that woman's accusations."

"Neither do you," Christy said, looking steadily at Ellen. "I apologize for letting myself be worried over what Shively might think."

Ellen waved her hand in a dismissive way. "It doesn't matter."

"We were all manipulated by a master," Christy said. "Me, Shively, Detective Patterson. She did it so beautifully that we were all taken in."

Ellen frowned. "Who are you talking about?"

"Natalie DeBolt," Quinn said. He was sitting straighter, watching Christy with bright, considering eyes. He'd figured it out too.

Christy smiled at him. "Yeah. Natalie. She pretended that she and Ellen were lovers so the cops would think that the motive behind Brittany's killing was an affair gone wrong."

"What? Natalie? She's not gay!" Ellen said, looking shocked.

"No, she's not. Nathan DeBolt told me that early on," Quinn said. "He laughed when I suggested she might be involved with a woman. He implied she was a cougar who liked to do more than look at younger men. But there had to be a reason for Brittany's body to be found at your condo, Ellen. Sex was the easiest explanation."

"And one the police wouldn't look much beyond," Christy said. "Especially when there was no obvious link between Ellen and Brittany."

Trevor nodded. "Go for the tried-and-true. Sex, money, and revenge."

"Don't forget love," Christy said quietly. "Brittany was murdered for love."

By this time Ellen was staring at Christy as if she had started speaking in tongues. And perhaps to Ellen, she had. "Are you saying that *Natalie DeBolt* murdered Brittany Day and Jacob Peiling?"

Christy nodded. "I think so. That's why she was down at the police station this morning. She wasn't there because she was trying to free Aaron or keep him from being re-arrested. It was because she was the one being arrested. That's why Nathan was so lost when Quinn saw him. First his son is named as an accessory to a murder, and now his wife is charged with committing two other murders, each one cold-blooded and ruthless. It must have seemed like his world had exploded around him, poor man."

"But Natalie is my friend! Why would she choose my apartment to kill Brittany? If she did kill Brittany. I can't believe this is even possible."

From the baffled expression on her face, Ellen truly didn't understand why she had been so cruelly betrayed. A deep sense of compassion made Christy cautious as she tried to explain. "You've been friends with Natalie for a long time, haven't you?"

"Yes, years. We met at EBU when we were both coeds. I introduced her to Nathan."

"Natalie isn't from Vancouver, is she?"

Ellen was frowning now. "No, she's from the Cariboo. The Williams Lake area. Why?"

"So she didn't come from money."

"No. Her father worked on a ranch in the area and her mother was a librarian in town. What are you getting at, Christy?"

Christy sighed. "Your friendship was important to Natalie, so she showed you the best of herself. You were someone who moved in the right circles, you could introduce her to the right people. She wasn't going to jeopardize your friendship by showing you her ugly side."

Ellen drew herself up, becoming every inch a Jamieson. "I refuse to accept this!"

Christy sighed again and rubbed the back of her neck. She knew it would be difficult to convince Ellen that the friend she'd trusted all her adult life had turned on her. She was about to try again, when Quinn said, "There is only one person Natalie cares more for than herself. Aaron."

"It's true she doted on the boy, but—"

"I don't think she knew about Aaron's involvement in Frank's death," Quinn continued, ignoring Ellen's interruption. "At least, not initially. By the time Aaron needed someone to vouch for him, a few months had passed. Who would be surprised if Brittany or Cara LaLonde came forward? He was regularly seen with both women, and had been for months. He just had to set it up and he'd be a free man. Without an alibi for the night in question, though, the evidence against him was certain to bring a conviction when he was brought to trial."

With a sigh, Christy said, "I agree with Quinn. A few days before Brittany came forward, she and Natalie visited Aaron in jail. I think Natalie had already been pushing her to provide Aaron with the alibi and the visit that day cinched the deal."

Ellen was shaking her head. Christy could see she wasn't buying any of this. "Natalie would not participate in such a conspiracy."

She's not listening, Frank said with a yawn. *The best way to deal with Aunt Ellen when she's like this is to give it up and move on.*

Roy shifted in his seat and Trevor frowned. Christy opened her mouth to disagree, but at that moment Ellen held up her hand. The imperious interruption was probably a good thing, since Christy had been about to reply to a comment Ellen hadn't even heard.

"Perhaps if you tell me more of the story I will be able to understand your reasoning," Ellen said, very much on her dignity. "What about this girl, Brittany Day? Why would she agree to be involved in this reprehensible scheme?"

"She was an addict," Quinn said. "Aaron got her addicted to coke—"

"Or maybe she was already addicted before she met Aaron," Roy said, pouring soothing waters.

Quinn shot a look at his father, eyebrows raised. Then he said, "Could be. It doesn't really matter who got her hooked, but that she was. Aaron was her main supplier, but with Aaron in jail, she needed a new source."

Trevor leaned forward. "Natalie?"

Quinn nodded. "I think Aaron told his mother who he got his stuff from and she became the conduit who supplied Brittany. Natalie threatened to turn off the tap if Brittany didn't provide an alibi for Aaron. So she did."

"And then she got cold feet," Christy said, shaking her head.

"With the help of Lorne Cossi." A muscle jumped in Quinn's jaw.

Christy grimaced. Her risky interview with Lorne Cossi was still something of a sore spot for Quinn. "Yeah. Lorne Cossi is not a nice person."

"Lorne Cossi? One of Jacob Peiling's grad students?" Ellen demanded. "What has he to do with this?"

"Lorne likes to coerce women into having sex with him," Christy said. "Usually he sticks to vulnerable undergrads, but he and Brittany shared an office and I think she was a bit of a challenge for him. He went hunting around for her weakness and he found it."

"Drugs," Roy said, shaking his head. "So he supplied her too?"

"No, but he knew that she was addicted and that she was neglecting her EBU work in favor of partying with Aaron. He threatened to go to Peiling if she didn't have sex with him."

"Not only Peiling, but her parents too," Quinn added.

"Poor girl," Ellen said. There was compassion in her voice and expression.

Christy nodded. "Yeah. Her money didn't matter to Aaron or Natalie or Lorne Cossi. There was no easy way out for her."

"So how did Cossi influence Brittany's decision to change her testimony?" Roy asked.

"He knew the alibi she'd provided Aaron was false, because she was having sex with him when Aaron was in the alleyway pushing Frank into the trunk of a car. Brittany had a choice. She could let the alibi stand and be blackmailed by Lorne Cossi for the rest of her life. Or she could revoke it now and take her chances with the legal system." Quinn shrugged. "She decided on the law."

"I think she may have felt guilty about lying, too," Christy said. She looked at her wineglass. "From the way her father described her, she sounded like a decent person who had wandered off the path. I'd like to think that she wanted to come back to where she ought to be."

"So she tells Natalie she wants to retract, what then?" Roy asked.

"I don't think she did tell Natalie," Quinn said. "I think she told Aaron. She went to see him the afternoon before she died. The alibi was still being investigated then, and if she pulled it, he would never be released. I think he told his mother when she visited him later that day and she handled it."

"She may have already had concerns," Trevor remarked. "Wasn't it Natalie who insisted Brittany swear an affidavit? Once that was done it didn't matter if Brittany was dead. The alibi would stand."

"And she couldn't retract it," Roy said with enthusiasm. "This is fascinating. Natalie must have been obsessed with getting Aaron released."

"I often thought he was the love of her life," Ellen said. "Until Christy exposed his participation in Frank's death, I have to admit I was charmed by him. I never saw his nasty side." She looked around the table. "I knew Natalie and Nathan were having problems. She was always respectful when they were out together, but I sometimes thought that perhaps she saw him more as a meal ticket than a husband." She paused, then lifted her chin. "But none of this explains why you think she deliberately chose to implicate me by leaving Brittany's body on my terrace?"

"You were her cat's-paw," Quinn said. "She needed to pin the murder on somebody. Who better than a Jamieson?"

"But—" Ellen shook her head. "We were friends. Longtime friends. I trusted her."

"Which may have been one of the reasons she chose your apartment. She could gain access easily. The super and your housekeeper knew her and wouldn't remember if they saw her around. They'd just think that she had come to visit and you weren't home to receive her. I think at some point she must have made a copy of your door key. When she decided Brittany had to go, she made use of it."

Christy nodded at Quinn's statement, then added, "She knew the layout of your suite. Where the furniture was. Where your bedroom was. Where she could stash Brittany's body and get away successfully."

"Surely she didn't kill Brittany elsewhere and drag her body onto my terrace!"

"No," Christy said. "She drugged her. Brittany was high when Natalie came to your apartment. That's why you heard the noise in your hallway. Brittany was so stoned that she couldn't walk straight. It wasn't yet dawn when Natalie let them in. Brittany didn't know there was a console table just inside the door and she stumbled into it in the dark. She hit the mirror above and it fell, causing the crash. Natalie hustled her out onto the terrace and whacked her with a plant pot to keep her quiet."

"Then Natalie hid behind the lounger and hoped you wouldn't come outside and inspect," Roy said. He shook his head. There was a look of admiration on his face. "Ballsy."

"It was November," Quinn pointed out. "The weather had turned. How many people go out onto their decks once summer is over?"

"True." A faraway look entered Roy's eyes. "Natalie must have freaked when Ellen got dressed and left. I bet she was hoping that she'd be able to do the deed and get out while Ellen was still asleep."

"Leaving me alone in my apartment with a body," Ellen said with a shudder.

"And no alibi for the time of the murder," Christy said. "Instead you were gone before she was and here in Burnaby long before Brittany was found."

"But the police found blood on my nightgown," Ellen said. She paled as spoke and her eyes darkened. "Detective Patterson hounded me about it when I was at the police station. I couldn't explain how it got there and she wouldn't believe me, because she said the blood spatter indicated I was near the Brittany when she was bludgeoned."

"I expect Natalie put your gown on once you were out of the apartment," Trevor said. "She finished Brittany off, then put the hairs on your pillow." He shrugged. "She realized she didn't have to rush, because she knew your housekeeper came in at noon. She had plenty of time to add artistic touches that would implicate you."

Ellen shook her head. "This is so very difficult to understand. Why did she kill Jacob Peiling? He knew nothing of Brittany's life with Aaron. How was he a danger to Natalie?"

"Lorne Cossi again," Quinn said. "Peiling knew about the student complaints against Cossi. He may even have known that Cossi was sexually interested in Brittany. He was aware that someone was blackmailing Brittany, and initially I think he figured it was Cossi, trying to convince her to sleep with him. Then he discovered Brittany and Cossi had already had sex. He put the date together with the alibi and realized that Brittany had lied."

"He told Brittany's father that he knew why she had died, and he thought he knew who had killed her," Christy said. "I suppose he did what we did, asked why someone would kill Brittany and then when he found out she'd lied about the alibi, he decided it had to be one of the DeBolts."

"But he was an academic to the end. He had to find proof before he could publish," Roy said, shaking his head.

"I'm pretty sure he thought Nathan was the killer," Quinn said. "But Nathan was a generous supporter of his program. He couldn't afford to lose that grant by accusing the man of murder then finding out he was innocent. He had to know for sure."

"Why meet with Natalie? Why not call Nathan outright and ask where he was the morning Brittany was killed?" Roy asked.

"Nathan would be furious," Ellen said quickly. "He would consider Jacob's question insulting. Jacob's funding would be gone immediately." She paused to consider, then added, "I expect he would talk to the president of the university and the Board chair about Jacob, too. He has a lot of influence when he cares to use it."

"So Jacob decided to pump Natalie for info instead," Roy said. He drank some wine. "Risky. What if they were both in on it?"

"I think Dr. Peiling felt guilty that he'd left Brittany pretty much on her own after she came to Vancouver. He'd promised Roger Day—one of his oldest friends—that he'd look after her, but he didn't." Christy stared at the wine in her glass. "It was too late to save Brittany, but at least he could put a name to her killer. Unfortunately, he underestimated Natalie." Christy glanced at Ellen, then away. "She is very good at making people like and accept her."

"So he didn't know Natalie was the murderer?" Ellen said. "That's why he ate the food she brought?"

Christy sipped some wine, then nodded. "He trusted her. He planned to ask her a few questions, enough to confirm his assumption that Nathan was the killer, but not to raise her suspicions. And if she did figure out where his questions were leading, he assumed that she would be horrified."

"So she shows up with food from one of his favorite restaurants and offers it to him. I still don't buy him eating it." Roy reached for the wine bottle and offered to refill Ellen's glass.

Ellen shook her head no, and sighed. "Good manners, Roy. Natalie would have presented it as a gift. Perhaps she told him it came from his favorite restaurant. If he protested, she may have said that the chef had made it especially for him. He would feel obliged to at least try it."

"Ellen is right. Natalie can be very charming when she wants," Christy said dryly. "She likes to give presents to people she wants to influence. She breezes up, hands the gift to the person, and says, 'Darling, I saw this whatever-it-is and thought of you. I knew you'd love it and I had to buy it for you.' Or words to that effect. The recipient is caught off guard and accepts the gift, because Natalie is standing there looking like an eager puppy who's just dropped a slobber-coated tennis ball at its master's feet. You think she means well and accept the gift, just like the puppy owner who doesn't want to touch the ball, but throws it anyway. It's only later, when Natalie asks for a favor and hints about what special friends you are, that you realize what's she's done."

Roy rubbed his chin. "Hmm. What about the EpiPen? Why didn't he use it?"

"When the first symptoms came on, she may have offered to help him, by giving him the injection. Once she had the pen all she had to do was make sure she kept it out of his reach," Quinn said. He accepted a top-up from his father.

"She disarmed him," Trevor murmured. His voice rose theatrically. "Then she struck!"

So did Roy, who emptied the bottle into Trevor's glass then stood up to open a second.

"What will happen to her?" Ellen asked.

"She'll be tried," Trevor said. "She—or her husband, Nathan—will hire a good lawyer." He grinned. "Probably my nephew, who's almost as capable as I was before I retired. His services cost the earth, but the DeBolts have the money."

"Will he get her off?"

Trevor shot Ellen a cautious glance. "That, dear lady, is up to twelve good people on a jury. But, no, given the evidence stacked against her, a very good motive for both murders and the deliberate, careful planning that went into the first one—no, I don't think she will get off."

"At least it's over and we can get back to living our lives," Christy said. She finished up the wine in her glass. "Now, I think we're probably all ready for dinner. It's one of Noelle's favorites. And Frank's." She smiled faintly. "My mom's chili." She scratched the belly of the cat snoozing in her lap. "You too, Stormy."

The cat yawned and stretched, then hopped off her lap to take up a station beside his food bowl.

"But first…" Christy hesitated, then said, "I know you don't want to go back to your condo, Ellen. You're welcome to make your home here, with Noelle and me." When Ellen opened her mouth, a polite refusal clear in her expression, Christy added hastily, "Despite what has happened before, we'd like to have you. You're family, after all." She stood up. "You don't have to answer right now. Think about it. The offer is open-ended."

"Thank you, Christy," Ellen said gravely. "I will consider it."

"All I can ask," Christy said. "Who's ready for supper? Quinn, would you call the kids?"

"I'll set the table," Roy said.

"What can I do?" Ellen asked.

Christy looked at her mischievously. She brought out the dish of meat and sauce she'd spooned out earlier and left to cool. After adding some of the hot mixture to warm it, she handed the bowl to Ellen. "You can feed the cat."

Turn the page for an
excerpt from

CAT
GOT YOUR
TONGUE

The 9 Lives Cozy Mystery Series
Book Three

Louise Clark

"Out with it, Dad," Quinn said. "Why are you phoning so late?" It was nearly two in the morning. Too late for a social call, so it was likely his father was phoning to unload some bad news. Beside him, Christy began to frown as she listened to his half of the conversation.

"We're at the *SledgeHammer* party. All of us." Roy paused.

"Yeah." Quinn was trying to be encouraging without being demanding. He didn't want to say 'spill it!' to his father, but that's how he felt.

"Trevor, Ellen, Frank, and me."

"You took the cat to a party put on by a rock band?"

There was a little hesitation, then Roy said, "Frank wanted to come. He's a big fan of *SledgeHammer*." His tone was belligerent.

Quinn resisted the urge to sigh. "Did something happen to the cat?"

"What? Nothing! The thing is, he found the body. Saw the murder, that is." Roy broke off and Quinn could hear the sound of raised voices in the background. Then Roy said, "I'm just talking to my son. I'll be with you in a minute." The voice in the background spoke again, the tone more urgent now, an edge of demand in it. "He's got nothing to do with this," Roy said, sounding annoyed.

"He's out of town. In L.A. No, he's not my lawyer. Do I need a lawyer?"

"What the hell?" Quinn said to no one in particular, because although Roy hadn't disconnected, he was no longer on his phone and talking to Quinn.

Christy sat up straight, her frown deepening. "What's happening?"

"I'm not sure." There was more background talk and Quinn thought, with some relief, that one of the voices belonged to Trevor McCullagh. "Dad said something about a murder, then he started talking to someone at his end. I just heard another voice join the conversation. It sounded like Trevor."

"A murder!" Christy's eyebrows snapped together. "Is your dad in trouble? Do you think Trevor is telling the cops that he's Roy's lawyer?"

"Possibly, but if he is at the party, he might be a suspect too," Quinn said.

"What's that?" said Roy, suddenly back on the line.

"I was talking to Christy, Dad. I woke her up when you called and she's here now. I'm going to put the phone on speaker."

"Don't do that! It's—"

Quinn hesitated, his gut clenching at the urgency in his father's voice. "Why not? I'm going to tell her anyway."

"I know, but… Better if you break it to her gently. Later. I don't have time to put everything that's happened into a nice package. There's a pompous ass of a West Van cop who wants to interrogate me about the murder. Trevor was only able to buy me a couple of minutes, so I'll have to be quick."

Quinn glanced at Christy, who was now staring at him wide-eyed with fear. "That's the second time you mentioned a murder. Who's dead?"

"Vince. *SledgeHammer*'s manager."

"Vince Nunez," he said for Christy's benefit. "You said Frank saw the murder. Who did it?"

Roy's voice lowered. "That's just it. We don't know. We

heard Frank demanding that someone stop and then the cat howling, so we all rushed out to see what had happened. There was Stormy, sitting with his paws on Vince's chest and yowling, but no one else was around."

"Did Frank not know the person who did it?"

"No. I mean, I don't know. Yes, yes, I'm coming!" The last must have been to the officious police detective from the West Vancouver police department.

When he spoke again, Roy's voice was even softer than before. "Here's the problem. Frank saw the murder being committed and he hasn't spoken since."

Roy hesitated and Quinn had a sense that his father was about to tell him what he wanted Quinn to shield Christy from.

His voice almost a whisper, Roy said, "We think he's gone, Quinn. We think Frank has left Stormy's body forever."

CAT GOT YOUR TONGUE

available in print and ebook

THE
9 LIVES COZY MYSTERY
SERIES

The Cat Came Back
The Cat's Paw
Cat Got Your Tongue
(More to follow)

Louise Clark is the author of cozy mysteries and contemporary and historical romance novels. She holds a BA in History from Queen's University.

For more information, please visit her at www.louiseclarkauthor.com or on Facebook at www.facebook.com/LouiseClarkAuthor.

Lightning Source UK Ltd.
Milton Keynes UK
UKHW010130111120
373160UK00004B/829